Past Imperative
Blue Light

Book 6 of the Danny Sharp Series

Time and Again

The Danny Sharp series
Time and Again

Book 1 Present Tense
Book 2 Past Imperfect   – Elusive Foe
Book 3 Past Continuous – Wild Wolds
Book 4 Present Imperfect - Fire and Flame
Book 5 Past conditional - Hunt and Hide
Book 6 Past Imperative – Blue Light

© Copyright Yen Rickeard
ISBN: 978-1-9993080-0-1
Published by iron sword. Contact via www.timeandagain.website

Yen Rickeard has asserted her right under the Copyright, Designs and Patents Act1988 to be identified as the author of this work.

Printed by Book Printing UK
Remus House, Coltsfoot Drive, Peterborough, PE2 9BF

Beneath the surface of Danny Sharp's seemingly normal life lies history darker than any of his new friends at Sheffield University could imagine. In his 'teens his home had been blown up, his mother maimed and his father missing. He and his school friend Kelly have secrets the world must never know.

His Aunt Moira is now married to the detective, Ken Raynes, who helped rescue Danny's mother and take the culprit Kevin Wilcox into custody. However, Kevin was deemed unfit for trial; his story was full of wild Celtic warriors, Iron Age chiefs and battles. So now Kevin is remanded in a psychiatric hospital, under the name Kuillok, the court stripping him of the name Kevin Wilcox because that man, five years younger than Kuillok, was a student working for Moira in Japan, unaware of any troubles

Danny has learned to live with the decisions he made a long time ago. He still mourns the loss, not only of his father, but of a second family he had scarcely got to know.

He has no idea how complicated his simple life is about to become!

Contents

Important People in the story.

C21st

Danny
Kelly James   Danny's school friend, his best friend
Tasgo Aed   Late Iron Age Warrior, lost in time
Chrissie   Danny's girlfriend
Gamma Halter   Danny's Grandmother
Freya Sharp   Gamma's daughter, Danny's mother
Moira Halter   now Moira Raynes, Freya's sister
D.I. Ken Raynes Moira's Husband
D.I. Purbright
Matt Davies   Student in Hull
Emma   Student in Hull
Bethany   Student in Hull
Pc Tony Parker
PC Jane Slade
Paul   Danny's Dad's friend, ex-army, now head of a security firm
'Jack'   works for Paul
Joseph Desmond Lawyer
Patricia Paxman Lawyer well known to Danny's family
Kevin Wilcox   Moira's young enquiring student
Kevin Wilcox   Imprisoned insane (5 yrs older than his student self)

Parisi

Seahome

Dugal	Dead **Chief**	Danny's Grandfather
Tasgo Aed	**Chief**	Dugal's grandson, vanished
Jago	**Chief**	Usurper
Kelwyn	paid man once bonded to Dugal	
Gamma	Dugal's consort, Freya's mother, Danny's Grandmother	
Dannaigh	(Danny) also Dugal's and Gamma's grandson	
Margan	older warrior	
Marrec	warrior	
Leir	young warrior, Marrec's son	
Cadryn	young warrior	
Brec	blacksmith once a slave	
Hod	Brec's slave	
Gatwyn	Brec's young slave (once called TheBoy)	
Moira	Dugal's daughter	
Pinner	older warrior	
Bahee	Pinner's daughter	
Treva	Bahee's younger sister	
Erient	Pinner's young son	
Armel	Farmer	
Cunedag	a 14 year old, absent.	
Cynwrig	an energetic 10 year-old also absent	
Kuillok	Kevin Wilcox, now departed.	

Cynmar

Brannaigh	**Chief**
Brad	his seconder

Prologue

September 24th 7.15 am two years ago. Yorkshire Wolds.

The two horses came over the hill at full gallop, neck and neck, turf flying from hooves, riders low over their necks urging them on. The going was soft, the track clear, morning air cool, sun bright. Danny was riding bareback, not even a rug or blanket between him and the horse. He had forgotten the freedom, the joy of it. The exhilaration.

The horse seemed to like it too.

At the end of the long straight someone had stuck a telegraph pole across the track, perhaps to stop vehicles using it. He knew Kelly would jump it, while he would have to slow and let the horse pick its way over the ditch at one side or the other. He had never once managed a safe landing from a jump without a saddle.

He felt good. Today might just be the day. The track wouldn't be too hard a landing if he fell.

Kelly must have read his mind, because she dropped back to a canter and called out, 'Not today, not this month.'

He slowed too, and they trotted up to the obstacle, and round it.

'Will they have stables at Oxford?' he asked her.

'Bound to. Lots of rich kids, Oxford. Swanky.'

'Style over substance?' he suggested lightly. He knew she wouldn't be intimidated.

She grinned at him, 'They'll need a stable lad. Free riding.'

'Won't you be too busy for riding?'

'Extras, you've got to have the extras. Plain double first gets you nowhere at Oxford.' She was teasing him now. He didn't mind. She would get the double first too, he was sure of that.

'Are you all packed?' she asked.

'I'm only taking the one suitcase. Going by train.'

She looked at him, surprised.

'I've got rooms near the station. It's easier.'

'One suitcase? Everything? Winter clothes and all?'

The horses were walking now, enjoying the respite after a run.

'Can always buy more,' Danny said carelessly.

Kelly laughed, 'Rich kids at Sheffield too then!'

'Well,' he said uncomfortably, 'was hoping to hide that.' He wasn't looking forward to that side of it. If anyone bothered to look him up on the web, they would know. He was hoping to get away from the past. 'I even thought of not going as me. A pseudonym.'

She looked puzzlement at him.

'After, you know, everything. The papers, TV, all that. Notoriety.' He said, mouthing every syllable.

'It's been three years. They've forgotten.'

He shrugged. 'We still get snooped. Now and then. Dustbins gone through, you know the stuff.'

She did, only too well.

He went on, 'Easier if I had another name.'

'But, I mean,' she protested, 'you can't, can you? Unless you're giving up Danny Sharp forever. You'd have a degree in the wrong name.'

'Could fix it with the university,' he said wistfully. It still seemed attractive in some strange sort of way. 'Attend under the new name, get the degree under my own.'

'You do make things complicated,' she complained.

'I like them simple. Uncomplicated. Without the adjectives.' Under her impatient stare he went on 'Rich? Mysterious?' He grinned, 'Handsome? Orphaned?'

'Not orphaned!' she put in quickly.

'You know, sort of,' he shot back. It still hurt to think it, let alone say it. His father gone. His mother missing for so long. It hurt to think of it. Metal instead of bone in her shoulder. The artificial hand that she insisted on calling bionic enhancement. Not his fault, they all agreed on that. He still felt guilty.

'So,' she was asking, 'if not Danny Sharp, who? What would I call you?'

He shouldn't have even mentioned it, but Kelly was the one person he felt he could share anything with. But now it came to it, he was finding it

2

even harder than he had thought it would be. He bit his lip. She was watching him. He had started, he had to finish. 'Aed,' he said. 'Tasgo Aed.'

She was horrified. 'No!' she yelled. 'You cannot be serious!' Her horse sidled nervously, feeling the violence of her response. She was furious. 'No! You can't! Danny, seriously, you cannot!' Her horse was prancing sideways now and tossing its head, but she could deal with that and still shout at him. 'You!' she spat it, 'You are not Tasgo!' You can never be Tasgo! You shouldn't want to be Tasgo!'

He had expected her to be surprised, and maybe a bit angry. Anger was often her first line of response. He had hoped she might find it amusing. He hadn't expected fury.

'It would honour him,' he started to say, 'to keep his name alive after so long,' he would have gone on, but Kelly wasn't having it.

'He's history!' she snapped. 'He doesn't belong here! You Idiot!' she snarled. 'You absolute idiot!' Suddenly she was off down the hill towards the stables at a fast canter.

He had so wanted it to be a pleasant parting, a happy moving on for both of them.

He kicked his horse into a gallop and went after her, shouting 'I'm not going to! It was just an idea!' but he knew it was no use, she was already too far ahead, and too angry to listen.

Giggle in the Dark.

Present day. May 5th 22.30 Hull

'This is spooky' Emma giggled as another light came on ahead of them, and the one behind went out.

'Standard energy-saving,' Matt told her as they came to the next door, and he tapped in the security code.

It was as quiet as the grave. The door swung open on soundless hinges, then slammed shut behind them with a clang. Bethany was beginning to be a bit troubled by all the security. She was glad to see that no security key was needed to get out. Matt was only slightly geeky, but she wouldn't want to get trapped underground with him for too long. He was a third-year, and supposed to be a real brain, but so far she hadn't seen any trace of it. She'd only come along to keep Emma company.

Another corridor, more spooky lighting to show them the way.

'Where exactly are we going?' Bethany asked again.

'You'll see,' he told her with a grin. 'This place has heavy security, but I've got the book!' He waved it, a little black-bound notebook. 'I used to work with him after he...' he paused dramatically, eyes twinkling, '...transformed!'

Emma gave a little scream of delighted terror.

'Who?' Bethany asked.

'Kevin,' he said. 'You must have heard of him. Kevin Wilcox? Went off to some conference in Japan and came back a changed man. Maths whiz, with a bent for electronics. Mad as a hatter!'

Bethany felt sudden disquiet. What were they doing down here with this guy they hardly knew? Emma seemed to be quite at ease with him, but Emma wasn't big on common sense. Bethany wished she hadn't had that second glass of wine. She hadn't realised how big the glasses were. Must have been a third of a bottle in there. Too much.

Matt was saying, 'Not that he was solid sane before – but got the grant for this...'

They had come to another door and this time Matt had to look up the numbers in his black book.

The door opened onto a lab; electronics, Bethany was pleased to note, no dissecting tables, no glass jars of unknown chemicals, no racks on which to torture prisoners. There was a glass cuboid, about the size of a shower cubicle, also a whole load of cables and black boxes. The shower cubicle had a big barrier with a sign on it.

SAFETY BARRIER
DO NOT OPERATE EQUIPMENT IF BARRIER IS OPEN.

There was also, in the corner behind the shelves, a comfortable couch, a table lamp and a coffee-making machine. A possible love nest in the making, thought Bethany. Well, if he was hoping for a wild threesome he was going to be disappointed.

Emma was exploring the racks of electronic equipment with excitement, as if it were the set of some sci-fi movie where strange and wonderful things were about to happen. Matt had taken over the office chair and was scooting it from place to place, turning on equipment, and adjusting settings. He almost looked as though he knew what he was doing.

'So,' asked Bethany, 'what happens here?'

'Well,' Matt drew the word out long, 'usually...' then he turned to her with a big grin, 'not a lot.'

Just a ploy to get them down here then, thought Bethany.

'But,' went on Matt, with what was in fact quite an attractive twinkle in his eye, 'there's this!' Like a magician he produced what looked like a painted Easter egg, a bit small, and worked over in black and silver.

Emma bounced over to him, anxious to get his whole attention. 'What is **that**?' she demanded, as if it might be of tremendous value. It was very pretty. Exotic, like a piece of jewellery.

'No idea,' laughed Matt, 'but Kevin was real uptight about it. On about it all the time. Had it made by some craftsman somewhere, but it didn't arrive until this week. It's in his book, look!'

He showed them a page, and there was the little egg, being held in a vice and attached to cables. And here, in the middle of the pseudo-shower, was the very vice, all cabled up ready.

'But what does it do?' Bethany asked yet again. 'What's he researching? What's the room for?' Why all the security? was her final unspoken question, and a cold shiver ran down her spine.

Matt chuckled. 'Let's find out,' he said, lifting the safety barrier and then opening the glass door beyond.

Emma was thrilled, this was different and exciting. This was what she had come to University for, not the parties and the wild drinking, though that was proving quite exciting too.

Bethany on the other hand felt sudden fear, not like her at all. Had that last drink tasted a bit funny? She wasn't sure.

Matt stood the egg in its little cup, secured the vice round it, backed out and turned to his banks of equipment.

'Do you know you're doing?' Bethany asked him.

'Sure, I've been down here dozens of times, with Kevin.' He laughed 'He was going to change the world. Move over Dr Who, here comes Kevin from Hull!'

'Cool,' breathed Emma. Somewhere something began to hum, or to whirr.

Bethany pulled the safety barrier back in place. 'I'm not sure we should be doing this' she said.

Caught in the Act.

About 2100 years ago, a week before Samain. Cynmar (now Hull)

Esk was more than happy with the voyage so far. The boat still had wine to trade, but if he was as fortunate with their next stop as the last, they could take it home with them and drink their fill over the profits.

He had set sail with the full intention of this being a simple trading voyage, but his crew turned out to be better than he had thought. It was always wise to have strong seamen, ready to fight, especially when you were not sure of the lands you would be visiting. You never could tell when the proposed trade might turn to pitched battle when they saw the value of your goods, and greed proved to be stronger than trading instincts. But on this trip it had turned out the other way round.

He had done decent trade with the first village, and the second, but the third had brought down some wonderful British trinkets, swirling brooches and swords with beautifully crafted handles. They had brought them right down to the shore, for him to look at. They were beautiful objects, and he had seen the look on the face of his own strong man as he took up one of the swords and felt the balance and swing of it.

Esk had looked into the trusting faces of the shore men and realised that he could count their number on the fingers of one hand. They had broken a few heads and taken the lot, for the cost of a few bruises.

The same had worked for the next village too, though they had been rather less trusting, and there were cuts and bruises on both sides.

Now, they had reached the next town, and with a steady breeze along the shoreline could land and leave with ease. It looked like another gift. As they closed with the shingle shore he could see women at work, bringing down trestle tables, and covering them with cloth on which to display their wares. A couple of warriors were coming down to the waterfront, swords hung at their hips, but that was to be expected.

The crew had got it off to a fine art by now.

Esk hailed the men ashore, and asked if they would trade for good Gallic wine. Who wouldn't? They were welcomed to land, and as the boat grounded, enough of the crew leaped into the water and waded to dry land to form a defence line in case of attack.

They put out the plank for Esk to walk down and jump the last yard into a retiring wave. He hardly got his feet wet as he went to meet the locals.

The leader was Branaigh, and his young second merely Brad. It seemed that in this land all their names were 'brown', of varying degrees.

After introductions he walked with them to where the women had set out an array of cloaks and shawls. No rustic work, these. The colours were bright, the weave tight, and they had been napped to a soft smooth finish he had rarely seen. He would willingly trade for these. He called for the small wine vessel to be brought, so that they could taste the quality.

As they did so, Esk asked casually where the men were.

They paused for a fraction too long before Branaigh said, 'Close by,' and held out his beaker for more of the wine.

Over the third cup, young Bran let slip that the men had gone along the coast to the next village, where apparently there had been some trouble, he didn't know what. Perhaps Esk had seen something?

Esk smiled. He knew full well what the trouble had been, he had the goods to prove it. If the warriors had gone to investigate his last attack, then the gods were surely with him. He eyed the woman who was pouring the wine. A perfect addition to the crew. They'd need some entertainment on the way back.

'We'll take the cloth,' he told the shore-men.

'And we'll take the wine,' agreed Branaigh.

'I don't think so,' smiled Esk. The guard for the boat had wandered nonchalant up the beach behind him. Suddenly they all had swords drawn.

The woman screamed, and ran. The men ran too, no doubt to get spears. Esk's crew bounded after them. The woman screamed again, a deliberate sound, not terror.

Then the world fell apart. Fighting men, shouting, bellowing anger, rising out of the wood pile, leaping from behind the hayrick, boiling out of the doors of the huts. They were everywhere, dozens of them.

8

Esk spun on his heel.

'The ship,' he called, *'to the ship!'*

Out of every hollow and hidden dip, shield shelled, local warriors were rising. From behind him the sound of battle, in front, fighting men fully armed. From somewhere arrows flew and his crew still on the boat were falling, screaming. Esk turned and ran, along the beach, away.

Footsteps echoed his in the shingle sand. In the soft mud that lined the little river he turned and found fury in his footsteps. Copper-red hair and sworded steel, a man leapt at him, death bladed.

The world ended with a flash of blue light.

Magic Tricks

Matt was playing with switches, twiddling knobs. An electric smell sharpened the air. Hair began to stand on end.

Suddenly the shower cubicle was filled with a blue glow. Blue lightning flashed blindingly brilliant and with a loud bang and clatter the lights went out.

Tasgo fell through blue fire into darkness. He landed hard against a flat surface and some sort of smooth wall. The sword had vanished from his hand, leaving it stinging. The beach had vanished, and the battle. The sound of sea was silent. For a moment there was eerie quiet, as if he had become suddenly deaf.

Like a soft dawn, light was fading into being round him.

The smooth wall he was leaning on did not exist. He could feel it holding him up, but he could see that it was not there. He could see through it to a more distant wall beyond, a real wall, and shelves of black boxes all tied together with smooth rope. Boxes and shelves, and nothing between them and him. A nothing which was holding him up. He moved his hand on the smooth non-existent surface. It was real enough to the touch. Somewhere a woman was screaming.

He whirled, hitting head and hand on some sort of structure, reaching for the knife in its sheath.

No knife.

Revealed, now that he had turned, there they were, three people, staring in shock at him, two women, one man. One of the women was doing the screaming.

Tasgo leapt backwards, away from them, and smashed against a hard wall. A wall which wasn't there. He struck out with his hand, hit hard on something which could not be there. He could see it was not there.

Nothing but distant shelves of boxes tied together with black rope, at a distance, not here, not here where he hammered with his fist.

They were not armed, the people. They looked as shocked as he felt.

He stopped, stock still, trying to see, to understand.

The woman had stopped screaming. The man's mouth was moving but Tasgo could hear no sound. He lashed out at the invisible barrier to his left, felt the hardness vibrate, heard the sound of his hard blow. There was nothing there though. Nothing he could see. Nothing!

In seconds he had found the limits of his movement. He was in an invisible box, held hard. He could feel it, but not see it. He was trapped.

Panic stormed through every limb. Fear screamed. He clamped them down, put them in their own invisible boxes. There were three people and they looked as scared as he felt. Were they trapped in their own invisible boxes?

Was he dead? Had that Waesuck turned and stabbed him without him even knowing?

No. Not possible. Someone behind him? A spear?

He ducked under the structure, there in the invisible box with him. He was praying to every deity he knew, that ahead there would be no obstruction to his passage forward towards the people.

No such joy. The box was complete on every side. There was no escape. He was trapped by magic, held for ever. The words, '*a thousand years*' whispered in his head, and panic leaped free.

He threw himself at the barrier that was not there. He hammered hard. He screamed frustration and rage, hitting in frenzy, knee and elbow, hand and heel against something that was not there, yet held him fast.

He battered himself against it again and again and again, till he fell, momentarily exhausted, to the floor. Tears of rage and frustration coursed down his cheeks.

The woman who had screamed suddenly started to laugh. She was a good-looking woman, blonde hair in some exotic style, clothes clinging. Some sort of siren? He had heard of them, but never wholly believed it.

'Matt! You idiot!' she was shouting, the laughter still escaping hysterically between the words. 'You had us going there! You really had us fooled.' She was throwing herself at the man.

So not inside their own boxes then. Was this some sort of hell, where all the demons and dark spirits would mock him for his shortcomings, for his failures and mistakes? Tasgo drew himself together. He wasn't going to be an easy prey.

'Oh my God,' Matt said again, still sitting in the office chair.

'How'd you do that?' Emma was demanding. 'For a moment there I really thought ...' She was looking with admiration from Matt, whom she had her arms round, to the man who was dragging himself up from the floor after his performance. Under the odd get-up, he was quite a hunk.

Bethany was feeling lightheaded. Had it just been a trick then, some sort of magic trick, with this man hidden somewhere till the lights went out? If so it had been a bravura performance. Quite an actor. Though she couldn't see for the life of her where he had been hidden.

Her eyes met his through the glass wall. It might all be an act, but the emotion she saw there seemed real. He was trapped and scared.

He was terrified.

She stepped forward and pulled the warning safety-arm out of the way. The glass door swung open, sending reflected lights scattering around the room.

Warily, filled with adrenalin-fuelled caution, Tasgo stepped out of his invisible cage, practically into the arms of the second woman, she of the dark hair and serious expression. He was jumping to no conclusions; he was keeping his distance in every possible way. She too was backing off quickly. She seemed as rattled as he was.

'Oh my God,' breathed Matt, yet again, as the figure came closer to him.

'Hello handsome!' Emma was moving from Matt to the newcomer reaching out to run her hand over his arm, feeling the muscles under the skin, ignoring the expression on his face. 'Where'd you come from?' she was asking.

Tasgo understood not a word, only the inflection. All right, he thought grimly, wondering how much was on offer, and what the price would be. He put an arm round her waist and pulled her to him, ready for anything that might happen next. To his great relief, she was definitely real, warm flesh and blood. He had expected the slight resistance, but now she was simply melting in his arms.

12

Rather disconcerting, that; she didn't even know who he was, what he was capable of. But then, she was obviously pretty drunk. He could smell it on her breath.

The other woman had stepped back, out of the way.

Tasgo held onto his prize. At the very least she could be something of a hostage.

'Oh my god!' Matt muttered once more.

Holding Emma close to him Tasgo looked across at Matt and Bethany. *'Am I dead?'* he demanded. They just looked at him. They too were pretty tense, almost as panicked as he had felt. He softened his tone, he tried to look more relaxed. *'Are we all dead?'* he asked.

Bethany looked at Matt. 'What's he saying?'

Matt finally moved, coming up onto his feet, eyes still wide in shock. He had thought the blue lightning would have been an excitement for the girls, one that might have brought its own rewards. This had never happened before.

'I need a drink.' His voice was shaky.

'Haven't we drunk enough?' Bethany wanted to know. If this was Matt's idea of a joke, she didn't like it.

'Not yet.' Matt had decided on a plan of action. He didn't know what had just happened, but he did know it was his fault. The only sensible thing to do at this stage was to get absolutely slathered, and leave the rest to the grey light of morning, when he might be able to cope with it. Or better still, the whole problem might have resolved itself without his input.

He headed for the door. Emma, with Tasgo's arm still romantically firm around her waist was ready to follow, and Tasgo wasn't going to differ.

To his surprise, what he had seemed part of the wall opened, and they all went through. The perfect geometry of the tunnel revealed was an amazement of magic, a light that moved along with them. The door that fitted so well. He watched carefully the movement of the handle, the turning of the door on its hinges.

The corridor seemed to go on forever. Was it hewn out of the rock, or created by men's hands, or was it pure magic, like the light always with them despite the darkness ahead and behind? Was the tunnel coming into being ahead of them, and vanishing behind?

Emma giggled and prattled, but she wanted Tasgo's hold to be looser, she wanted to call teasingly to Matt, or chirpily back to Bethany, who was following on without joining properly in the general excitement. Tasgo didn't want to scare her unnecessarily, he loosened his hold. In the tunnel she would be easy enough to capture again. Instead he held her hand. She seemed to like that.

All his senses were heightened by fear and incomprehension. He didn't know where they were or where they were going, but it was away from magic boxes and the whisper of a thousand years.

Long corridors and doors, doors on either side but mostly doors through which they passed, one after the other, in a seemingly endless stream. Matt was leading the way, moving faster and faster as if he were fleeing something.

They came up stairs and suddenly out into a room made of light. Coming towards them was another group, the splitting image of their own. One like Matt, another like Emma, another Bethany seeming to half fade against darkness, and finally a figure in more familiar clothing, so similar to his own.

With sudden hope Tasgo yelled *'Dannaigh,'* and leapt towards the figure leaping also towards him.

Suddenly the image was splintered as another invisible wall made itself evident by giving way before them, sending images flying, to let them out into – an impossible day. Full of dark shadows and brilliant lights. No sun. All the light came from enclosed spaces full of, of figures without heads, impossible shoes, bright interiors built out of whiteness and light. Tasgo felt dizzy. The stuff of dreams or nightmares, or both combined. Lights that swept over them and were gone, lights on the move. A mad place made entirely of magic.

From somewhere a heavy beat pulsed. There was music, patterns of sound, and that was where they were heading, through heavy doors into enclosed spaces. This space he recognised, despite the lights, despite the invisible walls that sent back images of the people inside, despite the volume of voices.

This was a hall with ale! This was the end of a feast, a celebration! At last something he could understand! But so many people in one hall! Matt shouldered his way through the throng, with Bethany and Emma close behind. Tasgo pushed up closer to Emma, got his arm round her waist again. It would be easy to lose her here. He wouldn't want to lose any of them. They were all he had.

Matt reached the bar, with Bethany beside him and Emma crowding him, still with what he was trying not to think of as 'the Creature from the Lagoon.' Matt realised that he would be the one buying. But the Creature was peering over the counter at the array of bottles with amazement, and looking down the bar at the glasses and the drinks in all their colours, like a kid in a candy store.

Red wine was being poured into balloon glasses for the lasses next to them, and without so much as a by your leave, Tasgo grabbed one, and lifted it as if to toss it back. As cries of anger went up, he merely sniffed it, and graciously handed it back with a big smile to the young woman beside it.

'Vino Gallo!' he proclaimed, and she laughed.

'Vino gallo,' she replied, lifting the glass to him as if it were a toast.

Tasgo turned to the barman and cried, 'Vino Gallo!' with an expansive gesture that seemed to encompass everyone in the bar, not just his companions. The barman knew better than to accept that, but Vino Gallo was what they got, in large glasses.

Tasgo loved the glasses. The fine magic material, here but not here, the size of the glass, the taste of the wine, the impossibly slender stem which somehow held up the whole goblet of wine. It was probably, he thought as he tasted carefully, the best drink in the world. And although some distant memory of stories about how drinking or eating in the land of the dead was to land yourself there for a thousand years, the sheer relief of something he understood was more than enough to smother it. Matt paid with a card, a move entirely lost on Tasgo; they all drank.

Tasgo downed his glass almost as fast as Matt.

With good wine inside him, the comfort of an ale hall round him, and a woman tucked to his side as a possible bargaining ploy, Tasgo felt he was getting back in control.

He tapped Matt on the chest to get his attention, then laid his palm on his own chest. *'Tasgo Aed!'* he announced, then with an enquiring smile, he gestured to Matt.

Matt was giving nothing away. He wanted no trail leading back to him. 'Jake Thakeray,' he said, giving the name of the president of the student's union.

Bethany was having none of it. 'He's Matt Davies,' she said, then smiled, determined not to be nervous. She put a hand at the base of her own slender neck and said, 'Bethany,' and, pointing, gave away Emma's name too.

Bethany was confused. If Matt had got a friend to play the part of the 'appearing man' why was he now lying about his own name? Perhaps it was all one of Emma's games, though she hadn't thought Emma that clever. Whatever it was, Bethany was intrigued. She would play along, at least for a while. Nothing as interesting as this had ever happened before.

Tasgo turned back to the barman with an expansive gesture, and shouted 'Vino Gallo!' once more. Bethany caught his attention.

'Where are you from Tasgo?' It was a strange name.

In answer he slapped his chest again, *'Tasgo Aed!'* Then he smiled at each of them in turn, giving their names, before bellowing again for *'Vino Gallo'*.

When he turned back he had something else in mind, he was looking into her face for some sign of recognition. *'Dannaigh?'* he asked, *'Moira? Freya?'*

Matt caught the barman's eye and ordered more drinks. Tasgo had been disappointed by the lack of response to his question. He was thinking hard.

'Dannaigh shapp?' he tried hesitantly, *'Freya shapp? Moira?'* Moira had used a title too, he was having trouble remembering. *'Moira alter?'*

Matt turned with sudden excitement. 'Halter foundation?' he cried.

Tasgo turned to him, hope in his face, *'Moira alter!'* he agreed.

For the first time since the blue light had crashed the stranger into the chamber, Matt felt the world was with him, not against. 'He's a bloody exchange student!' He looked Tasgo in the eyes, 'Exchange Student?' he demanded.

Tasgo didn't understand that, but he did know that Matt knew at least some of those names. *'Dannaigh shapp?'* he demanded again.

'You're Danny Sharp?' demanded Matt, somewhat befuddled by relief and by drink.

'Danny Sharp,' agreed Tasgo eagerly, using Matt's pronunciation and taking the repeat of the name as confirmation that Matt knew Dannaigh.

'Bloody Hell! He's Danny Sharp' yelled Matt.

'Who's Danny Sharp?' Bethany wanted to know.

'They only own the bloody department! They finance the research!' Not entirely true, but near enough. Matt was home free. If some rich kid wanted to dress up funny and play stupid games, Matt had to be off the hook.

Tasgo could see the joy and relief. He had fallen amongst friends, or at least amongst those who knew his friends. He raised his arms to the barman, letting Emma free at last. *'Vino Gallo!'* he demanded including the whole bar in the gesture.

Matt shrugged. 'He's good for it,' he said.

'I'll need a card,' muttered someone else behind the bar, as drinks started to be poured. You didn't have to ask students twice when offering free booze.

Twenty minutes later, the place was thrumming. But a prolonged pantomime of money and payment by card had finally reached the conclusion that Tasgo didn't have one. And Matt was well aware that his own card was never going to cover the riot that was going on round them.

There was only one solution.

Celebration and Speed.

May 5th 23.43

After the heat and noise, the night air was cool. Tasgo had no idea why they were running, and he was amazed at the speed the women could make while wearing those insane shoes. Bethany had stopped to slip hers off her feet, and fallen behind, so Tasgo had slung her over his shoulder so they could catch up. When he realised how little she liked it he put her down, and they ran side by side. She was breathless, but laughing now. They were all laughing.

At last the folk chasing them seemed to have given up, and they dropped to a walk. Tasgo looked more closely at Bethany's shoes. The only conclusion he could draw was that they must be some sort of weapon. A stamp from one of those would go right through a normal shoe, possibly right through a foot, or deep into a chest. He must remember to be very respectful to the women.

They were walking down a narrow chasm between tall shapes. There were fewer bright lights here, and no walls made of light. It was still the most alien place Tasgo could imagine. Twilight was mixed with darker shadow, or, in patches, was bright as day. The ground was smooth and hard, unreal, the walls around them were high and flat. There were strange lines on the dark ground, and every so often a stake jutted up with some strange symbol on it, or occasionally some sort of box.

There was nothing natural about this place. Nothing he could understand. The one thing he was certain of was that these people knew Dannaigh Sharp, and he was not about to be separated from them.

He could smell the sea, though there was no sign of any body of water. Heavy, throbbing sound was coming from one of the dark shapes around them, and its position was marked by brilliant lights. The noise spoke of some great festival, there might be a horde inside. Maybe the lights gave an indication of what sort of festival, but he couldn't make them out.

18

The far end of the chasm began to flicker with blue lights. They reminded him of the light that had thrown him from the battle field to here, and he stopped. So did the others.

Some weird thing swam by the end of the road, crossing it in a sparkle of blue lights. As it vanished a distant siren started, like a string singer, but louder, higher and more urgent.

With sudden haste they were moving forward, and in a few scant moments they were going in under brilliant lights, and into a cacophony that vibrated deep inside his chest. As they descended into a sea of moving bodies and flashing lights, Tasgo felt certainty close in on him.

He was dead.

There was no place like this in the world he knew. There could be no place like this in the world he knew.

Somehow, he had died.

As an afterlife, it was amazing. Everything was made of light! It was a chaos of colour. Sound, there was enough rhythm and variation for it to be music, it practically picked you up and made you move! The women! They were half naked, showing their legs, and their shoulders, and moving to the music in a way that could hardly be imagined.

Emma was drawn immediately to the dance floor, trying to get Matt to go with her, but he seemed strangely deflated. Tasgo wasn't!

With an arm round her waist he went out with her to join with all the writhing bodies. The arm round her waist didn't last more than a moment. The music took her. It had taken everyone. Each danced on their own. The moves they were making, the sexiness, the invitation! Tasgo had eyes everywhere but mostly on Emma. He started copying her every move. Laughing, she egged him on, getting wilder and wilder. They were clearing their own space. He could feel the music taking him over completely, filling him with energy, making him wild. It was a release, a release from tension, a release from terror.

He had lost track of Matt and Bethany, but as long as he had Emma within grasp, he no longer cared. If this was what death was like, why had they ever feared it? If this was death, he would live it to the full!

Whatever the celebration was for, it was something massive. For a scant moment he wondered if this was his own funeral. Certainly it was going to be breeding new life before the night was over.

Emma and he had cleared some space in the crowded room, now another woman entered it. The way she was dancing was a clear invitation, the gyrating hips, the pelvic thrusts.

Emma was a pallid competitor. Her wild gyrations were a chaotic form. The new one was far more obvious, Tasgo couldn't resist. He was right behind her, copying her every move, often a little late, because who would have thought she would ever do *that*?

A ring was forming round them, Emma on her own now and Tasgo shadowing the stranger. There would be a few choices to make, some local customs to be gauged. Were they going to perform here in front of everyone, or were there some quiet corners where they could be alone?

Suddenly the circle was scattering, and a man came through with swift strides. Tasgo could smell the anger, the hot jealousy.

The man's mouth moved, but there was no way anyone could have heard what he said above the roar of sound. Tasgo turned to him, smiling, ready, still dancing. The man was shouting words that were just noise within noise. The woman had stopped dancing, she was shouting too, at the man.

Then the man pushed Tasgo.

Dannaigh had told him, here they do not fight. He had made it clear, and so had Moira.

So Tasgo ducked, rammed a shoulder into the man's waist and came upright with the man over his shoulder. It was harder to dance with a struggling stranger on his back. The man was strong, but he was in no position to do much harm. Still dancing Tasgo made his way to the edge of the floor, where there were tables and soft chairs. Ignoring the blows to his back, he dropped the man head first into a chair and danced away back into the crowd.

In the empty centre Emma still stood, dumbfounded. The sexy dancing woman was sparking fury. She pushed Tasgo too! She was shouting, who could tell what?

Tasgo shrugged. What else had she expected? He put an arm round Emma, who looked as if she might dash off at any moment. She wasn't going to join him in dancing though. She wanted to leave their spot in the centre. She was looking round for the others.

Regretfully Tasgo turned his back on the promise of action of one sort or the other, and went with her. She and the other two were all he had. They knew Dannaigh. When he found Dannaigh all would be made clear. He would be home again, even if that were somewhere entirely new.

Emma had a better feel for this place. Of course she did. She found Matt and Bethany with no trouble. She was screeching at them, something in which the word 'nutter' filtered through rather hysterical laughter. It was Bethany who was looking in sudden alarm beyond Tasgo.

Turning, Tasgo saw again the man he had dumped at the edge of the dancefloor. He had friends. One of whom was painted, a uniform dark paint, as though it were the skin itself that was coloured so darkly.

This new adornment surprised Tasgo, but not so much that he didn't see trouble on the hoof. They had taken offence, and he didn't really blame them.

Dannaigh had been so insistent. They don't fight where he comes from. Perhaps this wasn't where he came from. But - these people knew Dannaigh. Things weren't making sense.

Still, he turned to meet the aggrieved man he had dumped, stepping in front of Bethany, so that she would be protected, but also spreading his hands to either side to show he was unarmed.

Suddenly, as if from nowhere other men were approaching from other directions.

A quick glance assessed them. Not an immediate danger. Purposeful, but not aggressive. Working together, one was turning towards Tasgo, the other towards the incoming danger. This was interesting.

'Having a good time?' asked the bouncer, with a smile, but also with a certain detachment. He was looking mostly at Tasgo, while keeping the others in view. Tasgo didn't understood the words, but he smiled back. The bouncer was taking in how drunk Emma was, she was tittering drunk, but he already knew her. Matt was new to him, and obviously a long way past sober. That left the quiet brunette and the guy with a style all his own. He looked alert and with it. He looked dangerous, but not aggressive.

'Think maybe we've had enough now?' asked the bouncer.

The brunette was gathering her stuff, she was ready to go. Matt was backing off in a very pleasing manner. Emma was pointing at the angry incomers and saying, 'He started it.' And then with a giggle, pointing at Tasgo, 'He's so funny!' Confidentially, 'He's really, really funny.'

'Maybe take him home?' suggested the bouncer, looking at Tasgo, as if the message was really for him. Tasgo understood the ushering movement of the hands. As he threw an arm round Emma's shoulders he was taking his lead from Matt and Bethany. Whatever they did, he would do.

They went, all together, not in a hurry but not hanging about.

The man he had dumped in the chair was not so easy. He was ready for a fight. They would have to leave too, but the bouncers were professionals. The two parties weren't all going to leave together. If there was going to be a fight, it would be at a distance.

Outside, Emma was finding it all too funny. 'He was dancing,' she was repeating, 'he was carrying him and dancing!' Matt, looking back, saw the other group coming out of the nightclub and looking for them.

Once again, they were running.

Ache in the Bones

May 6th 05.57 Sheffield

It was raining. He was running.

The rain slashed hard and icy at his face. He was running as if all the hounds of hell were after him. Perhaps they were. He could hear the pounding of their feet behind him. He could hear their heavy breathing. He could smell their fetid breath.

His clothes were sodden, cold and heavy. They clung to him and slowed him down.

And now the long grass was matted with heather, he had to leap and bound, and they were better at it than he was. He could feel them getting nearer, louder, more eager. He could hear the snapping of their teeth behind his heels, closer and closer. His heart pounded. He was gasping. Any moment now the fangs would catch and…

With a start he was lying in the dark. In the darkness he could see nothing. His heart hammered. He dared not breathe or move. Not a flicker that might attract – he didn't know what. He didn't know where he was. He only knew with a horrid certainty that it was not his own room, or his own flat. He knew he had been dreaming, but wasn't sure he was now awake, and if awake, where or when. In the darkness someone, or something, was lying beside him on the bed.

In one swift movement he rolled off the bed and onto his feet, ready, ready for anything.

A muffled voice came from the darkness, a woman's voice, sleepy and uncertain. 'Danny?'

It was Chrissie, girlfriend of nearly a year. This was her room, in her shared house. A bedside lamp came on and she looked at him with surprise. The bedside clock said 05:58, nearly time to get up.

Chrissie said again, 'Danny?' her voice a mixture of concern and amusement.

Alarm fled from him. He realised he was standing stark naked and dropped his hands from their fighting position. He breathed, steadying his pulse, trying for normal.

Chrissie sat up, all concern now. 'Nightmare?' she asked, warm, caring. He had done this once before, when she was less certain of him. She had been alarmed then. Now she was all careful concern.

He managed a smile. 'Sorry,' he said, adrenalin still coursing through his veins. He ached, not muscular, but deep in the bones, a feeling of loss, of duty unfulfilled.

She was holding the duvet up, in an invitation for him to return to bed. He knew she would want to comfort him, to mother him, but he knew where that would lead, and there wasn't the time, pleasant as the thought might be.

He sat on the edge of the bed, leant over and kissed her, a kiss that lingered, that promised more, until the alarm went off.

He pulled away. 'Got to run,' he said, swift but showing reluctance even as he reached for his clothes.

'Bloody task master!' she told him, falling back into the warmth of the covers. She didn't try and stop him though, and ten minutes later he was out of the door into the early morning light. Running would settle the alarm that lingered in his bones, the sense of loss that flooded back into him whenever he remembered how much he had lost, and now had to live without.

Another Day, Another World

Tasgo woke to a comfortable bed, and better still, a woman snuggled up against him. Looking beyond, he saw they were in a box, like a sleeping stall, but with a roof to it, and part of one wall was either open to the elements, or it was made of light.

Still here then, in – wherever?

The woman's hair was dark. Bethany then. Even better. She was the more sensible, she would make a good mother if they had made a child. If it was possible for him to make a child here. The room was full of strange things. Patches of brilliant colours on the walls suggested various images. An alcove off had one of those tight-fitting doors. The floor was covered in clothes and blankets and sleeping bodies, Emma and Matt. He was glad that he and Bethany had the prime spot.

He could survive here, make his way, if he had to. Better though to get back to where he belonged. If Dannaigh and Moira had done it before, it could be done.

He was wondering how the fight had finished, back on the shore near Cynmar, before the blue light had taken him. He hoped he had managed to kill his target before whatever it was that had happened, had happened.

Had the boat been taken? The crew could yield or die as they liked, but the merchant had to be taken, one way or another. He wondered what the rest of his men had seen, what they thought had happened. He wondered whether they had picked up his sword and knives, and he felt at his neck where Dannaigh's parting gift had hung every hour of his life since Dannaigh had given it to him until – this. Whatever this was. The gift was no longer there. Like his knives and his torc, it had vanished.

Bethany stirred, and he lent to kiss her shoulder. She turned drowsily, and woke with a start. Startlingly, she screamed! Not loudly, but enough to wake the others. She was pulling away, dragging the bedclothes with her, covering herself up, and looking shocked and alarmed. Surely she had not been that drunk? She had not seemed that drunk, neither drowsy nor unwilling, last night.

The others on the floor were hardly responsive, the man groaned, and the woman pulled blankets over her head.

Tasgo lay still for a moment, giving Bethany his most inviting look. She was eying his strength and muscles and taking in the scars. Tasgo thought she must have noticed them earlier, he could recall her questioning fingers exploring. But now they seemed a new, and unwelcome, wonder to her, and she was backing away among the detritus on the floor.

He sat up, throwing the cover off, and she threw some article of clothing at him to cover his nether regions.

'Bloody Nora!' she said, and without understanding the words, Tasgo gathered that was not good. He knew he had been pretty drunk last night – the drink seemed stronger than he was used to – but surely he hadn't had that much? At any rate, if he had not performed well last night, he could rectify that right now. He got up, reaching for her, and she leapt away as if he was the last one in the world that she would want. She had seemed eager enough last night, he remembered, more than willing. She had been amazing.

Why the sudden reversal? She was coy as a maiden.

With a sudden rush she was into the alcove, and through another door, unseen by him, opposite the one he could see. It slammed shut behind her.

On the floor at his feet, Emma was looking up and giggling. It had done well enough last night, but he realised that if giggling were her main asset, he could easily tire of it.

Matt muttered, 'Good god man, put it away.' Matt's head was throbbing, and the light was too strong. Worse, here was that guy from last night, as real as daylight and twice as obvious. Wherever he had come from, he was definitely still here.

Tasgo was looking around, seeing opulence, the thick bedcover, pleasing colours, though rather pale. Everything looked new, and precious. Shelves were full of strange things, and dark slabs of – something smooth and shiny - lay scattered around the place.

He found his brecks, half under the bedding, and pulled them on. His tunic was missing, probably under some of the debris on the floor. He found a couple of his carry pouches, the knife had obviously cut its way free, the pouch was a ruin. His precious scabbard had also failed to make the journey here with him.

Turning to find his tunic, he found an unnoticed opening to another room.

With a warrior in it! Dannaigh?

Not Dannaigh. The stranger saw him at the same time, had turned towards Tasgo just as he, Tasgo, had turned to him, and was assessing him, as Tasgo was too. Tasgo had no weapon, but neither did the other. A strange tingle ran down his spine. He could almost feel the magic at work. As he moved, so did the other. Exactly. He raised a hand. So did the other. He lowered it.

He was in command, it seemed. Of both of them.

He rolled across the bed, and lost sight of the other. The room through the doorway was exactly the same as this one, he could see more of it now. He lifted a handful of the blanket and pulled. He could see the blankets in the other room move too. Was he controlling the copy of himself, even when he could not see him?

He moved round the bed so that he could see his copy. It looked as curious as Tasgo felt. Cautious, he moved closer to the doorway, meeting the other there.

He had seen his own image in still water. He had seen it, distorted, in a polished metal pot. He reached out now and touched his own reflection in a plain sheet of magic.

He thought he looked formidable. A dangerous opponent, a good man to have as an ally. It was strange to see himself as others saw him. Unless the magic lied. It had all his scars right at any rate.

Enough of this, he needed to find Dannaigh. Or Moira, if she still lived. It was her name that had brought recognition in the man Matt. But that man had now subsided under the blanket on the floor. Tasgo could see a patch of his own tunic poking out from beneath Matt and Emma but decided against rousing both of them to get it. He could do that later, it was warm enough not to need it. And Bethany was already awake and up.

He stepped over their supine bodies, and tried the door through which she had gone. He could hear a strange rushing sound from beyond the door, which reminded him of mountain streams.

The handle was a simple enough lever, but the door did not open. He twisted pulled and rattled. Nothing happened. The door was closed to him. A small fear raised its head. He turned and tried the door behind him.

The handle dropped, the door opened. If he wanted, he could get out.

Stepping Out

Now that he was sure he could get out of the place he was in, Tasgo left the puzzle of the closed door through which Bethany had escaped him, and returned to look at the other two, lying on the floor. It was the man Matt who had recognised Dannaigh's and Moira's names. Now Matt had pulled some sort of blanket over his head and was feigning sleep. Tasgo guessed the man had a headache, he knew he did, but that was no excuse. He gave a gentle kick to get Matt's attention. It only brought him a groan.

As Matt tried to snuggle back into oblivion Tasgo noticed one of his own shoes sticking out from the tangle of arms and legs, and yanked it out, moulding it back to a foot shape. A single strand of leather indicated the other, so he grabbed that too, and sat on the bed to put them on, with Matt directly below him on the floor.

Last night had been a mixture of horror and elation, of dread and hope. As he put on the shoes he was trying to work it all out, but it still made no sense. After the sheer terror of the invisible box of his arrival, the celebration and the noise, the wild running together, none of it made sense.

He was still unsure whether it had been his own funeral he was attending, a celebration of his life. He didn't feel dead. He felt very much alive, even if he was Underhill. Well, if he was dead, he was dead, and it was time to make his way here in Underhill. And if he wasn't dead, he had to find a way back. His only hope was to find friends, Dannaigh and Moira. Even Ken would do. They would explain, they would show him the way to get back to where he belonged. Unless of course he really was dead. Either way, he needed their help, and it seemed Matt was his main hope.

Emma was stirring now, sitting up, pulling her clothes into shape, trying to ignore Tasgo as she did so.

Tightening the lace to pull the shoe round his foot properly, Tasgo smiled at her. *'Dannaigh Sharp?'* he prompted.

Emma was more concerned with sorting herself out, so he prodded her lightly with his foot, and asked again.

'Whatever,' was her response as she got up from the floor. It was Matt she was more interested in. 'Thanks for an interesting evening,' she said bitterly, tossing aside blankets, looking for her shoes. The giggles of last night were replaced by hangover, and possibly regret.

Tasgo found this unhelpful. It was not how he was used to being treated, but then, he was now Under the Hill, and everything was different here. Dugal had said so, Gamma had said so, and Dannaigh had shown it in his ignorance, being habitually out of step with the world above. Tasgo certainly found everything here extremely confusing. Now he had his shoes on, however, he felt ready for whatever this world would bring. It was time to take control.

Emma had found what she was looking for, was putting shoes on her feet and was obviously planning to leave. Tasgo stepped into her path. Smiling, he asked once more for Dannaigh Sharp. She should have noticed the way he was asking, expecting an answer. She barely glanced at him.

'No idea,' she told him and tried to push past.

He didn't push back, he was a guest here. He merely blocked her passage.

He tried *'Moira Alter?'* He was still smiling. She looked at him then.

'I have no idea,' she told him, shortly, 'and care even less. Right now I need a shower, and a change of clothes, so I'm going home.'

Except Tasgo was still in her way. These three were the only hope he had of finding Dannaigh. Bethany had already escaped him, there was no way he was going to let either of these two get away from him until he had found Dannaigh, or Moira.

Emma was nettled at being baulked.

'Shove off,' she told Tasgo, trying to edge round him, beginning to lose her temper, because he was always there, however she moved. With seemingly no effort he was blocking her path, and not even looking at her. He was looking down at Matt and saying the list of names again. He had no doubt that Dannaigh and Moira were important here. The fact that Matt had recognised them last night proved it true.

Emma tried to push Tasgo aside. He looked at her then, no longer smiling. His left arm went swift round her waist pulling her tight to him, moving her feet a staggered step towards him. She gave a startled gasp, leaning back, trying to escape him. His left foot stepped forward between hers and he moved his weight firmly onto it, sending her backwards and letting go with his arm at the same time. The body push was slight, but her weight was no longer over her feet. She toppled and fell, shocked, onto the jumbled blanket. Tasgo stood over her, looking back at Matt, waiting for an answer.

Matt ignored Emma's resentful screech, her babbling about assault, calling on Matt for protection. Matt had a much clearer view of his position. He could see the scars on Tasgo's chest and arms, sure signs of someone who was used to things getting physical. He had seen the efficiency in Tasgo's push. He lay where he was, pulling protective thicknesses of material over his body. He was apologising for not understanding what Tasgo wanted.

Tasgo appreciated the compliance of position and tone, but he could tell that the gush of words was not a positive answer. The lack of a common language was going to be a problem.

He sat on the bed. He needed Matt as a willing helper, not feeling threatened, but knowing his place, as helper. The woman was going to prove more difficult, she was getting to her feet, indignant. He kept her in sight as he went through the list of names again, one by one, slowly, watching Matt's response to each.

Emma made a dash for the door – at least, that had been her intention. Once again the interloper was in her path, standing in her way. She gave him a piece of her mind, and another shove, though this time she was stronger in her stance. When he closed in to lay hands on her she tried to slap his face. So hitting was allowed as well. He didn't retaliate in kind, it wasn't necessary. He merely blocked the blow, scooped her up in his arms, moved her across where Matt lay, and deposited her in the corner farthest from the door. She would have to clamber over Matt or the bed to get out, easy to control.

Tasgo sat down again, picking up his tunic now revealed where Emma had been. As he pulled the tunic on, he was trying to work out how to make Matt understand the urgency of his need to find his friends. The woman was sounding more determined, she had taken a white slab from her bag and was waving it at him. It didn't look like a weapon he should worry about, but he was alert to it.

As Bethany came out of the shower, wrapped in a towel, Emma was snarling, with an element of fear in it, 'You let me out of here right now, or I'm calling the police.' It was Matt who was looking scared at the prospect.

Bethany grabbed clothes from a drawer, saying as she did so, 'Don't be daft.' The sooner the shenanigans of last night were put aside and forgotten, the better. She could see Tasgo eyeing her appreciatively as she did so.

'What?' she asked, as if she couldn't see exactly what the matter was, sitting there and enjoying the sight of her with the faintest of smiles. Both Matt and Emma started to answer her, so she raised a hand.

'Be back in two shakes,' she told them, disappearing back into the shower.

Danny felt a little easier now; Bethany had not run off, and she looked even lovelier with her hair wet and smelling of – of pleasant things. It didn't solve his problem though, how to tell them what he needed when the mere names were not enough.

He concentrated on Matt, but kept an eye on Emma who was the more likely to cause problems. He pointed to each of them and himself, with their names. He said *'Bethany,'* and pointed to where they had just seen her, and then mimed shading his eyes from the sun while looking all about for *'Dannaigh Sharp?'*

Matt was not concentrating on the mime, he was sneakily looking for his own clothes. He would rather be dressed when trouble erupted, or the police arrived. Last night he had hoped that morning would bring release from the deeds of the night. Now he could see he was deep in trouble, and it wasn't going to go away. Whoever, or whatever, this was, the thing from the swamp was here. He was trouble, and it was all Matt's fault. He found his shirt and tried nonchalantly to slide an arm into a sleeve whilst looking as though he wasn't doing anything at all. The thing from the swamp snatched it from him, with a firm *'Dannaigh Sharp.'*

'How should I know!' he protested. His head was hurting and he couldn't think straight. He needed a drink, water would do, his mouth tasted like a sewer.

Bethany emerged from the bathroom again, pulling a tee shirt down over jeans, looking great. She would have liked to brush her hair, but it wasn't important. She wasn't feeling proud of herself, one-night stand was hardly a bad enough description. It was a relief to think that she had washed all that away, along with the night of madness. She was feeling strangely alive but also ashamed. She hardly knew the man. She was aware she was dealing with that side of things rather than facing the worst of the reality.

She still had no idea what had really happened in the bowels of the library. She could still feel the shock of seeing the man appear in a flare of blue light. She could still remember the panic that had shown in that man, and transferred itself to her. That remembered feeling wasn't going to go away, but, in the sober morning light, she knew that for Tasgo it had been real. Absolute panic. Something was very wrong. And Matt had made it happen.

Also, she was going to have to run to make the hockey practice this morning, and she really didn't want to disgrace herself for a second time in 24 hours.

'Right,' she said, looking at Tasgo. He wasn't in a panic now. He looked very much in command of himself. She felt something lurch inside her. A tangible attraction, which she wasn't going to give in to. Tasgo was making his mime again of searching for Dannaigh Sharp. His lack of English was obvious. She thought she understood what he was trying to convey and nodded, before making sure of it. She repeated the name pointing, ending with Tasgo and then pointed away shading her eyes and saying, 'You're looking for this Dannay Sharp?'

Tasgo nodded back, pleased. It seemed he was getting somewhere.

'How do you spell that?' she asked. Seeing no response she shook her head. 'You don't speak any English do you?' she asked, getting a puzzled blank look. 'Not a word? Polish?' she tried, 'Romanian, Hungarian,

Dutch? French, Italian, Spanish?' in desperation, trying to make a joke of it, 'Venezuelan?'

Tasgo had no idea what she was asking him. They could all see that.

'Right,' she said, decisively. 'Dan A Sharp.' Tasgo watched as she turned briskly to a shelf, opened up one of the larger black slabs, hinging it up to reveal a smooth vertical surface, and a base full of strange sigils. Her fingers moved like summer lightning over the shapes. The vertical surface blossomed into colour with a little tinkly musical sound.

Tasgo felt a tingling sensation pass through him. This was magic. This was Underhill, the secrets his grandmother Gamma knew, though he had never seen her do anything as strange as this.

The screen filled with strange twisted shapes that made no sense to him, more sigils perhaps. He wanted to slam the slabs back together, to stop this happening. He was afraid, he didn't know what they were or why they seemed so dangerous.

Now suddenly the upright slab was covered in colour, with tiny images of people's faces. She turned to him. 'There,' she said, 'Dan Sharp, all of them. Which one is yours?'

Tasgo stared at her, at them. He felt cold, and alarmed.

She beckoned him. He didn't want to go near her, or it. He didn't want to appear weak or foolish either. She was standing there, quite at ease, but then she was in control of – whatever it was. Supposing that these were all the spirits of people, trapped there in the slab?

Bethany took pity on him, maybe he was stupid? That would explain why he had no English at all. He didn't look stupid though. She beckoned to him again, 'Dan Sharp,' she said pointing to the pictures.

Could Dannaigh's spirit somehow be inside this black thing, so small? Tasgo made himself move closer. Lines and lines of faces, in rows. None of them Dannaigh. He didn't know whether to be disappointed or relieved.

She moved slightly, and suddenly these faces flew up the screen and were replaced by others. Some of them were hideous, the stuff of nightmares, monsters. Most of them weren't. None of them showed the face he was so desperately seeking. The images shifted again so suddenly he found it hard to focus. Matt and Emma had moved closer behind him, he had few worries about them. He knew they were no real danger, and

34

he could reach the door faster, should they try an escape. But they seemed as mesmerised as he was by the rows of faces.

'Let's try Danny Sharp,' suggested Bethany, fingers flying over the keyboard. A new set, rack after rack of tiny faces. Too many images, too fast for Tasgo. He was scared that these were spirits, or people somehow trapped, he was scared what all this sudden movement might be doing to them. Suddenly his eye lighted on a face. As words leapt to his lips, it dashed upwards and was gone, replaced with others.

'Yes!' he cried, pointing and then looking above the screen as if that would be where it was now.

Bethany scrolled them back more slowly, until Tasgo pointed. 'There!' he shouted. There it was. Dannaigh's face, older than he had been the last time Tasgo had seen him. Not surprising, seeing the amount of time that had passed. Dannaigh had filled out, his character was blazoned on his face, a strong face, intelligent, wilful, decisive. Only too sensitive. Tasgo remembered his own face, seen in the magic sheet of material earlier. It was easy to see the two of them were related. The same colour hair, the same structure to the bones, only Dannaigh had a touch of the wild about him still.

Something moved onto the surface of the image and suddenly Dannaigh's face seemed to fill the screen, still too small to be real, but real enough for Tasgo to reach out his hand as if to touch the flesh and make it real.

'Second-year student Sheffield, paramedic course,' proclaimed Bethany, words that meant nothing to Tasgo. A moment later the screen went black, and Bethany was standing up. 'Sheffield,' she told him, slamming the two slabs back into one, 'that's where you should be.' She transferred her gaze to Matt and Emma, 'I'm off,' she said, 'Hockey practice.' She narrowed her gaze to Matt. 'This is your doing,' she told him, 'you sort it!'

Tasgo liked the authority in her voice. She moved quickly towards the alcove, picking up a small bag and a large one. She was going to leave – to find Dannaigh?

Bethany saw Tasgo coming after her. She couldn't have that. Not with the hockey crew. They'd leap to conclusions. He'd be in the way. She'd never live it down. And it was Matt's problem, his doing.

She stopped, putting both bags into one hand. 'You,' she told Tasgo, jabbing a finger at his chest, 'stay,' with a jab at Matt, 'here.'

Tasgo smiled, looking quizzical, and came closer. She told him again, more clearly. She used the universal hunter's signs for 'stay' and 'sit' or 'stay low' as she spoke. She was authoritive. Tasgo liked that. He also knew what to do with women who thought they were in control. He said *'Yes, sweetheart,'* and took a submissive pace away from her. Emma giggled, there was a vindictive edge to it.

Satisfied, Bethany turned and went out. Tasgo was a half-step behind her as she went through the door.

One woman who knew what she was doing, who had, in moments, shown him Dannaigh's face, was worth a dozen Matts.

She stopped. He had known she would. He moved a half-step back, a grin on his face, daring her to try and stop him. It was a gentle grin, a playful one, he liked her and wished her no harm. At least that was what he hoped it conveyed. He could see it was less than convincing. She told him again, trying for stern, that he should go back.

With a gentle tilt of his head to the side he let her know he understood. Then he signed to her, she and he, would go together to find *'Dannaigh Sharp.'*

'No,' she told him, and then used the signs again as she told him to go back. His smile faded, but he looked patient.

She dropped the bags. 'You,' she told him, miming to the words, 'go back in there. Stay! I go, I come back. You stay.'

He cocked his head, patient, not moving. She picked up the bags, she understood now that he wasn't going back, that he was going to follow her out. She wondered whether he was pretending not to understand. She wondered just how ignorant he was. She led the way out of the flat, Tasgo close enough behind her to hold the door open for her and follow her through. He was glad she had given in so easily, though he had expected more resistance.

On the landing by the lift, at the head of the stairs they had climbed last night, or rather, earlier this morning, she stopped, looking out through the windows that lined the stairwell to the green space beyond with various paths through it. She took Tasgo's arm, and pointed out and beyond, while standing close to the lift doors. Behind both their backs, she pressed the button to call the lift.

Through the windows, the campus edge was laid out below them. To her right the building that held the student union, which she pointed out to him. At last the lift began to whirr, it was always slow, probably to encourage students to take the stairs and keep fit. She had only used it once, to bring all her bags and stuff up when she moved in. Now she was miming to him that they would make their way along the path below, into the campus proper, and then turn right.

Behind them the lift reached their floor with a grinding sound, and a ding, and the doors began to open. Tasgo heard the sound and looked, his hackles rising.

The solid metal wall, a great expanse of metal which he had already seen and marvelled that it had only one seam down its shiny surface, was splitting open. The metal was vanishing, dissolving as the gap widened! But now he could see that it was not entirely magic, the metal was in two parts, sliding away from each other, though where it was going, given the solid wall on either side, was a mystery. That must be where the vanishing or dissolving was really taking place.

One step gave him a view of what was beyond the door. A small room, the size of a sleeping stall, free of any furniture, entirely empty. Nothing to be alarmed at, he told himself, fighting down alarm.

Bethany was tugging at his sleeve, turning him back to the view as though the steel wall and the revealed room were of no concern at all. 'There' she told him, pointing energetically at the sheer edge of a building, a solid block of stone. Then *'there'* using his own excited word when he had seen Dannaigh's face. Try as he might, Tasgo could see nothing but a huge block of stone, a vertical cliff, and the parched grass on the ground beyond. She came behind him, so that she could point over his shoulder more accurately, to show him – what? He could see nothing of interest. Behind him he could hear once more the sounds of the moving walls, and at the same time he realised that Bethany was gone.

Turning, he saw the metal sliding back together across the entrance of the small room, enclosing Bethany inside it. He leapt forward, but she had timed it right. For a split second she thought he was going to thrust himself into the closing gap, but fear inhibited him, he was too slow. The doors had shut, the lift purred.

Tasgo hurled himself at the metal, his fingers thrust vainly at the edge between the two pieces of metal. There was no purchase. Friction alone was not enough to tear them apart. The sound of his wild effort, pounding at the metal as if it would give way to him, echoed down the lift shaft. Bethany remembered the wild fury of his panic when he had appeared within the glass cubical, the strength with which he had hurled himself against the walls. Luckily his assault now entirely covered the sound of the doors opening for her on the ground floor, and of Bethany stepping cautiously out in case Tasgo would hear and come racing down the stairs towards her.

Finding both the hall and stairs free of danger, she raced to the outer door, and then out on the path that led neither to the Union nor to the playing fields where she would shortly be.

Back at the top of the stairs, Tasgo stopped wasting energy on the metal. It was a small room, there had been no other way in or out. She would be coming out soon. He only had to wait. But this was Underhill, a place of light and magic, or so Dugal had said. He glanced back at the door to the flat, now closed behind him. He looked down the stairs, to the path she had indicated they would use. Still empty and silent.

Then he glimpsed her, the only moving thing, not where she had said they should go, an entirely different direction, running out of sight under trees. How had she managed that?

He spared a tiny glance at the doors to the small room that should have held her, but already his feet were on the move. He flew down the stairs, leaping them three or four at a time, hurling himself round corners, keeping it under control, a fall would not be good now, down to the bottom. The lever on the door held him up for seconds, and then he was through, off and running in the open air, eating up the space between him and her.

The path finished at one of those hard, dark surfaces, the sort they had run over during the night, the sort that the weird thing flashing blue had glided down so effortlessly.

Bethany was not there, not in sight anywhere.

38

She had told him to turn right so he turned left, still running fast. There would be no tracking her down in this landscape. It was like hard stone. She would keep to the hard stone. His heart was hammering, because she had tricked him, she had fooled him, and if he lost her...

Well, he knew the way back to the place he had been, where Emma and Matt still were. A poor fall-back position.

Stroke

60 miles away, to the west of Sheffield, mist was rising off Damflask reservoir, but that would soon burn off. Danny was still warm from his five-mile run to meet the bus, but now getting out of it into the cool air meant he needed to keep moving to keep warm. While he was getting the blades down to the water's edge, the others were stretching and arranging their bags or taking a swig from water bottles, but coming naturally together in their various rowing teams. The warm-up was short and easy, by the time they went back for the boats they were all ready, the team moving together without words to their positions to lift the long shell off its rack and carry it down to the water. Chas gave the familiar orders and they held the hull out and let it drop gentle into the water. Danny and Chas held it while the others picked up their oars and stepped nimbly into position in the boat. Chrissie stepped lightly into the cox's position, and Danny, as stroke today, got in to sit facing her, their knees almost touching as they exchanged a private smile. Chrissie hadn't run the five miles he had, the bus had picked her up from the same door Danny had left twenty minutes earlier.

Now they pushed off from the edge and floated out into water singing its liquid song against the hull, the distant call of a curlew sharp on the air, a feeling of readiness, of expectancy as the eight rowers became one team. From the bank Chas gave them the orders of the day, and Chrissie brought the loudspeaker to her mouth.

'Number off when ready,' brought the numbers one to eight from the appropriate mouths. 'Whole crew, from backstops, are you ready?' brought a slight shuffle from somewhere up the hull, rocking as someone shifted weight. A light breeze had taken them off the landing point and they were ready. 'Paddling light,' Chrissie commanded, 'Go!' And they were off.

Danny was concentrating on his stroke, trying to get it perfect, and the tempo even. He had practiced being stroke on land, but this was the first time they were asking him to take the position. He knew he was being tested, assessed. They wouldn't be thinking of making him a regular stroke, his technique wasn't good enough. Besides he was the shortest member of the team, the others were all six footers. His place was lightweight, in the bow, being an engine. So trying him out as stroke today might mean they were considering him for the first team. His eyes met Chrissie's, and she looked encouragement at him, she was calling the strokes.

Lost

Tasgo stopped running. He had lost her, she had eluded him, and he was lost. He was feeling dizzy from finding the same vista every time he turned a corner. Built boxes that stood in lines facing each other, every one the same, only the flat grey ground holding them apart. It went on and on for ever, a magical maze, always the same, no trees, no open meadows.

He had lost her, his main hope. And now he was trapped in this riot of recurring images, identical at every turn.

The sliding metal and the small room revealed, yet another box, were still in his mind. How could she have gone, unseen, from that to where he had seen her, outside, running?

He would be more careful next time. If he was given a next time. She had escaped him, she couldn't do that twice.

He tried to retrace his steps, but he must have made some error. He didn't arrive back at that cliff which held Bethany's sleeping place. He felt dizzy from all the tracks and corners, all the buildings always subtly different, in essence the same. Worse, those monstrous chariots which could move by themselves were sleeping along one side of the hard tracks which ran between the buildings. He had seen one roar suddenly into life and move off, thankfully away from him. An image leapt into his mind of the impossible thing that had glided past in the night, the low thrum of its voice echoing, the bright coloured lights that reflected everywhere, as if it were more than a thing, as if it leaked into the darkness, was part of it. He told himself as he jogged past other resting vehicles that the smooth grey stuff was merely a track, a road, made smooth and hard. Seeing the vehicle glide away, it was no wonder the track was dark.

He told himself he needn't panic. He wasn't lost. He had come a limited distance.

Matt and Emma might still be in that place where he had woken, if only he could find it again.

He pictured the size of the rooms he had been in, and the height of the building. How many more nests might there be on that tall cliff, like seagulls on their ledges, but hemmed in, enclosed, in boxes, big boxes? He stopped looking at the surrounding buildings, letting his mind reach out through all the turns and straight running he had done. He felt his way through them, feeling dizzy yet again, back to the source, the start, getting a feel for which direction to go. He turned and faced that way.

Keeping that direction in his mind, he padded off, back the way he had come, down roads oblique to his purpose, making every turn bring him back towards that invisible line that connected him to Bethany's sleeping quarters.

As he ran, he looked for trees, they would be taller than the inevitable buildings which still surrounded him. He looked above the buildings, relieved at last to see their tops in the distance, with the promise of green grass, and deep shadows.

Arriving at the next junction, he found at last a more natural scene, but not the one he had been hoping for. There were trees, true, and grass, but beyond them no tall cliff of nesting boxes. Instead a lower wall, another building, half hidden by shrubs and trees. He moved forward, crossing the dark road, onto the grass, into the shade. The building ahead wasn't as tall, but it was huge. He walked towards it.

Druids had once told him the ancients had built huge temples of stone, capped them over with stone roofs. He had not imagined that they would be as big as this. The walls were not of large stones, as described, but of small ones, orange-brown in colour, put together in complex patterns. Large square surfaces of magic, something clear as water, solid as steel were built into the design.

Worse, to one side, at a distance through the shade of large and ancient trees, the strange monsters of the night were prowling on what must be another track. No flashing lights, no beaming eyes pinning down their prey. He recognised in their growling movement the source of the background hum, the movement of air, the purr and growl of their passing. There must be hundreds of them, though only a few were visible, passing at frightening speed beyond the trunks of trees. They moved like individual members of a herd, keeping to their aligned path, their natural territory.

Even from here Tasgo could see it was not a track like the ones he had just been running on. It must be wider, larger. He had not crossed anything like that this morning, so the place he was searching for must be this side of it. But last night, heady from drink, and dancing, and running together, and being chased, last night they had crossed a wide road, dark in the darkness. They had crossed one or two like that, maybe three or four, he had been intent on keeping with the people who had recognised Dannaigh's and Moira's names, and everything had seemed strange and disjointed and impossible, full of shifting lights and dark spaces, shapes that made no sense.

But they had crossed a space like that, and after a period of dark shadows and distant music, they had come to their point of respite, the safety of closed box rooms in a cliff dwelling. He moved, parallel to the road, looking for any clue as to where they might have crossed, if indeed they had.

People passed on other paths among the massive buildings, the grass, the trees, but he waited for a lone person. At last one came, walking slowly, head down. He seemed to be caressing a small stone tablet.

Tasgo wandered into his path, but the man seemed not to see him, was going to step round him without even noticing, even as Tasgo was speaking. Finding Tasgo still there before him, blocking his way, he looked up, a little startled.

'Greetings,' began Tasgo, carefully polite, 'I am looking for Dannaigh Sharp. Matt or even Emma would do. Bethany?'

He got what he had expected, a total lack of understanding. He saw that the piece of stone in the stranger's hands was as smooth as the one Bethany had used, and glowed white, with black squiggles. The man, young but scrawny, not a warrior, never looked directly at Danny, didn't seem to hear the words. He stepped to one side, thumb paused over the screen, and nodded back the way he had come, and mumbled something, moving on, texting again. Tasgo had the feeling that he was already totally forgotten, had never really been noticed. The words he hadn't understood, the nod of a head was hardly significant.

He was horribly aware that he might never find his way back. He was trying to tamp down rising panic and make a new plan, to find instead the place where he had arrived in this strange place.

He knew it would be by water, because last night he had seen reflections, smelt the sea air, heard the slap of waves. The land seemed flat, so there was no downhill, but he guessed East, and South, as it would be in Cynmar. That meant he would have to cross the wide track, with its monsters.

That was a real problem. He was amazed at the speed of the things moving along it. He knew now they were not monsters, he had seen the wheels. No horse to pull them, nothing to push them. What could there be that could even keep up with them? It could only be magic. He had seen the people trapped inside, enclosed entirely. They brought back to him the chaos of the previous night, the terror and the amazement. His nerves were already jangled, putting him on edge. He would have liked to move further away, to be out of sight of them, but he knew that he would have to cross this to find his way back to where he should be.

He treated the track like a river, one dangerous to cross. He walked along the nearer bank, under the cool safety of the trees, looking for a place to try his luck. Speed was going to be his only chance.

His eyes gauged distances, brain disbelieving the speeds. As his feet hit the tarmac the distant car was suddenly almost on him. Heart hammering, his legs pistoned him forwards, horns blared, he felt the air blast him, the vehicle brushing past so close as he cleared the first lane and belted into the second. Screeching brakes, howling horns, he hurled himself clear and kept running into the empty space beyond, hurdled a wall into greenery, raced past the building behind it, to the back, leaping high to grasp the sharp-edged planked fence, forcing it downwards as he soared over it.

Breathing heavily he stopped in a green space. Behind him was the snarling sound of disappointed monsters, the crunch of metal, followed by voices raised in anger or dismay. He held his hand out to see the physical effects of near destruction. He was trembling.

He remembered then how Dannaigh had so often seemed out of step, how he failed to recognise the most obvious threats, and so often seemed afraid for no reason. Now he could see the difference between

Underhill and real life, he realised how much he had underestimated Dannaigh. He was beginning to wonder whether he could cope as well as Dannaigh had. But then, Dannaigh had had Tasgo to help him through. Once Tasgo had found Dannaigh, things here would be easier.

With a fence between him and apparent mayhem behind him, Tasgo walked away from it all, down a narrow path between a building and another fence, out onto a quieter trackway for those scary vehicles. Forcing himself to walk not run, he moved forward. He would search out the sea's edge, he would find the place where he had fallen into the chaos of this world.

Coming out onto another of those wider roads, with vehicles of various sizes pelting past him, he fought dismay. But even as he was trying to summon up reserves of courage to try and cross, the vehicles were slowing, all of them. Not far from him at either side of the black track, people had gathered, and now as the vehicles stopped people on foot surged across the road in safety.

Tasgo hurried to follow suit, taking advantage of this miraculous halting of high speed. He darted across the open black space before him, weaving through the static but growling vehicles beyond. Reaching the safety of the edged paving beyond, he had time to see the white stripes on the road where the people had crossed. How this magic worked he had no idea, he was just thankful for a safe crossing. He was silently calling on all the gods to help him find Dannaigh or Moira or Ken soon. He could feel the way the air itself was wearing him down, the smells that caught in his throat, the noise unceasing, the complete senselessness of everything. The wild joys of last night had not extinguished the terror of what had preceded it. He was drowning in magic. For a brief while it had seemed that Bethany was a rock to which he could cling. But already he had lost that one hope.

Hardening himself to the task, he made his way South and East. Throughout Parisi territory one thing was sure, if you went South and East for long enough, you would come to the sea. He put his trust in that being true Underhill as well. All he was finding was higher and larger buildings, everything hard-edged and stony.

As luck would have it, as he made his way through quieter streets, avoiding traffic and people, he was coming very close to the marina,

46

where they had been last night. And as luck would have it, P.C. Tony Parker was just coming out of the bar where they had drunk wine so wildly. The barman of last night was with him, as P.C Parker was explaining that, of course, they would do their best, but the likelihood of finding the instigators of the near riot last night was pretty small, although they did have Matt Davies' name.

But the barman, looking over the policeman's shoulder, said, 'That's one of them,' pointing. And there he was, exactly as described, though possibly a little less imposing than the image Tony Parker had got from the bar staff. IC1 male, 1.7 metres, stocky and strong, light brown hair in plaits close to his head, but somehow not dreadlocks, the outlandish clothing with added tatters. They might have mentioned the odd footwear, but then, inside a crowded bar, shoes didn't show so much.

Tasgo heard the policeman's shout. It sounded like a command. The man was coming towards him with negligent purpose rather than attack, but after last night Tasgo was ready for anything. The man looked dark, dressed in clothing of a uniformly dark hue, bluish in colour, with many carry pouches, which made him look bigger. Some of the things attached to him might serve as weapons, but there seemed to be no sword or knife. He was bulky, he was walking strongly towards Tasgo, but slowing now as he approached. His voice seemed casual when he spoke, but there was authority behind it. He was asking a question. He was the nearest thing to a warrior, or what passed for one here.

Tasgo stopped, shoulders squared, ready for him, pleased to have found someone who surely would know the people he was asking for, or at least know of them.

Though he carried no weapon, and wore no torc, Tasgo spoke as one chief to the emissary of another, with his right hand flat against his left shoulder, showing himself used to weaponry, but not about to use it. *'I am Tasgo Aed, son of Aod, son of Dugal Dragon slayer,'* he told the man, making a single friendly step towards him as he went on less formally, *'I am looking for Dannaigh Sharp, or Moira Alter.'* He knew the words would not be understood, he made sure the names stood out.

'You're Dannaigh Sharp?' the police officer asked; there had been a confusion of names from the barman, but he recognised this one.

Hearing the name picked out, relief flooded through Tasgo. *'Yes,'* he said, *'I am kin to Dannaigh Sharp, do you know where he is?'*

The constable heard affirmation and a repeat of the name. His luck was in, the suspect had practically walked into his arms. Better to be cautious though, this was a big bloke, built for action and looking ready for it, though his voice was polite. 'Thought so - interesting clobber, mate,' said P.C. Parker, keeping things calm and friendly. Dropping mild amusement, he went on, 'You were here last night, weren't you? Group of you? Good night out, eh?' He gestured towards the frontage of the bar behind him, and the man standing there.

Tasgo didn't recognise the place. Without the bright lights and loud music, it was now a dull dead building like all the rest. It bore no relation to the wild place of celebration that Tasgo remembered. Though, looking at the barman, he might have seen that man before. But his nerves had been jangled, the weirdness of everything had made it all swim together and blur in his memory. Only the sharp sense of bewilderment, confusion, fear and alarm remained certain in his mind.

He kept to the most important thing, *'Dannaigh Sharp,'* Tasgo said, and used his hand to point out the meaning, *'You, take me to Dannaigh Sharp.'* He did it with a friendly smile, as if he would at once be obeyed.

'I'm PC Parker,' Tony Parker answered, not too worried about the confusing mime and filling in his name just in case that was what was wanted, keeping the talk relaxed, friendly. His partner was standing half way between Tony and the bar and was speaking to his radio on his shoulder as PC Parker invited Danny to join him with, 'Let's sort this out.'

Tasgo kept a distance between them. He was eyeing up the second man, younger and possibly fitter than the first. Not far away, as if hiding, the nose of a police car stuck out from behind the building. Tasgo could see the wheels, he could see the blue and yellow markings on the car. He made a guess at the flashing lights, and the ones that pinned down the target.

The second police officer sauntered towards him, ready to flank Tasgo on the other side. Tasgo still smiled. He raised a hand to shield his eyes from a sun that was hidden and asked again, *'Dannaigh Sharp?'* Then to make it absolutely clear he tapped his own chest, *'Tasgo Aed'* then pointing at the first warrior, gave him the name of *'Peasy Parker'* and then looked out once more for *'Dannaigh Sharp'*

Each of them was reconfiguring their thoughts.

'You're not Danny then?' Tony Parker concluded.

The other policeman said laconically, 'Fits the description.' The description included the loose trousers, the long top with tatters, though not the funny footwear. It also said 5'10" muscular build, could be armed and dangerous. All of that looked true too, he could see why, at night, the man might have seemed taller than he was.

Tasgo explained again, in friendly but unyielding fashion, that it was Dannaigh he was looking for, with the now familiar mime.

Parker was looking thoughtful. 'Do you speak English?' he asked. And then, 'Englesi?' Then, as Bethany had, he tried a few possible places his suspect might come from. To no avail.

'You know Dannaigh?' Tasgo asked heavily. He thought they must. He could not see Moira being unknown, nor Dannaigh. Dannaigh had been ignorant, above ground, but he had potential. No-one could ignore Dannaigh. In ten seasons Danny must have made his mark, was probably a chief, or maybe a Druid, who could tell.

'Could do him for petty theft,' the second policeman said judiciously, coming closer.

'Got any I.D.?' Tony Parker tried, 'Papers? Driving licence?' while taking a step towards Tasgo, hand out ready to catch an arm, take the suspect under control.

Tasgo understood the movement. He stepped away, out of reach. He put up a hand, palm towards the second man, a clear order for him to keep his distance. He kept attention on Peasy Parker, and tried once more, giving the names of *'Moira Alter'* and *'Ken Keeper of the lore'* as well as that of Dannaigh. It had no effect.

It was a quiet Sunday morning, and they were quite close to the town police station. A few words on the radio had worked. A second police car swept in behind Tasgo.

No lights flashed at him, but he recognised the shape and the colour. Alarm flashed through him like the slash of a sword. It coursed through his veins to all parts of his body bringing power and readiness all the way to his fingertips. He made two careful steps away, drawing the two men in blue after him as if attached by invisible cords. The policeman's command to stay where he was meant nothing to him, no more than the background hum of a city on a sleepy Sunday morning. His eyes were all on the monstrous vehicle as it spread wings to either side. Men appeared as from under those wings, apparently growing in size as they stood, men dressed in the same heavy blue, with pouches and pockets and possible weapons. The wings closed with heavy clunks. The men started to walk forward, with the unhurried pace of warriors taking in the situation. Were they merely men? They had come from the monster as if spawned by it.

Men or monsters, he wasn't going to panic.

Four of them. One too many, if they had weapons, but... if magic were involved?

His heart was hammering out a war beat, ready for anything.

Tasgo turned to Peasy Parker, but didn't speak, he let his hands set it out. You and me, they said, then a shrug and a spread suggested that was acceptable. They stabbed at the new comers and their vehicle and gave a decisive rejection, both hands pushing their presence away. He was watching Parker's face, keeping the others in the edge of his vision. Parker understood what he meant, but it wasn't going to happen like that, it was in his face.

The men were coming closer.

Tasgo wasn't going to be taken. He bolted, and suddenly they were all running, closing in on him.

Fast Foot

Tasgo was obviously fitter than his pursuers. Two of them gave up almost immediately. Peasy Parker was the most determined, but Tasgo was pulling away from him with ease. As he powered along the streets panic was beginning to fade. He did not know who they were or what they wanted with him, but he recognised an attempt to take him. The men in blue had latched onto him, like warriors onto their prey. He wondered what it was about him had made them pick on him to attack. He even weighed, as he ran, the possibility that being taken might be the quickest way to find those in control here, people who would undoubtable know Dannaigh and his family. But being taken by them wouldn't be the best way to find those in charge. Until he knew better what was going on, who they were, he would not give in to them. It was easy to escape capture. Only Peasy Parker was behind him now, falling ever further behind.

Suddenly a police car swam into view ahead of him, flashing dangerous blue light. The same pattern of blue and yellow, the same one as before or another one? He couldn't tell. It had to be another one, there was no way the ones he had left behind could have got so far ahead of him. He came to a stop, looking back beyond Peasy Parker. There was only the one vehicle there, its half-hidden snout still peeking out from where it had been hiding at the start. The second one it seemed, miraculously, was now ahead of him, and swimming towards him. Peasy Parker was slowing now, obviously getting his breath back before coming closer.

Tasgo looked about him. He still had a moment in which to make decisions. He saw trees and a glimpse of green grass. Turning, he sprinted towards terrain on which, Lugh help him he hoped he was right, the flashing monster could not travel. He raced across a wide section of that dangerous dark track, and into a green space, where people walked as though there were no dangers, no horrors, no warriors who might attack. Wailing rang in his ears, following.

Changing direction he ran on, legs and heart pounding different rhythms of urgency. He leapt a raised bed of bushy plants, sped across more tarmac and into the gaping mouth of a narrow alley, which swallowed him. A narrower alley, a mere slit between huge buildings, offered protection, and he jinked into it, running as if his life depended on it, which it might well do. It opened into a different sort of track, made of stone, on which walked people without care or fear on their faces. He joined them. Glancing back into that narrow cleft, no pursuit followed him. He walked for a short while among those loitering, not one of whom seemed to have any task or work to hasten them on. Getting his breath back, he picked up pace to something that he could keep up for miles, for hours if necessary.

The city swallowed him.

At first he ran at random, not knowing where he should go or what to do next. Eventually he came into another green space, this one a patchwork of differing crops, each section hardly enough to feed a single person let alone a family. It was a sign of reality he had not expected. Relief was intense, but he remained cautious. He lay down on one of the green paths between the plots, invisible amongst the taller plants. Looking at them he realised they were all as alien as the man-made terrain everywhere else. Whiskery plants that smelled sweet, strange fruit, smooth green and round, smelling of dangerous poisons, none of them anything like the crops of his home land.

He realised he was hungry, but he was not tempted by anything here. That whisper was still in his head, a thousand years. He needed to get back. He couldn't live here. A part of him was worrying about what had happened back there in Cynmar. Had they finished the job? Had they taken the captain and captured the crew? What had his warriors made of what had happened to him?

He ached with the need to find his way home. He was dizzy with the strangeness of everything here. What if this were not the underworld, Underhill? What if Dannaigh were not here?

He shook himself out of such gloomy thoughts. People had recognised Dannaigh's name. Matt had. Peasy Parker had. Bethany had showed him

Dannaigh's face. He sat up cautiously, looking around him. A lone man was working on one of the plots, otherwise it was still and relatively quiet. The all-pervading sound in the background was vague and distant. Somewhere a bird was singing.

He had to find Dannaigh or Moira. He had to make a plan and stick with it. He had lost any idea of where Bethany's sleeping place was, he would have to find the shore instead. And somehow, soon, he must find something to drink, and to eat.

He got to his feet. South and East. The sun was high in the sky, though hidden by clouds. He started walking. He was working out a plan, several plans, to deal with what might come next.

Fight for Freedom

P.C. Tony Parker was back in the car, the paperwork had been filled in. He had updated the description of the wanted man and checked it against records. Though he couldn't find anyone like him in the records, the man had run, rather than come back to the bar and sort out the events of last night. He clearly didn't want to find himself in police custody. As far as Tony Parker was concerned, running was proof he was guilty of something, and the policeman was frustrated that he had got away.

He was explaining this to his new partner, Jane Slade, filling her in with the morning's events so far, emphasising the strength and fitness of the man, aware that she might be getting the wrong idea about his own level of fitness. In the corner of his eye, down a side street they were passing, he saw the very man himself, bold as brass, trotting away down a side street.

He drove on past the end of the road, calling it in on the radio, working out his best route to get ahead of the man, working out the best place to get him cornered.

It didn't take long, a few tactical stops across the end of a street, where the car could be seen, forcing the target to take a different route. Meanwhile others had been enlisted, another car was coming in from the North.

Soon enough, they had him where Tony wanted him, running in towards the cemetery. Tony would drive up from the south, turning the suspect north, and once he was committed, the second car would arrive at the far end. He would be cornered between the boundary fence of the industrial unit, and the high wall of the cemetery.

Always satisfying when a plan works.

Before the second car appeared, Tony stopped his patrol car at a distance, and got out, hailing Tasgo with a shout of 'Stay where you are.'

Tasgo recognised the man. He had been reasonable, at first.

Tasgo stood, waiting to see what came next

Coming forward, Tony Parker made a hand movement to keep Slade behind him, 'He was talking to me, before,' he told her, 'or trying to. Let's give him a chance.' He sauntered forward, unchallenging.

Tasgo stood, warily, allowing him to get nearer. He knew now that he could outrun the man, but not the vehicle. The fence across the road was strange, but it looked strong. The nearby wall was too high to vault, too high even to leap and catch the top with his hands

'Danny,' Parker started, from a distance, his voice friendly and only just loud enough to carry, 'Let's keep it calm, okay?'

Tasgo faced him. He didn't understand the question, but Peasy Parker seemed unthreatening. Tasgo took a stance, showing he was a powerful man, a reasonable man. He showed his empty hands, and his confident strength, though he had little hopes of getting the man to understand his need.

Parker saw ahead of him a strong suspect, ready to run, ready for anything, possibly ready for a fight. 'We can sort this out down at the station,' he said. 'Just a matter of an unpaid bill, no-one's made any other complaint. Maybe it was a misunderstanding, eh?' Though how anyone could rack up a two-thousand pound bill by accident was beyond him, and highly unlikely.

Tasgo took a gentle step towards him. 'Peasy Parker,' he acknowledged. There was no other way to continue than to repeat his need to find Dannaigh Sharp or Moira Alter. He did it with the usual mime.

'Yeah,' said Tony Parker, sounding agreeable. Beyond Tasgo he could see the pulsing glow of reflected blue light, where the other patrol car had stopped out of sight. It was reassuring. He had a good idea that Tasgo could not understand what he said, but he was prepared if this was no more than a ruse. 'You remember last night? The bar? You were with some people, weren't you? Two girls and a bloke?'

These were all questions, not challenges. Tasgo was trying to make out what the man wanted. He was aware of the other person in blue behind Peasy Parker, still by that mad machine. Head on one side this person seemed to be talking to themselves, maybe making a spell, or an incantation.

Tasgo made it clear again, who he was, what tribe he was from. He doubted the man could understand. That man was still walking slowly forward closing the gap between them.

'What language do you speak?' asked the policeman. 'We can get a translator on line, make everything easier.'

Tasgo put up a hand, a definite stop sign, understandable in any language. He said, clear and distinct, *'Dannaigh Sharp. You must know Dannaigh Sharp.'*

Parker paused, then tried 'Dan A Sharp, is that you?' He was thinking it was easy for the man in front of him to cause some confusion about his name. That would mean he had history, was probably wanted, perhaps in hiding. Or just plain foreign. Apart from the strange clothes, he didn't look foreign, though his skin was as weather beaten or suntanned as any Mediterranean type.

Tasgo explained again. *'I look for Dannaigh Sharp. I am Tasgo Aed, son of Aod, son of Dugal. I am Dannaigh's cousin,'* with the hand movements to make it obvious.

The policeman was losing patience. 'Let's get back to the station, we'll sort it all out there,' he said, moving forward.

This time Tasgo didn't step back. He knew what Moira had said, and her mother Gamma, and Freya and even Dannaigh. They all said that in this place there was no fighting. But Toma, Dannaigh's father, had been a warrior, fierce as fury, sharp as ice. It was in Dannaigh too, though he denied it.

Tasgo looked Peasy Parker in the eye, ready, and Tony Parker realised it was going to get physical. It didn't stop him.

Tasgo let the man grab his left arm. Eyes firmly fixed on the other, he said *'No'*, while his right hand came up peaceable slow to rest on the policeman's chest. The force in it stopped Tony Parker where he stood.

'Let's not play silly buggers,' said Tony. The simple effectiveness of Tasgo's move, the controlled containment of the man, silent now and still, full of pent force and intent, warned him that here was more trouble than he could handle. He said, 'Don't make things any worse,' tightening his hold on the man's arm, reaching for his handcuffs.

Tasgo broke free. Simple as that. He stood there then, his face just a couple of feet from the policeman's. He wasn't going to give an inch.

56

Back at the car Slade told the radio, 'It's kicking off,' as she moved swiftly forward to back up her colleague.

'No need to get physical,' Parker told his suspect, 'we go back, we sort it out.'

'Peasy Parker, find Dannaigh Sharp,' Tasgo commanded him, raising his right arm to the ready position as he pointed to himself with his thumb. *'Me, Dannaigh Sharp,'* the fingers of the hand coming towards him, to show the arriving of Dannaigh, the only condition on which he would give himself up.

Tasgo could see the second figure coming towards him, Tony could hear her, he wanted it over before she got here.

The police man said, 'Danny, whatever your name, I am arresting you on the suspicion of...' as he made the official grab and capture move. It didn't happen. The suspect countered, caught, ducked under their arms fastening tight on each other, twisted, and it was Tony in the straight-arm lock, kept at arm's length, no blows sent or landed.

The suspect forced him to his knee, it was that or have his arm broken. *'Dannaigh Sharp,'* Tasgo said once more, firm, *'Find Dannaigh.'*

Wailing announced the arrival of the second police car, now behind Tasgo. He could see the second figure bearing down on him from the car in front. He stepped to one side, taking Peasy Parker off balance, and letting go of his hold as if tossing the man aside.

He didn't know who they were, but they were warriors. He was trapped between two boundaries he could not cross. Behind him the hideous sound of the monstrous vehicle was getting closer. Peasy Parker would be on his feet any moment, ahead was only one person in blue.

Giving in was not an option.

He leapt forward to the lone adversary. With one fast movement, ducking low, sweeping upwards with explosive force of all his major muscles, hitting with his shoulder and hurling high with his arms he had his opponent flying.

Even as he followed through the movement he realised something was wrong, his adversary was too light, the centre of weight higher than he expected, flying higher, further than he expected.

Not a he but a she, cartwheeling above him now, instead of falling from him.

As if time slowed he could see the arc of her flight, the way she was turning. She would land head first on the hard ground, a shattering blow, possibly fatal. Fatal was not an option when he had no idea who she was and what was wanted from him.

Already his legs were reversing thrust to bring his hands back under her, one hand catching the back of her head, the other between her shoulder blades, taking her weight, moving sideways with her so that her feet would tumble over and strike the ground first, striding one long pace to hold all her weight. Her heels struck down, he could feel her pushing down, arching her back, trying to get control.

Beyond her Peasy Parker was on his feet again, racing in fast. The woman was twisting as she fell, trying to grab Tasgo's arm, to take hold of him. Her feet were already on the ground, Tasgo let her fall, dancing away.

The new vehicle had roared to a stop, men were getting out.

Now they were four to his one. They hadn't used weapons.

He thought he could deal with them, but he didn't want to. There were always rules, he didn't know them here. He didn't know what they wanted from him. He didn't know what they were. Any physical fight carried with it the possibility of death, and death could not be undone. As the woman hit the floor and rolled, he could sense a new purpose from the men dressed the same. One of them was shouting loudly, a command that Tasgo could not understand.

Peasy Parker's first concern was the woman, she was rolling up, hand, then knee on the ground, she was unhurt. Peasy Parker was not satisfied. He came forward slowly, giving orders, using the name Dannaigh as he spoke in a calming forceful voice.

The others, from the vehicle, were converging on him.

One of them had something in his hand, it might be a weapon. 'Kill with a look' were words that slithered into Tasgo's mind.

He had already noticed a metal box on a stick by the wall, red with a sigil pattern on it. He turned suddenly, away from them all, and ran at it full pelt. Leaping high, his foot hit the top of it, hammering hard. The box crushed under the pressure, but it was enough to boost him higher, arms reaching high, and catching that distant handhold, heaving upward. Parker was coming in fast, leaping to catch his dangling feet, but Tasgo

58

was faster, hauling himself upwards, getting a knee on the top, struggling for balance, getting to his feet high above them, out of reach.

He stood there looking down on them as they gathered under him. He showed his hands empty, out to the sides, far from where his weapons would be. His heart beat was strong, but for now he was safe.

'I am Tasgo Aed' he told them, calmly and clear, *'son of Aod, son of Dugal Dragon slayer,'* useless details since they could not understand, *'Kin,'* he went on, *'to Moira Alter, and to Dannaigh Sharp. Ask them who I am. Tell them where I am, they will vouch for me,'*

For the first time he felt less sure of this. Suppose something had happened to them here, in the five years of their banishment? Suppose they might be dead, even though they lived a thousand years? Perhaps he had even fallen into the territory of those who were their enemies. *'Give my name,'* he told them, *'to Ken Rays, keeper of lore. He knows me well.'*

One of the men below him had gone to the woman, who was standing at distance. He could see they were talking, and then they were both moving off towards the vehicle, still flashing its lights in the distance.

Behind Tasgo was an open area, in which stones thrust up through grass and, near the wall, shrubs. If the stones had significance it was not great, the place looked unused. A large building dominated the area. Tasgo couldn't see any way out of the enclosure, though there might well be one. The wall was too high to climb back over if he dropped on that side, and he didn't want to get trapped.

The men outside were shouting at him, useless commands, he couldn't understand them. Whatever they were, whoever these men, and woman, were, he could not risk being taken by them if they did not know Moira and Dannaigh, or worse, were opposed to them in some way.

How to get word to Dannaigh and Moira, or even Ken?

He threw his arms wide and bellowed their names, hearing the sound soar, and echo. Over and over he shouted, so that someone somewhere might hear, and send word to the ones he was calling on.

Already one of his pursuers had gone away, back to the impatient monster, lights still flashing blue with frustrated anger. Tasgo turned and walked along the wall. The men walked below him, keeping pace easily.

Ahead was a corner, and a lower wall ran on for a short distance. The men in blue would have to go further if he took the turn. He started to jog, the top of the wall was wide enough, he made the turn.

Tasgo took a chance as the men moved away from him to find a place to cross the lower wall. He dreeped into the enclosed area.

Cut off from them, he ran, past unnatural flowers and carefully tended plots, over grass cropped unnaturally to an even length, past the huge and solitary building with an air of desolation about it.

It could have been pleasant if it were not for the strange buildings with sharp corners, and a distant unearthly wailing that seemed to come from everywhere at once.

Into sight came a gateway, an easy exit. Tasgo ran towards it, and out onto the street.

There it was again, that monstrous vehicle with the strange markings and the potential lights, flashing again blue, angry. One man came from it, less wise, or perhaps more powerful than the rest.

One thing too much.

Tasgo had been holding down fear of the strange, the unworldly, the magic, everything. Wise fear, he had not neglected it. He could not, would not, run forever. No point ducking back into the enclosure. There, he would be trapped.

Another of the monsters came in from the opposite direction. They seemed to have gained courage from somewhere. Well and good. This he knew how to do. He had no weapons, so he spread his hands wide as he moved towards them, and they moved in on him.

They were surprisingly easy, as if they had expected surrender. One of them moved forward to grab Tasgo's arm, Tasgo lured him closer by bending it back, then with a sudden twist smashing his elbow into the man's temple, leaping back as the man fell, giving the others chance to see sense and back off.

Instead they came at him together, as one, with practised moves. But they expected less practised resistance. He used their own moves against them, he struck low and dirty, using head, hands, elbows, knees and feet, calculated heavy blows, full force. They went down as easy as one two three. He danced free, none of them were much hurt, he expected them to rise again. They did so, but cautiously, keeping their distance.

Someone behind him was shouting something, and he turned to face them. The man was holding something in his hands, it didn't look like a weapon. He shouted again, a single word.

Amazingly, impossibly, two snakes leapt from the box, launching themselves at Tasgo. They bit with agonising force. They knocked him backwards off his feet. His whole body jerked, out of his control. Darkness hit him, absorbed him totally.

They had killed him! He was dead!

But he could still hear and see. He could still move! Then they were all over him, twisting him over, forcing his arms behind his back.

He bucked, and kicked, he head-butted. He forced one arm forward, dragging the man with it. He was writhing free, but the combined weight was too great. Their aim was to control his arms though, rather than holding him down. Something clasped his wrist. His knee connected with someone's face. In a moment he had rolled over, but coming to his feet was impossible. His elbow put another out of action for a moment, and he gained a knee to the ground, his shoulder barging someone away.

Suddenly he was free! They had all jumped back, away from him. As he leapt to his feet he heard again that ominous shout, and this time the snakes bit his back, low down.

Agony as muscles spasmed, and darkness took him once more.

They had killed him again. He could feel them on him at once. As he came to himself, taking command of his own body, it was too late. He was face down, and his arms constrained somehow behind his back. They were leaning heavily on him. He was taken. Shaken, he fought for anger to cover terror and pain, with only partial success.

With shock and horror he realised the truth.

He was dead. Really dead. He was Underhill where the dead live, and these people could kill him any time they liked, again and again. Moira and Freya and Dannaigh, they had all lied when there was no fighting here. Freya's man Toma was proof of it.

What had he done to deserve such a punishment? He couldn't think. But he wouldn't submit.

No point wasting energy while pinned to the ground. He lay still, gasping for breath, for understanding, for power to fight on when they tried to lift him. They could kill him as often as they liked, he was never going to give in. He would never submit. Not ever.

Damflask

Danny was aching now, every muscle in his body protesting. The last row was a test of a sort he had never expected. At the far end of the reservoir Chas had called from the shore, ordering the stern pair to row the boat, all the way back to the boat house. Just the two of them at the rear of the boat propelling the whole mass of the shell and all the bodies in it.

Danny kept the rhythm, but soon realised that the rower behind him, Potts, couldn't keep up the pressure, Chrissie had to keep them on course, which was hard work too. Danny expected Chas to countermand the order at any moment, for the rest to join in. When he didn't Danny lessened the power into each stroke, so Potts could equal him for the long haul.

That was when Chrissie had given the order to stop, and then started the whole crew to work as one again.

They arrived at the boat shed, him and Potts red faced and sweaty, the rest of the crew appreciative but jocular as they all lifted the shell out of the water, and carried it over to the rests.

Potts sat himself onto a bollard, gasping complaints. It had been a hard task.

Danny didn't complain, though he ached too. He helped lift the shell out of the water.

They were moving some boats down South for some trials on the Thames, so Danny busied himself helping to put the shells onto the trailer, stacking them up, fastening them down.

Voices came from the other side of the stacked trailer, Chas and Ray, and the coach, moving away from where the others were doing cool downs or chatting.

Chas was saying, '...didn't complain, looked like he could go on forever.'

'He slowed,' Ray countered. He was the senior man here, post grad, old player.

'Only to keep pace with Potts,' the coach said.

They were talking about Danny, they hadn't noticed he was on the far side of the trailer. He should move away, he shouldn't eavesdrop. But he wanted to know what they thought of him, really thought of him. He rattled the framework to give them fair warning of his presence, but they didn't notice.

Ray was saying something about attitude and stability. 'I asked him last night, after the do, what kept him going so strong when the rest of us were knackered. He looked me in the eye and said, all serious, 'I imagine that my mother has been kidnapped, in the boat ahead, and I can only save her if I keep going longer and faster than they can.' Set me back a bit. What can you possible say to that? Then he burst out 'Gotcha!' laughing like a lune!'

In the silence that followed, Danny remembered doing it. He had drunk too much, they all had. He had let his defences down and spoken truth when he should have come up with something mundane. He had recognised his mistake immediately. Hence the comeback.

Meanwhile Chas was saying, quietly, 'You don't know his story? When he was fourteen a gang of thugs blew up his house, killed his father and kidnapped his mother.'

Danny was already walking away as Chas went on, 'Then he and this detective went after them and got her back...' he didn't want to hear the tale told again, with embellishments, as Erged the Druid might say.

Taken

It was not far to the car, but they had already dropped Tasgo once, and he had come up fighting. It took the six of them to hold him down and get leg restraints on him.

'Whatever he's on,' one of them said, leaning heavily on the restrained form, 'he's strong as an ox,' They had to lean on him hard until the wagon arrived to pick him up. PC Parker tried to talk the guy down, firm voice, but quiet, explaining. It had no effect.

The blokes with the wagon had looked appreciatively at the mass of blue clad bodies holding the detainee down. They hadn't realised they would be needed as well, to get him the few yards to the back of the wagon. When he saw the van, and realised he was going to be put in it, he went berserk, even under the weight of the six of them. He writhed and fought every step of the way across the grass to the van. Despite the restraints he struggled so hard they nearly dropped him again. They had to open the door wide to push him through. He was a madman, violent and unceasing in his struggles.

When they finally managed to shut the doors on him, they could hear him hammering on the cage doors with his feet or his head. The van was rocking wildly.

'You'd better follow us,' concluded the driver, as violence continued unabated.

Tony Parker said, 'He knows how to fight, he's trained. He's foreign, and he **really** doesn't want to get arrested.' There was a pause while they all took in the implications. Then the driver said, 'I'll call it in.'

They drove, the van still rocking under the thunder of the assault. The sooner they got him to the station the better.

Suddenly silence fell. The van rode smoothly on. The two men in the front exchanged a look, and pulled the van in to the side of the road.

They opened the back of the van as the following car pulled up behind it. Through the bars they could see the prisoner. He was a mess. Blood trickled from his nose, was flecked across his face. He had somehow got himself into a far corner, restrained legs pulled up close to him, back against two walls, staring wide-eyed at them, not moving.

'Off his head,' said the driver, 'God knows what he's on.'

PC Parker thought differently. He was minded of a wounded animal in a cage, terrified. Something like a tiger came to mind. Dangerous when cornered.

They stared in, Tasgo stared back. Let them come at him. He dared them to come at him, he was ready, legs coiled to strike.

They closed the doors on him.

Alibi

As Danny walked away from the trailer, a car pulled in to the entrance of the compound, stopping carelessly right in the middle of the gates, blocking the entrance. Two men got out, one in a suit, the other only slightly less formal with a tie and sweater. They stood looking about them, and it was Chrissie who went over to see what they wanted, and no doubt ask them to move the car. That was Chrissie all through, friendly, pro-active, sorting things out.

As Danny put an unnecessary coil of rope back in its place, he saw the man in the suit show something to Chrissie, and, looking more serious, she turned and pointed to the boat shed, where Danny stood.

He felt his hackles rising, an unfamiliar sensation nowadays, and probably entirely uncalled for. Still he turned further away as if he had not noticed them, and picked up a boat hook, which might also be useful for unloading the boats at the end of their ride.

Turning back he saw that the more casual of the two was strolling down the edge of the water, while the one in the suit was coming straight towards the boat shed. With the trailer in the middle of the open space, they would be coming at Danny from two different directions.

Boat hook held casually in his hand, ready to fit into the trailer, Danny walked towards the suit, a questioning smile on his face.

'Danny Sharp?' asked the man.

'Who's asking?' Danny said, sounding friendly.

The man already had his warrant card in his hand, and held it up for a brief second. 'D.S. Purbright,' he said, tucking the warrant card away, 'South Yorkshire Police. You are Danny Sharp?' The second man was closing in on him too, from his right.

'That's me,' Danny said, serious now. Had something happened to his mother? That wouldn't warrant the cautious approach from two directions. 'What's happened?'

'We'd like you to come with us to the station,' was the evasive reply.

Over the man's shoulder Danny could see blue flashing lights coming down the road towards them without siren. 'What for?' he asked politely.

'We just want to ask you a few questions,' the man had come closer, but stopped with a decent space between them, as had his partner.

Danny smiled, friendly, 'You can ask me questions here,' he pointed out. 'How can I help you?' There was a palpable tension in the air. Chrissie was coming towards them now, pausing by Chas. The oncoming police car stopped by the entrance to the compound, and car doors slammed. Danny stepped over to the trailer, and slipped the boat hook into its place, an ostentatious show of trust and friendliness.

DS Purbright took that on. 'Where were you last night?' he asked.

Danny gave a laugh, took his eyes off the man to find Chas. 'Where was I last night?' he called.

Chas took it for an invitation, and walked towards them as he spoke, 'Town Hall,' he said.

'What time?' the policeman wanted to know.

'Eight o'clock, what's this about?' Chas answered.

'Till when?' demanded the officer.

'Oh,' Chas was amused, 'the speechifying went on till nine, and the partying until eleven, and the post partying,' he looked questioningly over to Ray, who had wandered over as well.

'Half midnight,' suggested Ray, carelessly.

'And someone could confirm this?' the policeman asked. Behind him two burley uniforms were walking their stolid way towards them.

'Oh,' Charles grinned, 'about six hundred, I'd guess, give or take.' The whole of the crew had gathered widespread around them, drawn partly from curiosity, but mostly because they were crew. They stuck together, all for one and all that.

The man in the sweater said, 'Easy to get lost in a crowd that size.'

'We were centre stage for most of it,' Chrissy told him.

Danny took pity on the man in the suit. 'Sports England fund-raising event. We were on show for the first part, along with more major players, then we were in the crowd shaking hands and answering questions and thanking for donations. Cameras recording all over the place. Check it out.'

The policeman was looking thoughtful. 'And after twelve thirty?'

Chrissie grinned at Danny, 'He was with me,' she said claiming him as hers.

'All night?'

She smiled warmly, and nodded.

'While you were sleeping?' the policeman was clinging on to possibilities.

She grinned mischievously at Danny, 'Not much sleeping there,' she said.

'What did you think?' Danny asked at last, curious, 'What was I supposed to be up to?'

'Partying,' the detective said, dour. Then he gave in. 'Sixty miles away, in Hull.'

'Only an hour away,' the other policeman said.

'What about today?' asked Purbright, 'this morning?' he was looking at the sweat soaked and lake splashed clothing, the boats, the tired bodies well exercised. He already knew the answer.

Again Danny looked at Chas, and Chas gave the times. 'Seven till fourteen, only we aren't away yet.'

A phone sounded in the second policeman's pocket, and he stepped away to take the call.

'I'd still like you to come down to the station with me, Sir,' Purbright said, 'if you have the time. We can get you a cuppa too, if that's needed.'

Danny wasn't sure he wanted to go.

'What's happened,' he asked, 'No law against partying is there?'

'Fraud,' the policeman told him, pleasantly, 'someone's been taking your name in vain.'

'Looks a lot like you too,' put in the one in a sweater, looking up from his phone call.

Chas didn't take the implication lightly. 'You can check the footage, we were all at the do. And he's been crewing all morning.'

As the two uniformed officers came up behind Purbright, the second detective put his phone away. 'They've got the man Sir, Hull's got him.' He looked at Danny, no sign of apology in his face, 'Not you after all,' he said, somehow it still sounded like an accusation.

The man in charge didn't let his eyes leave Danny's face as he asked, 'They're sure it's him?'

'It's him alright,' came the answer. Danny felt relieved even though he knew he had done nothing wrong.

Purbright gave an apologetic smile. 'Sorry to have bothered you then Sir, it seems it can't have been you.' He smiled again, sympathetically, then went on, 'We'd still like a statement, Sir, to rule you out of the investigation.'

'He looks a lot like you,' the other man said heavily.

Chrissie was looking worried. It must have been a photo that they showed to Chrissie earlier.

'Can I see?' Danny asked. 'Good to know what my imposter looks like...'

Almost as an apology, the paper came out folded, and opened to reveal a startling likeness to himself. It was a grainy head and shoulders, so the hair was vague, some sort of curls perhaps. The eyes could have been Danny's own, the nose though was pushed a little to one side, and there was a break in one of the eyebrows, an old scar.

Otherwise, well, it did look amazingly like himself.

Then he was recognising, with disbelief, what he was seeing; the nose, the scar across the eyebrow, the look of purpose on the face. It was impossible though. Impossible, but his eyes moved down to the top of the shirt – a slash necked tunic, over-sown with fine wool. He looked back into those eyes, that vigilant face, seeing the tension in it.

What Danny thought he was seeing was impossible, he knew that, but he also knew it was true.

He felt the bottom fall out of his stomach, his heart skipped a beat.

'Someone you know?' suggested Purbright, seeing the shock on Danny's face.

'Tasgo,' Danny breathed, eyes still taking in the proof that his mind refused to accept. 'That's my cousin Tasgo.'

The implications were hitting him hard. The portal to the past had been destroyed, utterly destroyed, four years ago. Tasgo could not have come through it. But here he indisputably was. Tasgo, Iron Age warrior, here, in the modern. On his own. A quick prayer that he was alone, a warrior band would be too much, it would be fatal, it would be...

Tasgo, on his own, amid the modern? How would he take it? Not well. Not well at all.

70

He dragged his gaze from the proof to Purbright's face. Words already spoken were echoing in his ears. 'Fraud,' 'they've got the man,' 'under arrest.' Tasgo. That wouldn't have been easy, that wouldn't include fraud. Tasgo would have no idea who the police were, what they did. He would have thought... He would have done...

Words came incoherent to his mouth, 'He doesn't speak English,' not the modern stuff anyway, 'he's - he wouldn't know, he'd think...' Danny's brain was skittering away from the obvious. He couldn't say the obvious, it would only make things worse. He mustered anxious thoughts into words, 'Tasgo is my cousin,' he said clearly, speaking fast, because the dangers were real, 'he doesn't understand – how the world works. He'd think they were trying to kill him. He doesn't understand English. He wouldn't know what they were saying. He'll... he'll fight for his life.'

His hand was in his pocket, he had already found his phone. He squeezed the buttons three times quickly, sending out an alarm call. 'Where is he?' he demanded, tension rising in his voice,

'All right,' calmed Purbright, 'take it easy...' he didn't understand the danger.

'He'll think they want to kill him! He will fight for his life! He knows how to fight, and he will resist...'

'Why would he think that Sir?'

'Because...' how to give the immediacy of danger? 'Because he will! He doesn't understand!' Not the modern day.

It would all seem madness to him, the cars, the streets, the houses, the shops, the food, the people! 'He doesn't understand! Anything!' The man wasn't taking it in, Danny calmed his voice, tried to be clearer, 'He isn't normal, he,' inspiration struck, '...he's vulnerable, he doesn't know... what the police are... what he's supposed to .... He shouldn't be here! Not on his own. He's a vulnerable person, he has - learning disabilities.' His learning would be fine it was just that he was totally ignorant about anything and everything that was happening to him. Danny felt guilty using the words, but they gave a picture that the policeman might understand.

All the crew were staring at him now, perturbed, worried, cautious. Danny could feel his own heart hammering in a way it didn't during exercise. He took a deep breath as the policeman asked him, 'Why would he think anyone was trying to kill him.'

'He's vulnerable,' Danny was winging it, trying to cobble something together that the police would believe, while not making it sound worse than it was. The first thing was to stop anyone being hurt or killed. It might already be too late for that. 'His family, they were afraid for him. They taught him to defend himself, they thought he'd be... that people would take advantage of him, abuse him, I don't know, ... So they taught him to defend himself. Only he's strong, he doesn't know his own strength.' He looked the policeman firmly in the eye, 'Someone could get hurt, perhaps him, perhaps someone else. If your officers arrest him, if they try to put him in...' If they tried to put him in a cell, there was no perhaps. People would get hurt.

'You have to let them know,' Danny urged the officer. 'People will get hurt, maybe killed. He's strong and he knows how to fight!'

Purbright was watching his urgent movements, his agitation, and his control of it. He wasn't doing anything about it. Danny shouted, trying to get the urgency through to him, 'Warn them! Tell them! You could have major injuries, even death. He won't give up! He will fight for his life! Tell them!'

The policeman nodded towards his colleague, and looking over Danny saw that the second man was already on the phone. Relief flooded in, but anxiety remained high. 'I have to get there,' he said, 'Now. He doesn't understand a word of English. I can explain to him...'

'We've got interpreters,' Purbright assured him, 'What language?'

It stopped Danny in mid thought. He took a breath, and remembered Gamma's gambit five years ago. 'It's a rare dialect of a proto-Indo-European language, there are only three people in the country that can speak it, apart from Tasgo. Me, my Mum and Moira Raynes.' Ken Raynes could a bit too, but Danny thought it better not to drag his name into it. He had got his rank back, no need to compromise it again.

'How come?'

'How come what?'

Purbright was patient, 'How come your cousin doesn't speak any English?'

Pitfall.

72

Luckily his phone started ringing at that moment. He grabbed it out of his pocket, looking to see who had answered first. It was Paul. As Danny put the phone to his ear Paul, or whoever was on duty for Paul, was saying, 'Danny Sharp?'

'Yes,' said Danny, 'I need …'

'What's the weather like Danny?' interrupted the voice on the phone, stopping Danny in mid word. Damn! It was years since they set the emergency system, he had been sixteen, and stupid. He had almost forgotten the codes, but not completely, 'Cloudy, no chance of chocolate,' he said meaning he was not in immediate danger, but needed some urgent assistance.

Purbright said again, 'How come your cousin doesn't speak English, Danny?'

Paul's substitute asked, 'Is someone with you?'

'Yes,' Danny said, taking a step back from the policeman, 'A man's been arrested,' he looked at the policeman, 'Where will they take him?'

'Who's that?' countered Purbright.

'Help,' Danny told him, knowing the man on the phone would hear that word in a different context, that it would trigger reactions. He went on, 'for you as well as Tasgo.' Then to the telephone 'Tasgo Aed, he won't understand what is happening, he'll be terrified, and he knows how to fight…' The man at the other end of the phone would know how to fight too, had probably been with Danny's father in the Middle East. Danny was wondering how many people had been injured already, and how badly. 'Hull, don't know which station.' To the detective he asked, 'Which station will they take him to?' It was the other policeman who said, as if shutting down something, 'He's already at Clough Road,' which Danny relayed to the phone, going on quickly, for everyone, 'If he's in a cell they should keep him there, not open the door, not for anyone, not for anything.'

'They've got a doctor coming,' the man in the sweater said, still holding his own phone to his ear, 'they can tranquillise…'

'No!' Danny shouted. Tasgo wouldn't understand, he would go berserk! What would he think they were doing to him? Tasgo was a firm believer in magic, in spirits, in the supernatural. Someone poking a needle into him…

Purbright said firmly, 'Give me that', stepping forward and reaching for Danny's phone. For a brief second Danny thought of keeping hold of it, defying the man, but he needed to work with him, not against. He handed it over, thinking hard.

Keep calm, work out what the problem is, fix it. That was his father's mantra, before the explosion had taken him from them.

Everything was the problem now. Tasgo trapped in a cell, not knowing what was happening, that was foremost. He needed to get to Tasgo, as soon as possible. No delay. He needed to be travelling.

Meanwhile D S Purbright had introduced himself on the phone and was demanding to know who was on the other end. The answer seemed to surprise him. He asked, 'Why would Mr. Sharp need your services?' The answer made him look sharply at Danny.

Danny said, loud, for all and sundry, here and also at the far end of the phone, 'I need to get to Tasgo fast. Before anyone else gets hurt.'

Purbright was looking at Danny with a strange expression now.

Danny had no idea what the man who wasn't Paul was saying. He looked to the second policeman, still on the phone, presumably to Hull Headquarters, or Clough Road. 'Is he in a cell?' Danny demanded. 'Tell them not to open the door, not for anything, not till I get there to explain to him.'

The two uniformed officers were watching and listening with patient faces, waiting for whatever they had been called to do, backing up the two plainclothes men. There would be nothing Danny could do on his own. He would have to be persuasive.

Purbright said, tentatively, into the phone, 'We could do that...'

Frustration was rising fast in Danny, helplessness did not fit well. 'I have to get to him,' he said, loudly, 'he'll be anxious, if he can't get free, he'll harm himself!' not in the way it was usually meant. Others would be more at risk, if Tasgo could reach them.

To Danny's surprise Purbright was handing the phone back to him. As Danny lifted it to his ear, Purbright was turning to the uniform officers.

The man who wasn't Paul said in Danny's ear. 'We'll get someone in there, help keep your man isolated. The cops will get you there. Any other info for our man?'

Danny blinked. How would they manage that? Purbright moved over to the other detective, took the phone from him and started moving towards the exit, beckoning Danny to follow. The uniformed officers were waiting for Danny to move. They closed in on either side as he started to forward. Chrissie was looking more than concerned. The whole crew were watching, dumbfounded.

'Call Moira,' he told her, phone still to his ear, 'and tell Martin I won't make tonight's session.' Danny helped Martin organise the Brazilian Jujitsu sessions. Danny was a black belt, lowest level, he didn't want to let Martin down, but this was far more important.

Chrissie was demanding to know what was happening. Walking away from her, flanked by two policemen, Danny would have liked to know that too.

High Speed

High speed in a police car, lights flashing, siren as and when needed, was scary. Purbright had checked with the driver that he was trained for high speed pursuit before they got in the car. Danny was glad. It meant that although it looked like he was driving like a maniac, every wild surge onto the opposite side of the road, or the wrong side of a barrier was calculated and planned. It didn't help to sooth Danny's jangled nerves.

Purbright was in the back of the car with him. If the second uniform had got in as well, Danny would have been alarmed, but instead he had gone with the detective wearing a sweater. As soon as the man from Paul's agency cut off his call, Danny's phone rang again. This time it was Patricia Paxman in person. The lawyer simply said, 'What's up Daniel?'

Danny took time to explain carefully how Tasgo had been arrested, he didn't know what for, but that he was a vulnerable person who had little understanding what was happening round him. He would react violently if he thought he was being attacked, and he understood no English at all. Could she please get him some representation at Hull police station Clough Road as soon as possible?

Could a lawyer insist that Tasgo was left severely alone until Danny could get there? How long would it take before they got there? He asked Purbright for an estimate as they swept past bollards on the wrong side of the road, siren blaring as they jinked back to avoid a lorry still coming at them.

Purbright asked the driver, as he braked hard then pushed into a stream of traffic. 'Forty-five, give or take,' came the laconic reply, hardly audible under the urgent scream of the siren. Danny thought the man was enjoying himself. He wasn't going to break into the driver's concentration to ask whether that was time elapsed or time of arrival. He simply told the lawyer that it would be less than an hour, and she rang off to see what she could do.

It was a relief when they hit the motorway, flashed into the fast lane, and overtook everything on the road, siren only coming on when someone wasn't using their mirror and the car had to lose speed until they moved out of the way. They raced past traffic as though it was at a standstill.

Purbright tried to worm more information out of Danny. His questions were direct and to the point. Danny's answers weren't. Purbright would jump to conclusions, he had seen it happen before.

'What's your connection with the security firm?' Purbright asked.

'My mother's an archaeologist. Sometimes the digs are in places that weren't exactly safe.' He went on, unnecessarily filling gaps to keep the next question at bay, while appearing to be helpful. 'That's how she met my father, in the middle east, when all that destruction of historic sites was taking place. He was in the army then.'

'Where's he now?' Purbright would be wondering why Paul's man from the agency had called, and the lawyer, but not his parents.

'He passed away,' Danny said. Not died, never say die. In Danny's mind his father was still out there, still alive, but unreachable. 'Five years ago,' he went on, filling in the unnecessary details. Then, 'He and Paul were in the same unit, they were… mates. And Paul, he said he'd promised Dad he'd take care of us, if anything… They were like that, mates. All of them, together…' Again that feeling of loss, of being alone in the world, bereft of family, despite his mother, and Moira, and now Ken Raynes, who was something both more and less than family. He wouldn't mention Raynes. Danny had decided the police force was not like the army. In both they stuck together, but it seemed to him that loyalty gave way to ambition too often with the police. Perhaps he was just biased in that belief.

Purbright was framing another question so Danny went on, 'That's why Paul gave us a package deal, I guess. Never had to use it before.'

'Not even for Tasgo?'

Tasgo couldn't be avoided. There was no explaining Tasgo, but Danny would have to think of something, something vague enough not to tie them all in knots of fiction. Keep to the facts as much as possible. Give as little as he could.

'There's no explaining Tasgo,' Danny started, 'He's never been… ordinary. His mother spoke this rare version of an ancient language. He only ever spoke that. He doesn't understand… almost everything. He lives in a world of his own, simple things.' He turned to look at Purbright, to let him see the honesty and truth of the next. 'He doesn't know what 'police' means. He doesn't understand English. He couldn't obey a command, because he wouldn't understand it. He can't 'resist arrest' because he doesn't know what 'arrest' is. He would just see weirdos in odd clothing, trying to make him do something he doesn't want to. And his parents would have told him not to, not to take orders from strangers. He's vulnerable.' Vulnerable because he was here, instead of there. Now instead of then.

It still seemed impossible, but that had been Tasgo in the picture, unmistakably him. How had he got here? How could that be possible? Major problem, but stick with the immediate. He got in before Purbright could put his next question. 'What have they arrested him for?' he asked.

'Fraud,' said Purbright, a little too off hand.

'How could he possibly have committed a fraud when he can't speak a word of English?' demanded Danny.

Purbright smiled at that. 'They nearly drank a bar dry, nigh on started a riot.'

That was consistent, drink and riot, that would be Tasgo.

'How?' Danny demanded, 'How could he do that when he couldn't order a thing,' and certainly wouldn't expect to pay for it. Not even barter for it. He was a warrior, welcomed everywhere, with open arms by friends and wary courtesy by others. Purbright wasn't giving an answer, so Danny went on. 'If it's just a matter of a bar bill, we'll pay it, it's some simple misunderstanding.'

He could see Purbright assessing that. 'It's not just the bar bill,' he said quietly.

'So, what else?' demanded Danny, best to know the worst. He probably already knew. If they had Tasgo in custody, people would have got hurt.

'We'll see when we get there,' was all Purbright would tell him.

Danny hoped no-one was dead. There would be no escape from that.

Surprise

The Humber bridge sailed past, and they wailed their way through Hull towards the headquarters. It swam into view just as Danny remembered it. The last time it had been Ken Raynes who was in trouble. Danny wondered why he hadn't yet heard from the Detective Inspector. The car shot past the public carpark and braked violently to swerve in through the gates beyond, skimming through as they opened. Straight past rows of police vehicles into a covered area. A door swung shut behind the vehicle, making the docking bay entirely enclosed. In the sudden gloom dark figures moved.

Danny's door was opened and he got out, straight into the firing line of a sub-machine gun.

Black and menacing it pointed straight at him. As menacing as the eyes of the man staring down it at him, a dark figure almost inhuman in its protective clothing. As menacing as the strong voices around him barking orders that shock made mere roar.

'...on the floor now!' became clear, shouted by the man facing him. Far enough away to be out of reach, finger actually on the trigger. Cold dread washed through Danny. They couldn't shoot him, unarmed and defenceless as he was. Could they? Could they?

'On the floor! Now!' roared at him.

He couldn't take his eyes off the mouth of the gun, pointed straight at him. Orders roared over him like ocean surf. It was real, shockingly real.

Danny dropped to his knees, then face down on the tarmac, hands level with his head, cheek pressed against the dirty surface that smelt of tarmac, filth, exhaust fumes, and humiliation.

'Do not move!' roared over him. What had happened? What had Tasgo done to bring this down on them?

The Detective and the driver were not being served the same. In the corner of his vision Danny could see them standing, hands on the top of the car, names demanded, being searched, being told to stand aside. One man took control of them both. Another came to Danny demanding his name. Heart hammering, eyes still anchored on the open mouth of the gun that never wavered, Danny told him, breath hard to find. What was this? Why this? Why him?

'Do not move!' Barked the one who had all this time kept the barrel of the gun pointed unwavering at Danny's body. Danny could see the little 'O' of its mouth pointed at him, ready to spit. He didn't move as hands came onto him, patting against his body, his arms his legs, moving away to order Danny to roll over. The man with the gun trained on Danny moved, so as always to have a clear shot as Danny was patted down on his front.

His phone, his keys, his wallet were all taken from his pockets.

If they were going to cuff him Danny would protest. He would refuse to co-operate. He had done nothing. The 'O' of that gun never wavered, it was fixed on him. They couldn't shoot a man for demanding his rights.

Only – they would be the ones left to tell the tale. They could say whatever they wanted.

The two policemen were being ushered in through a door, out of sight.

Danny hoped there was a camera watching this area, recording everything.

The man who had taken all his possessions stood back.

'On your feet!' came the demand from the man with the steady gun.

Danny moved slowly. With great caution he rolled and got a knee to the ground, then a foot. Carefully he stood up. They were both pointing their weapons at him now, carefully placed so that each had a clear shot, without risk of shot or ricochet reaching the other. Danny didn't raise his hands. This was their game, and he didn't want to play it. Anger was rising like a slow tide in him, but he wasn't going to show it. He wasn't going to make a stupid mistake like that.

Like magic the door opened behind the man who had so far hardly moved, as if the weapon and its fixation on Danny had held him in place. The man backed into the doorway, and his mate, on the other side of Danny said 'Move!' so Danny followed into the dark mouth of the doorway.

They frisked him again there, as if once were not enough humiliation. While they were doing it Danny, hands against the wall, protested, 'I've done nothing. I'm not a threat.' They didn't answer. When they had finished their more intimate search they both stood back. At long last the gun turned away from Danny as if disappointed. The other man's gun was already holstered. They told Danny to go ahead of them, then followed him through into the reception area.

It seemed crowded. There were too many people there, too many of them in the full protective gear and holding the same semi-automatic weapons. As he walked in Danny looked around taking it all, evaluating. Purbright and the Driver standing against a wall, keeping out of the way. The three armed men who had greeted them so violently, and another, to his left, set off with a good view of the room. On his right, further away, was the desk for booking in the newly arrested, almost hidden behind three uniformed men, with another behind the desk. There were three civilians as well, two sitting on hard chairs, a horsy looking woman and an older man, thinning grey hair and a face like a prune, folded in on itself in crumpled patches, eyes almost lost in the folds. The third stood at the mouth of a corridor, in the stand-easy pose, legs apart, hands clasped lightly in front of his crotch. He looked fit, he looked bored, as if he had seen it all before and knew he could handle it. He looked like Danny's father had, when he needed to. He looked ready, ready for anything.

Danny kept walking right into the middle of the room. 'Who's in charge?' he demanded, unawed. Not what any of them had expected.

There was a momentary silence, as if none of them was sure. Then the man behind the desk said, 'That'll be me.' He was the custody officer, a sergeant, the one who booked in and out, who supervised the treatment of prisoners.

'Why the guns?' Danny demanded, 'What for?'

The Sergeant took too long to answer, so he wasn't really the one making the decisions. 'We're on lock-down,' he said, coming at last to a reason, 'possible terrorist alert.' Danny felt his heart sink. What had Tasgo done? He remembered the false note when Purbright had said 'fraud'.

As the Sergeant had started to speak, his eyes had moved to one of the gun carriers behind Danny. Possibly the one whose gun had fixed so firmly on Danny, it was hard to tell them apart with all the gear on them. What would Tasgo have thought, faced with these? Monsters, demons?

Danny turned to this man, the one who was calling the shots.

'He doesn't understand English, even though he was born here,' Danny said clearly, for everyone to hear, 'so he couldn't have obeyed commands. He has only a very limited understanding of how the world works, so he doesn't understand what the police are, or the powers of arrest. He probably thought they were trying to kidnap or kill him. He's probably terrified.' More urgently, 'Can I speak with him now?'

'Doesn't look terrified,' someone at the desk said, looking down at a screen.

Danny hoped he was coming over as sure of himself but knew he might be sounding cocky. He took a calming breath and tried to lower the tension. 'I don't know what's happened to cause this over-reaction. He's my cousin, can I speak with him now?'

'He'd need sedation,' the duty officer said. 'He's violent. We managed to get the leg restraints off, but then he went crazy, we only just managed to get out.'

'He's terrified,' Danny told him, again, trying for calm despite his own fast beating heart. 'Once he knows I'm here, he'll calm down. I'll explain what's happening,' Only, he would have to know what was happening. He took a breath, 'I'm sorry he's been such a trouble,' of course that's what he had been, 'he's never been out on his own, I don't know how that happened. Something's gone very wrong. Can I speak with him?'

Mollified by a reasonable answer, the Sergeant looked at his screen again, and opened up a little more. 'He's out of it now, in a daze, not sure he's going to listen to anyone.'

'May I see?' Danny asked. With great daring he moved from his powerful position in the centre of the room, towards the Sergeant at his desk. Once again the sergeant glanced at the man with the gun for permission, then turned the screen so that Danny could see.

There were several pictures on the screen, different cells, but the biggest, the one picked out, showed an almost empty room. A shelf for lying or sitting on, an alcove with a toilet in it, the upper part of it obscured from the camera for privacy, and in the nearer corner, squatted

82

down, back to the corner, a figure, head down, steady as rock, just a smudge in the corner.

'Been like that for near on an hour. Spaced out. I would have gone and checked him, but...' Despite himself, his eyes flicked towards the man standing in the corridor, patient.

Danny looked at the figure on the screen, the hair in knotted braids kept close to the head. From here he couldn't even tell if it was Tasgo. But if it was, he wasn't spaced out. He was resting, conserving his strength, coiled ready to spring. He could wait like that for hours, if he had to.

'Let me talk to him?' Danny said, anxious, ready to move.

It was the man with the gun, Danny was thinking of him as 'Top Cop', who said, 'We'd like some questions answered first.' He still held the gun ready for immediate use, but he wouldn't fire it, not in here, with all these people. It still made him the dominant person in the room. He went on, 'Who is he?'

'Tasgo Aed,' Danny answered, he was ready to answer a few questions, not many. 'My cousin, a vulnerable person.'

'You are?' was the immediate response.

'Danny Sharp, his cousin, student paramedic at Sheffield.' He put in the 'paramedic' because it seemed to impress people, it put him in with the good guys. Not for this man, it cut no ice with him.

'If he's native why doesn't he speak English?'

'Because his mother didn't, and that was the only language he learnt.'

'Nationality?'

That was enough. Danny faced him, eye to shooting visor, 'British. Look, I don't know what your priorities are, but there is no danger here now. I don't know what you think he is or what he's done, but I know he's in there, alone, in the hands of men he thinks might do anything to him, anything! Let me talk to him, so he knows he's relatively safe. He's vulnerable, you have a duty of care to him too.'

The prune-faced man on the chair stood up, 'As legal counsel to Mr Aed, I must advise you that his needs are not being met at the moment, and that,' he smiled, adding more creases to his face, 'your investigation might advance a lot faster if you let the interpreter speak with the client.'

Legal counsel? Patricia Paxman had been quick! 'Good man!' thought Danny.

It was all taking too long. Tension would be building in Tasgo with every passing second. Then as a silence began to stretch, Danny realised Top Cop's dilemma. He didn't know what Danny was, what information or commands he might give the prisoner while pretending to talk him down. He spoke out loud, 'You can check on me,' he told the man,' I'm just an ordinary student, from an ordinary family, except, you know families, Tasgo's a misfit. He doesn't belong on the streets without someone to explain things to him. Something must have happened, it's obviously upset him. This is all just a misunderstanding.' How big a misunderstanding they must never know.

'Already checked,' said 'Top Cop', 'we know about you,' heavily as if it had confirmed something really bad.

Danny wasn't going to fooled into being defensive. 'So you know I'm okay,' he said.

'Explosion?' said the man. 'Father killed?'

Anger flashed through Danny, but he held it back, contained, forceful in his voice but not uncontrolled. 'Mother maimed,' he confirmed, hard, 'me wounded. Don't try and turn it against us! We were the victims, the victims of a madman, the one calling himself Kevin Wilcox.' He let anger spill over a little, 'I saw what damage that did, lived through it. If you think for one second that I would inflict that on anyone else, you don't know me!'

Prune face said, 'Perhaps Mr Sharp could talk to his cousin through the door? It has a slot wide enough for that,' he explained unnecessarily.

Surprisingly, Top Cop looked to the man standing in the mouth of the corridor that led to the cells. By the time Danny looked that way, there was nothing to show on that man's face except patient readiness. Danny had assumed he was another policeman, but now he thought he looked more like a soldier.

'Who are you?' leapt from Danny's mouth.

It seemed to amuse the man. 'Jack,' he said, 'Paul sent me.'

He didn't look like a Jack, whatever Jacks might look like. Danny felt his hackles rise, and didn't know why, except perhaps that the man was standing between him and Tasgo. Had this man somehow persuaded the

84

police to leave Tasgo locked in his cell, unmolested? It had seemed a forlorn hope to him when he had asked for it. There he was though, blocking the way to the cells.

Another thing to leave for later. Keep to the point, press on, he thought to himself.

'Do we go through or not?' he demanded, impatient.

Surprisingly the man called Jack asked mildly, 'You think it's safe?' Then seeing the surprise, he added, 'Paul wants you alive, unharmed if possible.'

Now that the guns were no longer pointing at him Danny thought he was in very little danger. But that was Paul. Long ago, he had promised Danny's father to look after the family, and so far he had had very little chance to do that.

'He's not dangerous,' Danny told them all, 'he's just lost and scared. Just defending himself, as he sees it.' An image that didn't quite fit the Tasgo Danny knew, but circumstances change things.

Top Cop said, 'You tell what you're going to say before you say it, and you translate for him before you answer.'

Danny nodded assent, 'Jack' stepped aside, and they walked into the corridor, a little crowd, the Custody Sergeant, 'Jack', Danny, Top Cop and the lawyer.

Greetings

The cover for the slot moved aside with a rasp and clang, leaving an oblong gap looking into the grim little room. From here Tasgo could not be seen at all. Danny imagined him in his corner, instantly alert, even if outwardly he didn't seem to move at all. He was still cuffed behind his back, so the corner would be best for him. His legs would be his weapons, He could lash out, using the walls as a base to push from.

Now that he was here, Danny felt uncertain. He had been trying to work out, all the way here, how he would deal with Tasgo. The truth was, he didn't know. It all depended on what state Tasgo was in, how terrified, how angry, how lost. He could still hardly believe that it was his cousin in here, two thousand years later than his life so far.

I'll tell him I'm here,' Danny told Top Cop, then called, 'Tasgo' tentatively into the cell beyond the gap. There was no answer. He looked to the men by the screen which showed Tasgo. One shook his head. Danny took breath, and then called out, firm and confident, 'Tasgo, it's me, Dannaigh.' Silence.

From the desk a policeman said, 'He's looked up.'

Danny looked at Top Cop and repeated, 'Tasgo, it's me,'

Now Tasgo was on his feet roaring! 'Run Dannaigh, Run!' He rushed from his corner to the centre of the room, facing the door. 'They will kill you! Run!'

He was a shock. Danny should have expected it, five years had passed. This wasn't the Tasgo of five years ago, a youth, tough and challenging. He had gained height, and muscle. He looked more like his grandfather Dugal, Iron Age Chief. He had breadth, and heft, and presence. He looked like a chieftain himself. Except his face was a reddened mass of bumps and new bruises. Dried blood caked his nostrils and above his mouth. Flecks of blood all over his face and hair. His eyes were rimmed red with anger and humiliation. He looked dangerous. He looked deadly, even with his hands pinioned behind him.

His roar was a roar of defiance, his words those of a brave man, his eyes belied it all. Terrified was too small a notion.

Danny felt for him, hurt and angry. His voice was sharp as he translated for Top Cop, and went on to answer Tasgo without waiting to voice the words in English first.

'*They won't kill me Tasgo. They won't hurt either of us.'*

'*Run!'* Tasgo yelled, an order, fierce, '*they will kill you too! Run!'* Danny could hear his frustration at having to repeat the order, the strength in his voice, thinking Danny was in danger and trying to save him.

'He says you'll kill me,' Danny translated, then went on '*No Tasgo, they will not harm us.'* Not anymore than they had. '*You are safe now, they won't kill either of...'* Tasgo's shouted answer stopped him dead.

'*They already have!'*

What! What?

'*Wait,'* Danny told him, turning to the custody officer. 'He says you tried to kill him.'

'They say a lot of things.'

Top Cop was watching Danny, seeing the anger, waiting for the outburst of a dangerous man. Danny tried for calm. He called in through the hatch.

'*They haven't killed you Tasgo,'* he said, '*look, you're alive and talking to me.'*

In the middle of the room Tasgo looked at him, no longer raging. Taken, but unsubmissive, he stood straight and met Danny's eye, ashamed, hurt but unbroken. '*Three times, they killed me,'* he said, bleak. '*Get out if you can.'*

What to make of that? Danny couldn't find words at first, then, '*When I leave, you will come with me. Believe it.'* He wasn't sure he could make it true, but he'd damn well try.

They were waiting for the translation. This time Danny let the anger show. 'What have you done to him,' he demanded, hard and to the point, 'three times? So that he thinks you might have killed him, three times!'

'Calm down...' the sergeant began, as if he were some drunk or wild creature.

'I am calm,' Danny told him, fierce, 'What have you done to him?'

'It's what he's done...' began the sergeant.

Danny stayed quite still, so they couldn't accuse him of being violent himself. But his voice, not loud, was a battering ram. 'What have you done to him?' he demanded again.

Prune face put in quietly, the voice of reason, 'My client does appear to have taken quite a battering, and if I may say so, the arresting officers don't...'

'You didn't see him,' the sergeant was having none of that, 'He did that to himself in the back of the van coming in...'

'What has been done to him three times?' Danny insisted.

From the Desk came a voice, one of the officers on this side of the desk. 'We had to Taser him. He was an immediate threat. In a frenzy!'

'Three times?' Prune face sounded mild, surprised. 'In what time scale?'

A silence fell.

'I'd like to see my client alone, now,' his new lawyer said, asserting himself quietly, 'with his interpreter.'

'I'm not opening that door yet,' the custody office said flatly. 'Not to let a civilian in with him.'

'He's calm now,' Danny told him, 'now that I'm here. I'll explain...'

And while the custody officer and the lawyer argued the ins and outs, and Top Cop looked on, Danny looked through the slot and explained to Tasgo.

'They're afraid of you, Tasgo.' So they should be. 'They are scared to open this door. They need to see that you are calm...'

'I am,' snarled Tasgo. Danny was silent, taking that on. Tasgo was a long way from calm, he was wild. Danny knew how that felt. Anything was possible.

'Translate,' ordered Top Cop.

'He's scared,' said Danny. It was true, even though Tasgo would never admit it. 'Give me a moment to explain he won't get hurt.' Not waiting for a reply he turned to Tasgo again. 'They won't open this door until they are sure you won't attack them. Don't attack them. If you attack them, you will die.' He could see the man with the Taser standing behind him, by Jack. 'I can get you free,' said Danny, he hoped he could, 'but it may take a long time. You must do what I tell you, at once, without pause or argument. Even if you don't like it.'

'I have to demean myself?' growled Tasgo.

'No,' despite his own agitation, Danny was going with calm but firm. *'You have violated the local customs, they need to see that it wasn't your intention.'*

'I have to grovel,' Tasgo said, flat.

'You have to show that you are reasonable. You negotiate from a place of power,' the cell was hardly that, but, *'they are afraid of you.'*

Danny could see the wild in Tasgo giving way a little to a sense of power. But Tasgo's voice dropped, allowing fear, shame and bewilderment to colour the words, *'They killed me Dannaigh. Three times.'* He couldn't understand it. Neither could Danny. If Tasgo were dead how could he be standing here telling Danny this? Even Tasgo must see that was impossible. Another thing to let lie for now.

'You aren't dead,' he told Tasgo quietly. *'Tasgo, you remember how often I was so stupid when I first came to you? How ignorant I was of things that seemed simple to you? This is my world. I know how it works. I followed your lead in yours, just do as I say for a little while now, and all will be well.'* Even if Danny could see no way out of this hole that Tasgo had dug for himself. In the corner of his eye he could see the officers at the desk looking at the screen. He could guess what they were thinking, looking at this big man and his confrontational attitude. One of them moved off quickly.

Danny put this aside as well. *'Say 'yes Dannaigh',*' he suggested to the big man quietly. He counted his own heartbeats waiting for the response.

He reached twenty-four before Tasgo said, surprisingly calmly, *'Yes Dannaigh.'*

Danny breathed again. He turned to the custody sergeant. 'I'll tell him to sit on the bench,' then turned and did so. Tasgo twisted to look at the bed. Then he walked smoothly and calmly and sat on it. The look he gave Danny afterwards might appear docile to others, but Danny could see the challenge in it. It wasn't going to be an easy reunion, but it was enough. As Tasgo had turned Danny had seen the state of Tasgo's wrists in the cuffs. He had been trying hard to free himself. He must have known they were steel, but still he had tried, beyond all reason. He wondered whether the lawyer had noticed that.

It took a few long moments to get agreement for what he wanted. He wanted the man with the gun out of sight from inside the cell. He pointed out that it wasn't needed, wasn't going to be used, and that while a Taser was also unnecessary, it would more appropriate to use that if Tasgo still proved violent. The custody sergeant was more than happy with that, he didn't want these armed men in his domain.

Danny turned to Jack, if that was his real name. 'You've got the role of bodyguard,' he said, choosing words which the police might accept, 'If he thinks you are in charge of keeping the uniforms at a distance, he'll feel safer. So if you'd keep your back to him, and look like you're barring entrance to everyone else...' He felt foolish giving instructions like this. He was trying not to look it too. But the truth that he was deadly serious must have shown.

He turned back to Tasgo, waiting with a face that gave little away. 'I'll go in alone first,' Danny told the custody sergeant, and then relayed it to Tasgo. The man who had left the desk came hurrying back with a riot shield, one of those plastic ones you could see through. The Sergeant took it, and holding it in his left hand, he unlocked the door with his right, pulling it open.

Danny stepped into the gap. Tasgo leapt to his feet. *'Don't come in,'* he shouted in alarm, *'they will close it against you.'* but Danny was already inside.

The air felt electric, it was all Tasgo – his anger and frustration- his humiliation. His defeat. His will to resist until death. Only he had already died three times, if he was to be believed. The cell reeked with danger. Tasgo's eyes went beyond Danny, to the people who stood outside, to the shield made of light.

Danny stopped. All the words Danny had thought of on the way here, while the detective kept asking questions, and he had been answering as best he could, saying words that meant nothing, that gave away nothing but his own anxiety, all those words were suddenly gone. *'I thought I'd never see you again,'* broke out of him. It drew Tasgo's eyes to him. *'I thought I'd lost you forever.'* All those feelings of loss and emptiness flooded back into him. Here was Tasgo, after all those years of emptiness, and he dare not advance and hug him, not with the watchers, and the handcuffs, and Tasgo's own brand of anger and challenge. Even as a

90

prisoner, taken, he was powerful, grandson of a powerful Chief, grown into the same sort of power. He also stank of ammonia. He had wet his pants, probably when tasered.

Tasgo said, *'Can you take the chains off me?'* Keeping to the point. It did what it was meant to do, it reminded Danny what he was supposed to be doing.

Danny stepped forward and put a hand on Tasgo's arm. He wanted to throw his arms round him, as Dugal had once done for him. Instead he turned, standing with Tasgo against all the odds, feeling suddenly complete. 'Let's have the cuffs off,' he suggested to the custodian.

The custodian looked unwilling, now that he could see the two of them together, side by side, Danny an inch taller than his cousin, though not quite so set with muscle and power.

Looking at Tasgo's battered face the lawyer said, 'I'd like some photos of this,' taking his phone out of his pocket. Too late Danny realised what was going to happen. He turned fast, his arm coming across Tasgo's chest, to resist Tasgo's reaction to the phone. The flash did its thing. Tasgo did not strain against Danny's arm, he stood. He stood his ground. Very quietly he whispered the truth of what he felt. *'We will kill them all.'* Venom keep close, ready for action at the right moment.

'No we won't,' Danny told him quietly and 'He's not used to the flash, it scares him,' to the lawyer.

The lawyer, unbidden, shuffled into the room, the antithesis of action and anger. 'Well,' he said, 'can't have that, can we?' His face puckered further, into a smile, eyes twinkling as though this was no more than a tea party. 'I'm your lawyer, young man,' holding out his paw, 'Joseph Desmond.' Then, as if only now realising that Tasgo could not shake his hand, he turned with a benign look at the Sergeant, 'Can we have the cuffs off, if it isn't too much trouble?' As if this were all normal, as if no weapons had been on display earlier, just another day at the office.

'Just stand,' Danny told Tasgo quietly. *'No-one is going to be harmed, not us, not them. These are the keepers of the lore.'* He felt Tasgo take that in, felt tension take a turn into something different, and just as wary.

The Custody Sergeant left the riot shield outside the door. He went behind Tasgo and undid the cuffs carefully, stepping back smartly. The lawyer had followed him in, and now the camera flashed once more.

Tasgo stood firm. His feet were planted on the ground as Danny had told him, but his muscles jumped at the sudden light.

'What is that?' Tasgo demanded quiet but sharp, bringing his now free hands to the fore. Danny wasn't fooled by the quiet. He had seen the tremor of fear.

'He's taking note of wrongs done to you,' Danny told him, 'Keeping a record.' Tasgo's wrists were purple and crimson, rubbed raw, bruised and already swelling. Tasgo glanced at them as if to remind himself of what had happened. He didn't rub at them, they were a reminder he wanted to keep sharp. The lawyer smiled up at Tasgo, finger raised. 'Just one more,' he said, as though he were a nurse, taking temperature rather than photographs, the camera flashing again, taking in the state of the wrists. Tasgo winced, but didn't move.

'And an interview room, don't you think?' the lawyer asked the custody Sergeant, as if asking for a slice of cake, to go with the tea.

'I stink,' Tasgo said, almost under his breath, still keeping his eyes on all the other people in his cell, 'and I need to shit,'

Shit.

This needed some thought. Even a retarded simpleton knew what a toilet was. 'In the corner,' Danny told him, 'is a – a thing with water in it. You sit on it and shit into it, then walk away. '

Tasgo looked at him in disbelief. 'You shit into water?'

'It's special water,' Danny told him.

'Special- you mean magic?'

'I'll explain later.'

'And while I have my breck's round my ankles?'

'Everyone else will move out. You'll be safe. Jack will guard the door, he's your honour guard.'

Danny turned to the Custodian, now out of the room, and explained that Tasgo needed to use the toilet. Unsurprisingly, everyone left Tasgo to it. Even Danny left, he needed to be sure of a few things.

Jack agreed to continue to act like a body guard, and wait outside the interview room. The lawyer, Joseph Desmond, was confident that no-one would be listening in to his privileged conversation with the client. Danny would rather have heard that from the police. But the lawyer also wanted the doctor to examine Tasgo. He gave Danny a meaningful look as he said this. Out of the corner of his eye Danny could see an uncomfortable shifting among the uniformed men.

It proved easier than Danny had expected. Once Tasgo had his brecks back on, Danny stood in the doorway and said, *'There's a wise one wants to look at your injuries...'*

'What injuries?' demanded Tasgo.

'You haven't seen yourself,' smiled Danny. *'It won't take long, and it's best to agree with the wise.'*

Tasgo shrugged. As Danny had guessed, the horse faced woman was the Doctor, and she wasn't in a good mood. She had been kept there for hours with nothing to do, and Danny guessed she had been unsettled by the guns and the tension. He knew he was. But she took her business seriously, and Danny was busy translating questions and orders as she checked that there were no broken bones, and Tasgo could count up to five fingers when she held them up.

'No effects of concussion?' she asked brusquely, and then seeing Danny pause to find the right words, 'like seeing stars?'

Foolishly Danny asked just that and Tasgo, wide-eyed, was looking round the little room. *'There are stars? What stars,'* he demanded.

'No stars,' Danny told him softly, *'I used the wrong word.'* But Tasgo was looking at him to see whether he was lying now.

Once Danny had explained that Tasgo had taken it literally, the Doctor came to her conclusion. No concussion, no broken bones. She wanted Tasgo to take off his tunic, but Danny said it wasn't a good idea, that Tasgo would read that another way. He would think he was in danger. He knew the Doctor and the police would get the wrong idea when they saw the scars. So she bandaged Tasgo's wrists, much to his surprise, and was telling the police that she'd send her report to them later.

'Copy me in on that please,' chirruped Desmond, all smiles as the woman demanded to be let on her way. The armed police were no longer in sight, Danny hoped they'd gone back to wherever they came from. He rather thought that they hadn't.

If they had thought Tasgo was a terrorist, they only had Danny's word that he wasn't.

Briefing

The moment the door to the interview room closed, and they were alone, Danny did what he had wanted to do since he first saw Tasgo, he greeted him properly. They clasped hands, and then embraced, Danny feeling a tremendous release in the absence of guns and police, Tasgo still tight with tension, and watching over Danny's shoulder as the lawyer sat a little recorder on the table and became another man entirely.

The lawyer spoke to Danny alone, in one breath. 'How dangerous is he, does he need medication, have you got a doctor's record of his mental condition?'

Danny took longer to answer. 'Now I am here he is safe, he doesn't need medication. His family is ... it's a bit complicated, they won't have seen a registered doctor. He just needs someone to explain what is going on, in simple language,' he added, trying for details to make the tale true, 'and to tell him what he should do in the circumstances.'

Tasgo was looking at the white bands on his wrists. He was interested in the elastic strip that fastened down the ends of the bandage.

Now Joseph Desmond spoke to Tasgo direct, setting out the facts. 'You're in a lot of trouble young man. They want to throw the book at you. Fraud, resisting arrest, assaulting police officers, grievous bodily harm, possibly terrorism offences. Tell me in your own words what happened.'

Danny translated, feeling relieved that he could now ask the questions he needed answered. *'We're in deep trouble Tasgo, you've broken the rules. You shouldn't have fought the people in blue. They are the keepers of the lore. What happened?'*

'I don't know,' was Tasgo's less than useful answer. *'It was a skirmish, no more, at Cynmar, cunning raiders. The leader ran, but I was...'*

'When you got here?' prompted Danny. Interesting as the way it happened might be, there were more pressing points to cover.

It brought Tasgo to a place he didn't want to remember. The panic, the terror that had consumed him were buried deep, he didn't want to know that paralysing fear again. Danny saw him bracing himself.

'An invisible cage, with walls of light. People watching. Things.' His eye's met Danny's, *'I couldn't get out. I was trapped by...'* by nothing. He took a breath and tried to sound untainted by the event, *'by a cage of light. She let me out, I...'*

'She, who?' asked Danny, butting in gently, hearing how badly Tasgo had taken it, not wanting to provoke emotions contained within it.

Tasgo managed a smile despite himself, *'Bethany, beautiful woman. I think we made a child...'*

What!

The lawyer saw the reaction and said, with a trace of his previous self, 'A little translation would be of assistance.'

Danny took the time to tell him, 'He's trying to tell me how he came here on his own, but it makes no sense. It scared him.'

'So I saw,' the lawyer commented. 'Take your time.' But Danny had seen him glance at his watch just before. Did they have limited time for this?

'You came out of this cage of light, Bethany let you out and then...' then they had sex, Danny was wondering how that would work out, and whether it was willingly or otherwise...

Tasgo said, *'They seemed – surprised,'* he offered.

'They?' Danny asked.

'Matt, Emma and Bethany,' Tasgo told him. *'We went through – through long caves and doors, like these doors,'* he turned to show the door behind them, closed and heavy. *'And then, then there was a celebration... Was it for me Dannaigh? Was it my own funeral?'* Alarm was showing on his face again.

'You're not dead, Tasgo,' Danny told him firmly.

'Please,' said the lawyer.

'He got picked up by three people, and they went to – some sort of party?' showing how he didn't understand himself. *'What sort of a celebration?'* he asked Tasgo. He remembered the funeral two thousand years ago, and the aftermath of that.

Tasgo obviously didn't know what sort of celebration, with an offhand movement of his hand he came back with, *'First there was drinking. Vino Gallo…'* with a wry twist of a smile. *'It was very strong, and there were lots of people there, a big gathering. Then we ran. There were lights everywhere, very bright, and headless people, and a - a Thing. It is some sort of chariot, but I didn't know then, it just swam, like a fish, a huge…'*

'Tasgo?' Danny brought him back from remembered terror to the here and now. And quickly, before Tasgo went on, he brought the lawyer up to date with, 'They got him drunk at some sort of party.' The headless people and the fishy vehicle he left for later. He nodded to Tasgo to carry on.

'Then there was a bigger celebration, with loud noise, music and dancing.' He leant forward, *'There was this woman Dannaigh, you wouldn't believe how she was moving. She might have been a high priestess or a goddess, or,'* reluctantly admitting the less poetic, *'a woman of pleasure, part of the fare. She liked me. I could tell.'*

Danny quickly relayed this to the lawyer with, 'Then they went to somewhere with lots of dancing. Sounds like they were clubbing.'

'There was a man who wanted her for himself. Do they paint here Danaigh, he was very dark, all over? Or perhaps very sun darkened, like some of the traders?'

'I don't know,' Danny told him, *'What happened?'*

Tasgo was looking very serious now. *'You told me that you never fight here Dannaigh. It isn't true. He pushed me, he wanted to fight.'*

'There was a fight,' sighed Danny, he should have known.

'No, I picked him up and put him down outside the dancing,' Tasgo paused, *'upside down it is true, but it was no fight.'* He smiled, *'He didn't like it. He came back with some friends,'* he could see what Danny was thinking and a smile widened, *'Strong-arms intervened, and we left. It was fun. We ran from the place of light into darkness, we went to a nest in the sky.'*

For Desmond this became, 'Someone tried to start a fight, but he refused. The bouncers stepped in and they left.' For Tasgo he asked, *'Nest in the sky?'*

'A cliff, partly made of light. She was like a maiden, Bethany, shy yet eager. She was…'

96

'*Leave that bit out for now,*' Danny told him. In this world for only a few hours and already bedded. That was Tasgo all right.

Tasgo would rather have dwelt on the pleasures, of which there had been a few, rather than the horrors, of which there were many.

'*What next?*' Danny demanded.

'*I tried to find you. Matt, he is a useless man, but he knew your name. At the drinking, he knew your name, and Moira's. I told him I was looking for you. Either he didn't understand, or he wouldn't let me know where to find you. I think he knew but would not say. Do you know this man - Matt?*'

'*Maybe, I know a lot of people.*' Danny had no idea when all this happened. It could have been last night, it could have been a week ago. Though how Tasgo could have remained unknown to the police for that long was beyond him. '*What happened next?*'

'*This morning, Bethany... she tricked me, Dannaigh.*' He sounded hurt, let down. '*She went into a small room, and the door closed on her. But then she was running away through the trees. Far away. How did she get there? I chased her, but she was gone.*' Tension was back in his voice. '*There are all these boxes Dannaigh, built, I think, lots and lots of... of big boxes all the same. Hundreds of them. They made me dizzy...*'

The lawyer coughed. Danny was too confused to try and translate. '*What size were the boxes Tasgo?*'

'*Big, as tall as my new hall but square with sharp...*' he stopped suddenly, tragedy in his eyes, silence on his tongue.

'*Tasgo, what is it about the boxes?*'

Tasgo glanced towards the lawyer, then looked nervously towards the door. Setting his eyes on Danny he asked, '*Who is this man, what is he?*'

Danny took the chance to let the lawyer know where they had got to. 'He's not making a lot of sense, he sees the world differently. He spent the night with these people, Matt, Emma and Bethany. Then Bethany went, and he tried to follow her... I don't understand what he is saying about boxes. Whatever it is, it scared him. Now he wants me to explain who you are.'

'I'm his lawyer,'

'Too complicated,' said Danny, 'he doesn't know what that means.'

'Does he understand the law?'

Sort of,' Danny said thinking hard, 'He doesn't know what our laws are, but he knows right from wrong...'

'Pity,' Purbright muttered, making a note on his iPad. Then clearly to Tasgo, 'I'm the one who will state your case clearly, to protect you from the worst interpretation of your behaviour, and to try to make all judgements as fair as possible.'

'Got it,' said Danny. Then, to Tasgo, *'He's a sort of wise man, a helpful one. He's on your side, he needs to know what happened next. About the boxes?'*

Tasgo had got over whatever had stopped him. *'What are they Dannaigh? So many of them, in lines, with the dark path between them? All of them the same?'*

It dawned then on Danny. *'Big boxes, really big? I think you mean houses. Not round like the hall at Seahome. Made of brownish blocks put together?'*

Tasgo shook his head. *'There are hundreds of them Dannaigh, everywhere, everything is boxes. Big boxes.'*

'I think you must mean houses Tasgo. People live in them.'

'As far as the eye can see. Round every corner. So many. There are not that many people, Dannaigh.'

Danny thought he understood. *'Cynmar is bigger than Seahome, right? I'm told Stonewall is bigger than Cynmar.'*

'It is,' confirmed Tasgo.

'This is Hull, it's bigger than any of those, than all of those put together, than all the Parisi, put together.

'Where are the cattle, the sheep, the grain to feed so many people.'

'Those are houses. We'll check it out once you are free. I'll show you.'

Then he had to explain it to the lawyer, how Tasgo had never seen a town, let alone a city, and was troubled by it. The lawyer put it down in swift movements on his pad, then asked, 'Can we cut to the chase. The police, the arrest, the assaults.'

Tasgo explained how the morning had gone, the seeking, and the threat. There was no need to describe the tension to the lawyer, he could feel it in the foreign words, the fleeting wonder and terror on Tasgo's face. Danny continued to translate more, and less, than the words. The lawyer asked few questions, always concise and to the point. He wanted

98

to know about P.C. Parker, how long they had talked, or rather tried to through sign language.

Tasgo kept telling Danny that there was no time for all this, that he had to get back, soon. Now. He was impatient but keeping it in check for now.

By the time they had finished, Danny had lost all track of time. The bleak little room had no natural light, there was no knowing what was going on outside. His stomach told him it was time to eat. He realised that Tasgo had eaten nothing today, and probably drunk nothing either. Tasgo was beyond such worries. The smallness of the room was oppressing him. He wouldn't think of food, and probably wouldn't be able to keep anything down if he did.

At first Tasgo had been content to sit in a chair, but by the end he was pacing the room restlessly. The last information the lawyer wanted, was where Tasgo would be staying when he was released. Something Danny had yet to think about, so dim and slight as that possibility seemed.

Moira had a house in Hull, which she let out to post graduate students. But she kept the attic rooms for herself, a tiny apartment, with its own cubicle shower and toilet. She called it her bed-sitting room. Danny couldn't see any other choice. Moira was in London, with Freya, who was giving a talk as part of a symposium. He was still wondering where Ken Raynes was, and why he had not answered Danny's emergency call.

At last the lawyer closed his recorder and iPad, and told them what his plan of attack was going to be.

Small Victories

Danny could hardly believe it, but they were walking out of the police station, all four of them, free as birds. Though birds could be caged too, he reminded himself. It hadn't been easy, and Danny's respect for their lawyer Joseph Desmond was immense.

He had come out of his crumpled corner wreathed in apologetic smiles. The police started by officially charging Tasgo with a multitude of sins, though the lawyer had advised against it. Tasgo was asking Danny what was going on now. It was clear he didn't understand. At least he was sitting, which took a lot of tension out of the proceedings. The police wanted to get stuck in with the assaults, but the lawyer, apologising for his own lack of understanding of the whole episode, persuaded them to start at the beginning with the 'obtaining goods by deception'.

Having shown that Tasgo had no money, no bank account and no bank card, and beyond that, no words, they were left with the fact that he had been encouraging the crowd, and must have known payment was due.

Danny had interrupted. They still had all his possessions, so he had to ask for a coin. He told them what he was about to do, then showed it to Tasgo, asking him what it was.

Tasgo took it cautiously, turned it over and peered at the marks on it. *'It's metal,'* he said at last, while Danny translated, *'not gold, too light for lead, perhaps silver.'* He puzzled for few seconds, then the penny dropped, he looked up bright with discovery at Danny, *'Is it one of those Roman things, that they use for barter?'*

Danny translated it as he spoke, changing the last bit to, 'Is it one of those Romany things, that they use for decorations on horse leather?' Then he added, 'He's never been shopping or had to pay for anything. He has no idea what money or payment is.'

The policemen looked at Tasgo dubiously. Joseph Desmond said, 'Part payment of the bill was taken on a credit card belonging to a Matt Davies, but there were insufficient funds for the majority. The full payment will be paid by Bacs today, together with a sum to be agreed by the business to cover any damage or cost incurred. A simple misunderstanding.'

He looked over the top of his glasses sorrowfully at his opponents, 'Nothing to warrant the following harassment and heavy-handed treatment that followed.'

He then pointed out that Police Constable Parker had been an 'exemplar of modern-day policing' to start with, quickly realising that he was dealing with someone of limited or no understanding of the English language and attempting to draw his client back to the premises in order to settle the monetary misunderstanding.

Danny was glad he was not translating it all for Tasgo. Tasgo might have laughed out loud at the description.

Then came a sorrowful lambasting of what followed. The harassing of a vulnerable person, who soon came to the genuine conclusion that he was the victim of violent attempts to kidnap and/or molest him. Even so, his client had not been as violent as he might have, being a strong young man, equipped to defend himself with a certain amount of basic skill. In the case of the police woman, Jane Slade, when he had inadvertently caused her to fall, he had also caught her, and saved her from a head injury.

He had ridden over protests at this, saying that he was aware that the police were under-funded and under-manned. He regretted that they had used so much man-power on a simple misunderstanding over payment of a bill, he had no desire to bring a formal complaint against the police, despite his client's obvious injuries. It was in nobody's interest to tarnish the reputation of the local police force, when charges against him could simply be dropped.

Danny wondered what the exact definition of blackmail was, and how close to the wind the lawyer might be sailing.

They didn't give in easily. Police officers shouldn't have to put up with violence against themselves. Arrest was not assault. Getting Tasgo out of the police wagon had been a case of violent manoeuvres and injuries taken on both sides.

It took quite some time for the lawyer to wear them down, but eventually charges had been dropped, against surety of the Lawyer himself, and Danny as well, that no further trouble would arise.

Danny had given his home address with his mother as Tasgo's residence, and Moira's tiny apartment at the top of her house in Hull as where he would be sleeping tonight. Paul's man, Jack went with them. Danny thought that was an important part of the agreement. They seemed to have faith in Jack's ability to intervene should Tasgo turn vicious.

So there they were, out in the evening air, though not completely free.

Free At Last

They stood outside Police Headquarters while traffic rushed noisily past on the main road. All the men with guns seemed to have gone, those trapped in the lockdown had made their way home. There were still cars in the car park, there was still the roar of traffic. The lawyer had left them, with a sudden bleak message for Danny, before he rushed away. 'Your cousin is a danger to himself and others, take care, Mr. Sharp, take care.'

Now that Tasgo was outside, free, the wild in him dared to raise its fears once more. Despite Danny's presence to explain things to him, there was no explaining the vehicles which charged at so great a speed, but without any means of propulsion. Tasgo shivered, and told himself it was the cold. He didn't believe it. He, warrior that he was, looked to Danny as a child might look to an adult for safety in a storm. He was ready to take on anything, anything at all, so long as he knew what it was, and how it might harm them.

Still full of tension and shock, the memory of the mouth of the gun imprinted on his vision, Danny was looking about them. He didn't know Hull well, so he asked Jack, standing on the other side of Tasgo. 'We need somewhere quiet, away from the traffic, somewhere green and natural looking. Somewhere we can reach on foot.'

Jack knew just the place. They crossed the main road, Jack with arm outstretched as if to order cars to stop, Danny holding Tasgo's arm and telling him when to run. What seemed to be the forecourt of a business quickly turned into a footpath, flanked on one side by scrub and trees, and on the other by nettles and brambles screening allotments. Danny could feel tension easing out of Tasgo as immediate threats were left behind. The road noise faded, and the evening twitter of birds covered what was left. Railing and a gate heralded a park with children's playground. Jack had led them to a good place.

Danny's mind was racing. Now that the immediate danger of Tasgo under police arrest, confined but undeterred, was dealt with, the larger issues remained. How had Tasgo got here? What to do with him now he was here? A view of green grass and distant trees invited them in.

The slow swing of a huge white blade in the sky took away all thought of safety and peace. A giant wind turbine stood near the huddle of an industrial estate across the river hidden behind trees. The blades swept silent round, slow, massive, unreal in their perfection and size.

Tasgo stopped dead.

Danny moved between him and the sight. *'It's not important,'* he said, *'It cannot harm us.'*

Tasgo demanded *'What? What is it?'* his voice tight.

'It takes power out of the air and gives it to us. Leave it alone, it won't harm us.' Behind Tasgo, beyond Jack, who had moved quietly closer, the path went round a small stone mound with trees round it. *'We'll sit over there,'* Danny decided, *'come.'*

For a horrid moment he thought Tasgo was too mesmerised by the giant blades, its huge tower of support, but at last he turned most deliberately, putting his back to the monster as he walked away.

Danny managed to get him sitting with his back to the thing, though it was hardly visible behind the screen of trees. Jack stood a little aside, like a good bodyguard, unobtrusive, always to hand if needed.

'Are you right?' Danny asked.

'Am I dead?' demanded Tasgo.

'Of course you're not dead!' Danny snapped before he could stop himself. Once more he met that challenging look from Tasgo, one that he had almost forgotten. Jack moved a leisurely pace closer.

'I am Underhill,' said Tasgo, not to be put aside.

Danny decided not to deal with that small matter yet. *'You are not dead,'* he said, making his voice quiet but firm. *'You don't feel dead, do you?'*

'They killed me three times,' Tasgo told him, *'they couldn't do that if I were alive.'*

'They didn't kill you. It's a… a weapon that, like a heavy blow, knocks you out for a second. That's all.'

'It was snakes, that bite,' Tasgo corrected him.

Danny shrugged, he didn't want to take time to argue that. *'How did you get here, Tasgo?'*

104

'I do not know, Dannaigh, you're the ones who come and go! Show me the pathway, lead me to the gate and I'll go back. Every moment that is wasted is dangerous. Jago is not to be trusted. He'll make something out of it! Get me back there Dannaigh...'

'Dugal will keep him under control, Dugal and Gamma.' Danny couldn't help a grin at the thought of his grandmother putting Jago in his place.

Then he saw the expression on Tasgo's face. *'What?'* he demanded.

Tasgo had gone pale, a ghastly white under his tan. He was on his feet now, as if ready for anything. *'You don't know,'* he said, barely audible. *'I thought you knew everything, everything that happened at Seahome.'*

Alarm rose in Danny too. What had happened in Seahome? What could be bad enough to turn Tasgo so pale. Trying to cool his cousin, keeping his own voice calm, Danny asked again, *'What?'*

'Dugal is dead, Dannaigh.' He retreated a step, as if Danny might be a danger. *'Dugal is dead and it is my fault.'* He was as wild as ever Danny had been. *'Is that why I am here? Dannaigh, is that why?'*

Danny was shocked. He could not imagine Seahome without its chief. He could not imagine the ancient without Dugal in it. And Tasgo was distraught. Danny threw aside every other thought or plan. He took command.

'I very much doubt it Tasgo. You had better tell me. Here, sit again...'

Tasgo didn't want to sit. Danny thought he was ready to run. Impossible thought. Tasgo would never run, he would always stand and fight.

'Tell me,' Danny said again, softer.

Tasgo braced himself, but his voice was broken as he started. *'It is my fault,'* he said again. *'I didn't intend... I didn't know.'* He stopped, and gathered some strength. *'It is my fault,'* he said for the third time. *'I wanted a new hall, a bigger, better home. There was this ash tree, straight as a spear, thickset, tall, a beautiful tree, Dannaigh, proud. I wanted it to make an inner circle of supports. I spoke to the spirit who lived there, I wanted her to know that it would be an honour, that everyone who saw those beams would thank her and revere her. I told her,'* he had to take breath then, *'I told her how her trunk would make the support and her branches the roof beams, for my new hall, when*

105

Dugal died.' Now it was out, he could breathe again, he could explain further.

'Dugal liked the plan, the old house had been reroofed several times, it could do with being larger. He said he wanted to see it done now, done and finished. So we went out with axes and saws, half the men of the village. We spoke to the tree spirit. Derven was there, he made offerings of oil and of bronze. We cut it down with care. It fell almost as planned. But the spirit was strong in it, it fell but somehow stayed attached, the trunk still...' He had to take breath, he could not look at Danny as he went on, *'Dugal took his axe and went to free it. He hit it with mighty strokes. The tether broke, and it fell to the ground.*

'Then the tree spirit remembered what I had said, and it flew at the Chief. We couldn't see it, but we could see him fighting it. He dropped his axe, he fell to the ground, struggling, I tried to help, I drew my sword and stabbed the air above him where he lay wrestling her, but I could not hit her. He died Dannaigh. He fought hard, but he died, because of my foolish words.'

For a long moment Danny could only stare at him, seeing his desolation. His mind was churning through the images Tasgo had presented him with. Dugal was well into his fifties, an old man who had lived a full and strenuous life. As if he had been there, he could see Dugal, on his back after strenuous hard work, bent arms grasping air, heart hammering, unable to speak. Flailing against massive pain. Heart attack. Major heart attack. Not how Tasgo saw it.

Danny took breath. *'No'*, he told Tasgo, gently, *'it's not your fault.'* But Tasgo had already made up his mind, Danny would have to find something stronger to change it. *'It was his destiny. He knew that when he agreed to build the hall with you. It was his destiny to step aside for you. It was the right time, while he was still at the peak of his strength.'*

'You think so?' Tasgo was finding it hard to accept.

'It was his destiny, and it was yours, to take over his role.' Danny didn't have to think twice about that. No-one but Tasgo could be chief after Dugal. Even Jago would have to see that.

Tasgo looked at him hard, assessing the truth of Danny's words. *'You are sure of this?'*

'I am,' Danny told him.

106

As guilt dropped out of Tasgo, energy flooded in.

'Then why am I here?' he demanded, 'I have work to do, I have to be there, to be in control! They will have seen me go Dannaigh. They won't know what to think! Take me back through Dannaigh, I have been here too long already.'

'I can't,' Danny told him. 'Our gate was shut for good. You have to tell me how you got here, and then we can see about getting you back.'

Tasgo looked bleak at that. 'I don't know how I got here,' he said.

'Tell me,' Danny urged, 'tell me what happened.'

So Tasgo told him about the raiders, working their way down the coast, and how Seahome had been called on to help, and had guessed their next port of call. They hardly had time to hide before the boat was in full view. Like Dugal before him, he had waited until the raiders had made it plain what they were. Then they fell on them as wolves on sheep. Only the sheep had spears and knives and swords. He was confident of victory though. He had been at the heels of their leader, he thought he had struck home, when the blue light came and took him.

At that he fell silent. They both fell silent, Tasgo trying not to remember what followed, Danny thinking fast and waiting for Tasgo to be ready to tell him more.

After a while, Danny prompted, 'What then, Tasgo?'

Tasgo told him, the tightness in his voice telling of the terror and the panic, while the words merely stated the facts. The invisible walls that had held him, the panicking people beyond them, details were lost in a fog of emotion. After that Danny got a picture of a tunnel with doors in it, a bit like a train perhaps, but a tunnel. He got downtown Hull, with bars and clubs, celebrations as wild as the aftermath of a funeral in ancient times.

The weird floating lights were, of course, police cars on the prowl.

The nest in the sky took a while to fathom, but at last Danny realised it was a block of flats, with glass near the stairs.

Danny did not bother with the details. He did not bother with Jack, who had drifted closer as emotion had flowed free. The important thing was that Tasgo had done nothing to cause the portal which had brought him here. Danny knew of no tunnels underground. Unless they could find out how he got here, it seemed Tasgo was here to stay. What to do with him? Without letting him learn how everything here worked, in case he could return somehow. He couldn't take modern knowledge back to the Iron Age.

Now Tasgo was leaning forward, *'How do I get back Dannaigh? I must get back, they will be thinking... I do not know what they will be thinking but it can't be good. How do I get back?'*

Danny had no answer to give him. His father always said, keep calm, see what's wrong, fix it. It would take more than Danny's wits to solve this. Meanwhile, Danny had some immediate tasks to fulfil.

'When did you last eat Tasgo?' he asked. The lawyer had made sure they got water, and Tasgo had gulped it down. Danny guessed Tasgo was still thirsty. Tasgo allowed himself to be side tracked, which proved how hungry and thirsty he must be. It turned out that Tasgo had eaten nothing today, and nothing the day before because of rushing to the battle. It seemed that last night there had been drinking, but no food. Tasgo had eaten next to nothing in forty-eight hours.

There was also the small matter of the brecks, smelling worse with every minute. And also Jack, standing close enough to hear their talk, but not able to understand it.

Tasgo saw Danny glance at Jack, and asked, without looking in that direction *'Who is he Dannaigh? He is one of them, isn't he?'*

'He is my paid man,' Danny told him, *'You needn't worry about him.'*

'I don't like him Dannaigh, he was there, in that place.'

'I know, I sent him there.'

'He was there before you came Dannaigh.'

'Yes,' better not get lost in explaining about telephones, best not mentioned at all. He turned to Jack. 'Is there a fast-food near here? Burgers or fish and chips?' Things they could eat with their fingers, without the use of forks. Light was beginning to fade, soon all the lights of the town would be coming on, another marvel for Tasgo to wonder about.

Jack nodded.

Danny had his belongings back now, and he forked out a twenty. 'Can you get enough for three?'

108

Jack looked at him, making no move to take the money. 'Paul said to keep you in one piece,' he said. And when Danny didn't seem to understand, 'I'll not leave you alone with him.'

That checked Danny. 'Are you working for me or Paul?' he asked at last.

'Both.'

Danny gave a sceptical huff. 'All's well,' he told the man, 'we just need food.'

'Where are you going, after?' For a paid man, Jack wasn't very biddable.

Danny answered him anyway. 'My aunt's flat,' and gave the address.

'Why don't we go there now? He can get cleaned up, and you can order a takeaway.'

It was a good idea. Jack put the address into his phone for a route, and they followed his directions. Danny tried to keep Tasgo from seeing too much of the screen.

Moira's

It wasn't far to walk, a side street close to the university. Danny could see Jack taking in details, like a good bodyguard. He had been useful, but Danny would be glad to be rid of him. He had seen far too much of Tasgo. It was just as well he couldn't understand a word of their conversation.

Moira's house was a semi, with space for parking on the front. Danny had a key to the front door in his pocket, but he paused to thank Jack for his assistance, saying he'd pay Paul whatever was due. Jack was stolid.

'You think you can manage him if he gets upset?'

'He's had a rough time,' Danny told him, 'once he's calmed down he's no threat to anyone.'

'Doesn't look like that,' said Paul.

'He's been lost where no-one can understand him, then forcibly arrested, tasered, humiliated, left in cuffs for ages...' Danny hadn't realised how angry he was, he made himself speak more quietly, '...of course he's upset. He'll calm down.' He was aware of Tasgo watching them eagle-eyed, hearing the conflicting tones. 'We'll be fine now,' Danny told Jack.

'Mind if I see where you're taking him?' Jack asked.

Danny could hardly say no. He didn't think Jack would take no for an answer. Tasgo was standing outwardly calm, that stance that could move into anything from a friendly hug to a devastating attack. He was watching how Jack and Danny were facing one another, he was standing ready.

Danny tried the handle of the door before reaching for his key. It opened easily, unlocked. Danny went in, and Jack waited to follow Tasgo inside. The television was on in the back room, Danny led them up the stairs, to the door at the bottom of the stairs to the attic. No key was needed here either, Moira seemed to have infinite trust in her lodgers, one of whom appeared suddenly in a bedroom doorway. A man of medium height and build with glasses and jagged pale hair.

'This is a private house,' was his greeting, crisp, with a Germanic accent. 'what is your business?' He wasn't taken aback by the way the three men turned to him, Jack and Tasgo almost coming shoulder to shoulder as they turned.

Danny cut in with a smile, 'We're going up to my aunt Moira's room, she's letting us sleep here. I'm Danny, her nephew.'

'Three of you,' the man was disgusted, 'I hardly think there is enough room for three.' His nose was wrinkling with distaste, it might just have been the smell, but Danny didn't think so

'It's all right,' Danny told him, 'Jack will be leaving shortly. My cousin's had an accident but he'll clean up all right.'

The man's chin rose, he hadn't introduced himself, and now he was retreating to his room. 'Moira did not tell us of this,' he said, 'I will phone her immediately.' The door shut firmly, not slammed.

They went up to Moira's room. It was a simple room, quite small. A futon served as sofa or bed, a fold-down desk took up one end wall, and opposite, next to a small cupboard for clothes, was the door to the shower and toilet. The sloping ceiling had the only window, a sky light allowing the faint evening glow to show all these things. Best not to turn the light on yet.

Tasgo looked around with satisfaction, it was a large sleeping stall, showing Moira's high status. It was all a bit strange, but then, they were Underhill.

Danny turned to Jack, still filling the doorway. Time to get rid of him. Danny would have to explain the shower to Tasgo, it would be obvious that was what he was doing, and no-one was so stupid that they didn't know what a shower was.

'Thanks for looking after us,' he said to Jack, 'We'll be okay from here.'

Jack was looking at Tasgo, 'You sure?'

'Perfectly,' Danny told him.

'Paul would want me to stay.'

'Not necessary,' Danny told him. Then tiring of all this, 'It's not me who needed protection, it was Tasgo. He may be big, but he's vulnerable.' A word he had never thought might apply to Tasgo.

Jack took a card from his shirt pocket. 'Call me direct,' he said, 'I won't be far away, I'm in Hull.'

'Thanks,' said Danny taking the card, and waiting for him to go. Jack paused, taking in the room, the only bed, the enclosed space. It could be called cosy, it could be called tiny, rather like a cell. He went, and Danny closed the door behind him.

Tasgo was already stripping off the clothes that reeked of sweat, battle, terror, and above all ammonia. He must have started while Jack was still here. Danny wondered how much of the scars Jack had seen. There were some new ones, but they didn't cover the slash where an axe had bitten through Tasgo's shield, smashing it and slicing flesh.

'What is there for me to wear?' Tasgo asked, standing naked, as if it were normal, which of course was natural to him.

Danny explained about the shower, simply by showing it. Tasgo watched with amazement as Danny turned a piece of metal and water fell from the nozzle above. Danny had to do it several times to show how easy and simple the control was, before Tasgo was prepared even to get close enough to try. That was good, because it took a while for hot water to wind its way through the pipes to the top of the house. Now it was nice and warm

When Danny showed him the soap, Tasgo sniffed it cautiously. He looked at Danny, wide-eyed. *'This is how Dugal smelt when he came back from visiting. He said it was the smell of happiness.'*

Danny grinned, *'Get happy,'* he told Tasgo.

Tasgo didn't look happy, but he stepped into the booth, and turned on the shower. Danny closed the glass door.

It flew open as Tasgo crashed out again, looking wild, wilder than Danny had ever been, when it had been his turn to be a stranger in a strange land. Danny caught him, contained him. Tasgo didn't fight against it. He was looking with horror at the shower. Suddenly it came back to Danny, Tasgo's words, being held in an invisible cage, a cage of light. Surely he couldn't mean a shower cubicle? That didn't make sense. A glass cubicle of some other sort, then.

He explained. He showed Tasgo how to open and close the door, let him do it himself. Eventually Tasgo got back in. He left the door open and started the shower. As steam began to fog the glass, Danny threw a towel on the floor outside, to soak up the spillage.

He went on to do things in a logical order. He phoned out for a pizza, with everything. He bundled Tasgo's clothing into a shopping bag, ready to take it down to the washing machine. He phoned his mother, but got 'unable to take the call'. He didn't phone Ken Raynes, though he was still wondering why he hadn't heard from him. . Now Moira was married, there might be something of Ken Raynes' in her cupboard. As he hunted there for something that Tasgo could wear, he thought about phoning Paul, on the usual line not using the emergency mode. He was wondering about Jack, why he was so keen to stay close, what he had been doing that he could get to the police station so fast. He was wondering who had decided that Tasgo was perhaps a terrorist. He didn't blame them for that, it had just been unfortunate. And scary. Now that it was over, he could feel how scared he had been, looking into the mouth of the weapon, knowing what it could do.

There was an oversize jumper that would at least cover most of Tasgo. It was Sunday, the shops were long past shut. He considered going on line and ordering some clothes for express delivery, only he didn't know what size Tasgo would be. Less tall than Danny, but wider. Powerful deep-seated muscles had broadened and filled Tasgo's physique. He looked formidable.

Danny sat on the futon, running it all through his mind again, feeling the powerful emotions. Six hours in all, since the police car had pulled into the boatyard. That was Tasgo for you. Every emotion under the sun, the possibility of sudden death, conflict, and - and a strange feeling of being whole again. He hadn't known how much he had felt the lack, the emptiness of estrangement. When he was feeling low he would tell people, his current girl usually, that he was missing his father, which was true. But it wasn't the whole truth.

He realised suddenly how long Tasgo had been in the shower. He could hear it still running.

He opened the door, to find that a single towel had been inadequate to soak up the water. The floor was awash. Tasgo was standing in the flow, eyes closed, turning slowly, soaking in the blessing that came in the form of warm water. The air was thick with moisture and warmth. Danny reached in and turned off the shower.

Tasgo opened his eyes, relaxed now, still relishing the warmth and the scents. The look he sent to Danny for the reason for the interruption, was warm and unchallenging.

'You've had enough, don't be greedy,' Danny told him, smiling. Tasgo at ease was a happy sight. It seemed that warm water had washed away all the tensions and soothed a troubled mind. That too was Tasgo all through. He planned ahead, but he lived for the moment as well. Danny found him another towel, and set about rescuing the shower area, wringing out the towel into the sink and mopping again and again, until the floor was practically dry.

A Simple Plan

Danny woke with surprise. His nerves had been so on edge after yesterday, he had been so full of worries and dangerous possibilities to be avoided that he had thought he would never sleep. Fear and tension were tiring though, and when he did drop off he had slept like a log, even though it was on blankets on the carpet.

Last night Danny had given up trying to explain, and Tasgo had given up expecting some gate to be opened now, immediately and at once. They had polished off a pizza, an unexpected food to Tasgo, full of taste, puzzlement and suspicion. Then Tasgo had settled half naked on the futon, and fallen at once asleep, so deeply and suddenly that Danny realised how fierce had been his terror, his joy and dismay that he was totally exhausted. So Danny had crept down the stairs, settled the fears of Mr Uptight, put Tasgo's clothes through a wash, and made a number of phone calls. To Chrissie's numerous texts he texted back

>Nothing for you to worry about. Looking after my cousin. Won't be back for a few days. XX D.< She would worry just the same.

This morning, Danny was making plans. Moira had texted that she would get here on the 12.25 train, there was a lot to do first.

He had hardly started, when Tasgo woke, and was amazed to find his clothes lying beside him, clean, dry and smelling of summer meadows.

His morning greeting, as he dressed, was, *'How do I get back home, Dannaigh?'*

'I don't know. I thought the gate had been closed completely, that we couldn't return to you, nor you to us, not ever,' Danny told him. *'Your arrival was a big surprise.'*

'Yes,' Tasgo agreed unhappily, *'a big surprise.'* Then he went on more thoughtfully, *'I didn't think you would be so difficult to find, Dannaigh,'* looking at Danny as if he were disappointed with what he saw. *'I thought you would be known to everyone, a chief or,'* he shrugged one shoulder,

'someone important. I thought I would only have to say your name, and someone would show me the way.'

Danny thought that would be true, had he stayed in the past. There he was Dugal's grandson, Tasgo's cousin, a warrior, though without a sword. He already had a reputation, though perhaps not one he felt proud of. *'There are more of us here, Tasgo, and we live longer. Here, I'm still young, making my way.'*

Tasgo nodded, accepting that. Then he set that aside and concentrated on what was more immediately troubling. *'When you told me, and Moira and Gamma, they told me too, that you did not fight here, it wasn't true. I have encountered the men in blue. And the women,'* he added, ruefully. *'Your father, when he came to us, he was already a warrior. He was trained in fighting. Why did you tell me something that isn't true?'*

He was being careful not to call anyone a liar, but that was what he really meant. Danny wished Tasgo had left his father out of it. He marshalled his response carefully too, for other reasons. *'It is true, generally speaking. Because of the people in blue. The* 'police'*. They are like... the force behind the lore. If disputes come to blows, they turn up. They stop the fighting. If people are fierce, they trap them in a small room, like they did with you, until they come to their senses. If folk have done damage, they are made to repay, or to spend a long time trapped in a room like that. They take it very badly if anyone tries to fight them. So most people behave well.'*

Danny could see Tasgo thinking that through. *'That is a cruel punishment, to trap them in a place like that. Better to make them bondsmen, so they can be useful and work their way to freedom.'*

That was quite an idea, thought Danny, state slavery, how would that go down?

Tasgo said thoughtfully, *'They let me go.'*

Danny smiled, at first look he had thought the lawyer Joseph Desmond was nondescript and harmless. He had proved to be a warrior with words. What Danny said was, *'We were lucky to get away with it.'*

Tasgo kept to the main point. *'How do I get back Dannaigh? What must we do to open a gate?'*

Danny had been facing that problem for years, for five years to be exact. Only - he had known that it would be wrong to do so. They had closed that portal for a good reason, to be in the past was to alter the past. To alter the past would alter the present, it would change the world.

It was a point that he understood and appreciated, but it stood beside another equally significant thing that his aunt had said. Whatever they did in the past was already done, it was, quite literally, ancient history. It had been done two thousand years ago. It was already woven into the present. Danny was inclined to think that gave them a let out. They could do anything, it had already been done. A small part of him though acknowledge that if they made a new portal, that would alter the past. It would change things. It was all far too abstruse and complicated for him.

One thing was clear though. Now that Tasgo was here, that in itself changed everything. Tasgo did not fit here. As far as Danny could see, he would never fit here. Everything would be magic to him. Even if he learned the language, he was unsuited to modern life. He had only been here twenty-four hours and look what trouble he had caused already! They had to find a way of sending him back.

'I don't know,' was all he could give. Knowing how badly that might be taken he went on quickly, *'Moira is the one. Moira and Freya. They're the ones with brains.'*

'Freya lives?' Tasgo was more than just surprised.

Danny gave a wry smile. The titanium and steel hand was going be even more of a surprise. *'She does,'* he said, *'but it has been hard for her.'*

Tasgo nodded and got back to the main point. *'And she will help open a new gate?'*

'If it can be done.' Danny cautioned.

'We could go back to the gate you shut, and open that again,' suggested Tasgo.

No chance. The equipment they had used to make the electromagnetic pulse that had stopped it had all been melted and fused. Some of it was still hidden in the cave, because they couldn't get it back through the narrow fissures in the rock.

Danny wasn't even sure they could make a new one. They had no idea where the old one came from. Gamma, Danny's grandmother, had simply found it by accident. *'It isn't that easy,'* he started, but Tasgo was in no mood for defeatism.

'Then we build a new one,' he said firmly. *'What do we need?'*

A whole pile more of space-time theory, thought Danny, another Einstein or Higgs. This wasn't helping. Tasgo had got here, there must be a way, an anomaly of some sort. He said, *'First we have to find out how you got here. Where you arrived would be a good start.'*

Tasgo thought he had an answer, *'Matt knows,'* he said, *'Matt and Bethany and Emma. Matt seemed to be the one in charge, but Bethany...'* she had been balm to his spirit, so alive, so beautiful, so lithe and passionate. He forced his attention back to the matter in hand. *'Either of those would be do. But,'* he had to admit it, *'I lost them.'*

'We'll find them,' said Danny, he already knew more than that. The lawyer had mentioned Matt Davies, the one whose credit card had maxed out. *'We'll find Matt, and he'll take us to where you arrived. But first,'* he said, *'we need to get you some new clothes, so no-one will point at you and laugh,'* he finished, remembering Tasgo saying much the same to him one day two thousand years ago. He could see Tasgo remembered it too, he was smiling.

Moving On

Tasgo lifted a sleeve to his face sniffing, looking at Danny over the top of it. *'Dugal used to smell like this sometimes, when he had gone off with Gamma. He said it was the smell of happiness,'* he added, somewhat bitterly.

'He had Gamma to show him around,' said Danny. He didn't add that Gamma hadn't taken him clubbing nor got him into any fights.

Now he was dressed in his own clean clothes, looking like a cross between a hippy and a prize fighter, ready for anything, Tasgo said, *'We should go to the gate you used to come through and mend it.'*

'You can't have come through that gate,' Danny told him. They were in Hull, where there had once been a settlement called Cynmar; the portal his family had used was in the basement of Moira's house, near what had once been Seahome. *'Tell me again, what happened when you fell into a cage you couldn't see?'*

Tasgo told him, but this time Danny was ready with questions. *'What colour were the walls?'* and *'What could you smell? Could you smell the sea?'*

The details were becoming clear. The unexpected blue light out of nowhere, falling into a glass cubicle, the long corridor, with doors, the colour just being 'dark'. Tasgo had still been in shock, in a controlled panic, everything too strange to take in. Danny got descriptions, of a sort, of the three people, Emma blonde and giggly, Matt a little older, and no warrior, about the same height as Tasgo, but not as muscular, not at all. Danny learned a lot more about Bethany, her height, the glossy dark hair, the fine-grained skin, perfectly coloured, her curvaceous body, her quick reactions, her sympathetic nature, her beautiful dark eyes, her full mouth and perfect teeth.

'I think you've fallen in love Tasgo!' smiled Danny, and Tasgo actually cocked his head to consider it.

'*I would have to know her better,*' he concluded, amused. It was good to see he could still smile about something.

Danny posed his next question carefully, '*Tasgo, she was willing, wasn't she? You didn't have to...?*'

'*Is that all you think of me?*' growled Tasgo, put out by the mere suggestion.

'*You can be quite,*' what was the best word, '*enthusiastic...*' was the nearest translation.

'*So was she,*' declared Tasgo, remembering the tender, questioning touch of her hands on his skin, the sympathetic wonder in her eyes as they looked into his.

Smells of cooking were wafting up the stairs, time was moving on. '*Good,*' said Danny, '*now there are a few words you need to know...*'

By the time the shops were open. Tasgo could say, 'I yam so ree. I donut speak in glish,' and knew the words for, 'yes', 'no' and 'stop'. He had undone his hair in the shower last night, and now it hung in wild abundance round his face. Danny pulled it back into a pony tail, which made Tasgo look too much like a pirate. Since he already looked odd enough in his brecks and tunic, Danny tied the hair quickly into a man-bun. It transformed him. He was a modern man, a fit and strong modern man. The bruises coming out all round his face, the little nicks where he had cannoned off hard edges and corners, were another matter. He looked like a hard man, possibly a dangerous one, but when he smiled, he looked confident, the victim of some freak accident, a man who had been hurt by something that could happen to anyone.

They set out.

Danny explained about zebra crossings and traffic lights. He warned that vehicles, he called them chariots, moved much faster than people could, so you had to have a large gap in the traffic, or to wait for the chariots to stop before stepping in front of them. What Tasgo was making of it all, he didn't ask. When they arrived at a suitable shop, Tasgo became subdued. Looking at the display in the window, Danny suddenly realised what the 'headless people' Tasgo had spoken of must be.

'*They are just posts to hang clothes on,*' he told Tasgo, but Tasgo didn't seem to believe him. In the Iron Age they cut off the heads of their enemies, Danny knew, and sometimes stuck them on poles to help guard their homes. Leaving their bodies headless. And Underhill was where some of them thought the dead went, or might do, once laid in their graves, or left on the field of battle. Too much history to undo in one go, he dragged Tasgo into the shop.

By the time they came out, Tasgo was in a state of bemused wonder. So many clothes, so many, many, days and weeks and months of work, all in one place, so many bright colours.

The underwear was a surprise to Tasgo, he liked the softness of the material. Although he was about an inch shorter than Danny, he needed larger size jeans. The attendant offered to have them taken up, be ready in just a few days, but Danny just rolled the excess length into turn-ups. The largest t-shirt only just fit across his chest.

It finished the transformation.

Tasgo still stuck out like a sore thumb, he had presence, he wore the bruises on his battered face easily, as if it were normal. He walked like someone ready for anything, as if daring the world to try taking him on. Danny realised that he was still in a state of high alarm, but could think of no way to lessen that tension. He remembered how his own first weeks in the Iron Age had been. He had managed to stay alive then, Tasgo would get used to this. It might take quite some time.

They walked out together towards the university. Everything Tasgo had told Danny about Matt, Bethany and Emma shrieked 'Students'. And they could stop at the Students' Union for breakfast. Tasgo was looking around him in a more focused way. Either he was settling down, or he was wondering if he was recognising places. When they reached the steps up to the union, it became clear.

'*I was here, yesterday,*' he told Danny, but he hung back as Danny led him in.

Others, finishing their breakfast, or grabbing a quick coffee on the go, looked at Tasgo. He was unmissable. Tasgo soaked up what he took to be admiring glances. Danny didn't disabuse him, Tasgo needed all the positives Danny could send his way. They ate breakfast with fingers, Danny had chosen suitable stuff. He thought Tasgo would find forks amusing, rather than a brilliant idea to introduce to the folk back home. He was wondering whether they would ever get Tasgo back to where he came from, because if not he would have to learn all the modern, if he was going to fit in.

Enough of the ifs, he thought as they finished eating and wiped hands and mouths clean with the paper serviettes. It was time to move things forward. Bethany had a room in one of the flats, and he led Tasgo in the direction of the Courtyard as a first guess.

The moment it came into view, Tasgo let out a cry and started running, he wasn't easy to keep up with. He never had been. But he stopped outside one of the entrances, looking up. 'Up there,' he said, 'high up, Bethany has her sleeping stall here.'

There was a security number pad beside the door, one to which they had no key.

It was still early in the morning, and the more eager students were leaving for morning lectures. Danny stood outside, explaining this to Tasgo, until he could see someone approaching the door from the other side. He timed his approach to meet them as they came out, holding the door for them then walking inside with Tasgo following.

Tasgo started up the stairs at speed. When Danny caught up with him, Tasgo was eying the lift doors with suspicion, and Danny suddenly realised what that part of the story had been about. He wasn't about to enlighten Tasgo. Instead he asked, 'Which door?' because there were several.

Bethany

It took a while for someone to answer Danny's knock. It was opened by a tousled head above a onesie, a rabbit suit. She took in Danny, with his welcoming smile, and then saw Tasgo's face, full of bruises, questions, wonderment and admiration of the woman he saw before him.

'Is Bethany in?' Danny asked brightly.

'What happened to you?' the girl asked Tasgo, taken somewhat aback but sounding sympathetic.

'He had an accident,' Danny told her. 'Is Bethany in?'

'Poor you,' she told Tasgo, and 'I'll see,' for Danny. She walked away leaving the door wide open. Danny stepped inside, blocking the corridor so that Tasgo wouldn't push in further. The rabbit girl knocked on Bethany's door, once, then again when there was no answer. She had begun to turn back to the two men when a sleepy voice answered. A moment's consultation through the open door, then rabbit girl turned back closing the door behind her.

'She's getting up, come on in,' she said, starting to move away down the corridor.

'S'okay,' Danny answered at once, remembering how Tasgo had said Bethany had tricked him and escaped. Standing in the doorway there was nowhere she could go.

Rabbit girl looked back, a little surprised to see them still standing there. As she looked at Tasgo with his battered face she seemed disappointed. She was obviously curious.

'Suit yourselves,' she said, walking away down the corridor, fluffy tail wagging slightly as she walked.

'Is she...?' Tasgo started uncertainly.

'No,' Danny told him immediately, it was so obviously a piece of clothing that he was surprised that Tasgo was going to ask. But maybe he had been going to ask something else more reasonable.

Just then the door to Bethany's room opened and a sleepy Bethany came out, wrapped in a sensible dressing gown. She stopped when she saw who it was, looking from face to face.

'So now there are two of you,' she said, almost accusingly.

Danny's smile broadened, he could see why Tasgo liked this woman. 'Yes,' he said, 'he's my cousin. Only Tasgo was brought up without any English, which made life rather difficult on Saturday.'

'Yes,' she said, looking at Tasgo, 'What happened to his face?'

'He got beaten up,' Danny offered. 'I'm his cousin, Danny.'

Bethany was still looking at the bruises that covered Tasgo's face. She was remembering Saturday, how Tasgo had picked her up and ran with her, how he had dealt with the man looking for a fight. She was wondering how he got in a fight, on Sunday after she had left. She was wondering how much Tasgo had told Danny about Saturday night, in her room.

She turned away from that to Danny, 'Danny Sharp?' she asked, 'Halter foundation?' and as Danny nodded, 'Is he an exchange student?'

'No,' Danny told her. He didn't want to get into that. 'He was just brought up not speaking English. Where did you find him?'

'We didn't find him,' she said, 'he just appeared. Suddenly. In Matt's lab.' She had convinced herself that there was a perfectly rational explanation for what had happened, she just hadn't worked it out yet. But now the question, put like that - there was definitely something odd about the question, and the cousin. She wasn't surprised it was all a bit out of kilter now, it had been right from the start.

'Can you tell us what happened,' Danny asked, 'Tasgo's not making a lot of sense.'

So Bethany, still keeping her distance, one hand on the door to her room, told them how Matt inveigled them into going with him through some sort of catacomb, into his lab, and how Tasgo had arrived in a flash of blue light. Telling it made her remember the things she had been trying hard to forget, or at least ignore; the strange light, his sudden arrival, how terrified Tasgo had been, frantically, desperately, terrified. She looked at him again, a different man now he was no longer frightened. His smile at her was warm, it made her heart beat faster, but he looked like a man who would not be easily frightened. He looked like a man who would fight off any attackers, a man who would be in control, not the one who got beaten up. She looked quickly away, back at Danny. She concertinaed the rest into a few terse sentences, the less said about that the better.

Danny wasn't interested in what happened after. He asked about the lab, where it was, how to get to it.

Bethany told him where, down by the old town, the municipal buildings, a door in the basement that just seemed to be a cupboard or something.

'And Matt has a lab down there? Danny asked. That didn't seem right, the University was all up here, not the old part of town.

'He said he shared it with someone.' Someone not entirely sane, she remembered now, and again a shiver ran down her spine.

'It's Matt Davies, isn't it?' Danny asked, 'Do you know where we can find him?'

'No,' Bethany was sure now that something was very wrong. 'You're not in trouble with the police, are you?' she said suspiciously.

'No, nothing like that,' Danny told her, hoping it was true, 'just trying to get things straight for Tasgo.'

Bethany's eyes met Tasgo's, and she remembered the gentle touch of his hands on her skin, the warmth of his arms so strong, yet so tender.

'Were you hiding in there?' she asked him direct.

Danny answered, 'You thought he was hiding?'

'Either that or there was another way in...'

'Must have been,' Danny told her.

Bethany was still looking at Tasgo, remembering how terrified he had been. If he had simply come from another room, why would he be terrified? Suddenly she really didn't want to be doing this, to be talking with these two strangers, inside her own flat. She felt naked beneath the dressing gown, and vulnerable. 'I have to get ready,' she said, 'lectures. Hope it all works out,' she told them, showing them the door without coming any closer to them...

Danny didn't want to go. He wasn't sure they could find this lab from her description. On the other hand, she didn't have to tell them anything, and they knew now where she lived. He turned back, and found Tasgo, his shoulder nonchalant against the wall, enjoying the sight in front of him.

'*We go now,*' Danny told him firmly.

Disappointment showed on Tasgo's face, as he reluctantly let Danny push him out of the door. 'Perhaps we could buy you a coffee later?' suggested Danny turning back to Bethany, now ready to close the door on them quickly and firmly. She wasn't looking at him, she was looking at Tasgo.

'Sometime, maybe…' she answered, as the door closed rather too quickly.

'*We scared her,*' muttered Danny as they took to the stairs, and heard Tasgo chuckle.

Turning he saw the smile on Tasgo's face. '*What are you looking so smug about?*' he demanded.

Tasgo smile widened. '*She wants me,*' he said, self-satisfied.

'*Don't count on it,*' Danny told him, realising as he said it that it was probably only too true. Then, '*We have more important things to think about.*'

Tasgo obviously agreed, the smile faded and as they turned the corner of the stairs he asked. '*What did we learn?*'

Danger

Moira arrived by train as promised, shortly after twelve. She took a taxi and met them on campus. Tasgo greeted Moira with the hug that he had failed to give Danny, but then, both he and Tasgo were not as tense now and conditions were more favourable. They ate outside, where trees and grass helped hide the buildings around them. Tasgo asked politely about offspring, and Moira confessed to Lily, now four years old and quite a handful.

'Just the one?' Tasgo was surprised. Then, worried, 'Ken still lives?'

Moira laughed at his surprise. 'He does. For us, I think one is enough.' If it puzzled Tasgo he gave no sign of it. He was still too tense and full of alarms. Danny was glad they hadn't had to go into town again, with all the overload of senses that would bring.

While they ate burgers, Danny brought her up to date. When Danny told her that Dugal had died and Tasgo was now chief, he thought she might shed a tear or two for her father, but no. 'He was a good man,' she said, 'and a great chief. You won't let him down, Tasgo, I'm sure he will be proud of you. Congratulations.' Tasgo didn't claim it was his fault, he thanked her as a chief would.

She didn't seem disappointed with what they had found out. She knew exactly where to go.

It was downtown. Despite Danny's misgivings, they walked. Tasgo kept a wary eye on the people, the shops, the vehicles, the headless bodies in the window displays, the vertiginous scale of the buildings. Despite Danny on one side of him, and Moira on the other, he was alarmed and ready to react. Nothing Danny could do or say would change that, so Danny did nothing but walk, easy, with confidence, in the hopes that it might rub off on Tasgo a little.

The library was open, and nobody batted an eyelid as the three of them walked in. Someone at the counter greeted Moira by name, and

Moira told her she was showing some researchers around. It was a good size library, a maze of book shelves, computer terminals and table tops, many occupied by students and books. It was the place where Moira worked, or rather part of the place. In a far corner was a door marked 'Staff only'. Moira led them through and down the stairs to the rest of the library, the real books. A big sign facing them at the foot of the stairs read,

STOP
DANGEROUS BOOKS

Moira smiled.

Danny said as they passed it 'Dangerous?'

Moira smiled. 'A joke, you can read it two ways, with or without added punctuation. There is an argument that most books are dangerous.'

'Most books?' queried Danny.

'They can carry infectious ideas, or make people think. They let you see things from a different angle, some people don't like that.'

Tasgo was looking about him warily. On either side high cliffs crammed with books were jammed up to each other. There was a winding mechanism to shift them apart, but Tasgo didn't fathom that. To him they were just strange structures, complex walls that left a corridor through which they could walk. The way was dark, despite the light that came on magically over their heads and faded away after they passed.

A chasm opened up to their right and left, and Moira turned left, towards a door at the end of the chasm. She had to use a keypad to gain access.

Tasgo moved with caution now, ready for anything, as though danger lurked at every doorway they passed through, every side door that remained unopened. He was uncomfortable, though having Moira and Danny with him should have been some comfort. They seemed to understand the strange lights from the ceiling, like miniature suns filtered through an orange haze. They seemed not to understand the danger that lay ahead. Moira opened another door, and Tasgo stopped.

'This is it,' he told Moira tensely. 'It was here.' He was wishing for a sword, a spear or even a knife, anything that would serve as a weapon.

128

But what good were weapons against magic? The length of the tunnel, the doors closing behind him, had alarmed him. Neither Moira nor Danny seemed prepared enough for the dangers ahead. He was so tense Danny could feel the energy coming off him, the readiness, the fear.

These were tunnels, just like the ones Tasgo had moved through two nights ago.

Danny made a show of looking at the walls and doors with relaxed interest. He had not seen this part of the library when he had come with his parents, when he was quite small. He had marvelled then at the expanse of books, now he wondered when and how this warren of tunnels had been built. Was it just for the books? They were quite near the marina now. Why weren't they underwater?

'Used to be dry docks, before the war. Covered over and used as shelters.' Moira told him, opening yet another door.

Instead of a wall, big loading-doors were to their left. Ahead was another door, needing a different number key than all the rest.

Tasgo halted entirely as the door opened and he could see in. This was it, the place where he had landed, from a small height, into an invisible cage. He grabbed Moira's arm as she was going in, drawing her back.

Inside stood all the boxes tied together with dark, smooth ropes. He could smell fear in that room, he could smell danger. They shouldn't go any closer.

'It is here,' he told her, making his voice firm. 'This is where I fell into a cage that cannot be seen.' To make sure of their understanding, of the danger there he added, 'Bethany, Emma and Matt, they were all afraid.' The edge to his voice showed they hadn't been the only ones.

Moira turned to him, 'It must have been horrid Tasgo, but you're safe now.'

'We shouldn't go in,' he told her, still holding her arm. She could feel how tense he was.

She stepped closer to him, 'Don't worry, this is a place where I work, I know it well.'

Danny stepped past her, through the door.

The electronic boxes, the resonance chamber, it could have been used for anything. They were just black boxes with dials and adjustments, put

129

together for any purpose, but to Danny they reeked of the set-up that had gone into the cave hidden below Moira's house, to destroy the connection with the past, to kill the portal and put out the blue flame forever.

This was the dark place where five years ago Moira had worked with Kevin Wilcox, foolishly letting him play with ideas of time travel and worm holes. This was the place where Kevin Wilcox had learned everything he needed to know in order to destroy Danny's childhood home, to injury Danny's mother and to send his father into oblivion. He turned back, bleak, to look at Moira.

This was the place where somehow Kevin Wilcox had turned himself into Kuillok, evil sorcerer of the Iron Age.

He thought then of the months he had spent nearly five years ago, being unaware that Moira and Ken were working with Kuillok behind his back, finding a way to close the connection between now and then.

Unaware of Danny's misgivings, Moira was more concerned with the present, and with Tasgo. *'We have to find this Matt person,'* she said, *'He did something that caught you and brought you through. We need to know what he did.'* She was leading Tasgo back the way they had come.

Moira already had Matt's address, she had been busy with her laptop on the train. She headed for a taxi rank, but Tasgo's reaction to the proximity of the vehicles was obvious. They decided to split forces. Danny and Tasgo would go back to the university, she had a time-table for his course, so they might catch him coming in or out of lectures, or in the library, working.

She would go to Matt's home address and meet them back on campus later.

Danny had done a little homework while Tasgo slept, so he took a different route back to the University. He thought some physical exertion might calm Tasgo's anxieties a little, so they set off at a dogtrot. It gave Tasgo less time to take in what must be for him impossible things, and it made good use of the extra energy adrenalin was giving him. They trotted through back streets almost empty of people and traffic. They reached more residential areas and took to the cycle track alongside a large ditch. Green grass and flowing water seemed to be having a soothing effect, though the water flowed in an unnaturally straight line.

They had to cut across to reach another cycle path that ran parallel to Beverley Road. When they turned the corner Tasgo stopped dead. Dread and horror filled his face, he was pale. Danny could see no cause for alarm. It was just another street, much like the others, but Tasgo was filled now with overwhelming emotions. He was trying hard to control them, to keep courage as he turned to Danny. His voice was little more than a whisper, as if to speak the words might make them true.

'Is it all,' he got out, *'all like this? On and on? Everywhere? Is it all like this, Dannaigh? Your whole world, boxes?'*

In an instant Danny's imagination made the leap into what Tasgo was seeing. A world entirely man-made, tarmac roads, cliffs of glass, stone and brick, houses like boxes set together like a Lego town. Tasgo had been fighting the reality, but now it had overcome him. The sheer quantity had become too much. The largest group of buildings Danny had seen back in the Iron Age had been no more than a village by any modern standard. This last turn had been one too many. Tasgo had obviously been hoping for some sort of respite, a more natural view. It had been building up in him over time, so many streets, so many buildings, on and on, seemingly forever.

Once when Danny had been overwhelmed by emotion, Dugal had encompassed him, enfolding him in his cloak, shutting out the world, giving him strength. Danny couldn't do that for Tasgo, he didn't have the strength or the power. Instead he stepped close, his own face filling the centre of Tasgo's view, his hands on both Tasgo's shoulders, giving strength and support.

'No, Tasgo. This is a town. A big town, bigger than any you could imagine, but it doesn't go on for ever. Outside there are trees and fields, crops and woodland. You will see, later. And now we are going back to where Bethany has her nest in the sky, where there is some grass and trees.'

Tasgo met his eyes, but was still looking bleak, as if he could hardly believe what Danny said.

Danny was relieved when they found the cycle path, paved but bounded by weeds, sprawling ivy and rough bushes so thick that you almost ignore the buildings beyond, behind the tall fences. The greenery seemed to sooth Tasgo a little, as they padded on.

Turning a corner they came upon a more open space, carved out of the surrounding properties. Stunted trees, a few bushes, a fire pit surrounded by what might have been grass, now beaten to bare earth. A few rocks large enough to sit on had been added, and the rubbish bin, which had been ignored by those who had dropped the fast food packaging and the beer cans. It looked tired and used.

Danny hoped Tasgo would take it as a promise of better things to come.

Tasgo took it badly. He stood and looked. Silent he stared in sadness, till anger rose in him bringing energy. Tense and terse he swivelled his angry gaze onto Danny, waiting beside him.

'Who?' he demanded, 'Who has done this?'

Danny withstood it for a moment, then turned and looked again at the area, trying to see it as Tasgo might. It was the last remnant of a woodland, marooned and clinging on to life as best it could. The stunted trees held few leaves. The shrubs were grey with dust and dirt.

Tasgo was still waiting.

'We're in a town,' Danny told him, and was going to say how such a place would be a treat for children, but Tasgo cut in,

'They have killed it,' tight with anger Tasgo cut through anything Danny might say. 'The spirit of this place has been trampled on. It is dying.' He looked again at the desolation. 'It has already died.'

'Not quite,' Danny said quickly. 'Children keep it alive. They come here and share their lives with it. When they are here it is a happy place.' He hoped that was true. Or at least partly true. Or at least was enough to cover over the pain that Tasgo so obviously felt. Yesterday had been full of terrors for him, and he wasn't over it yet.

'Remember,' he urged Tasgo, 'what a fool I was when first I came to you. I could not see things as you do. I didn't understand. You have to trust me, Tasgo.' Danny remembered Moira's words, all those long years ago. He spoke them quietly now, it was the best he could offer. 'I will never knowingly let any harm come to you.'

Somehow they made it to the university without further incident, even though there were a couple of busy roads to cross.

Students spilled out from the lecture hall, Matt was not among them. Danny spoke to some of them. As they turned eyes to take in Tasgo's

132

injuries, or just as noticeably failed to look his way, those who confessed to knowing Matt also confessed that he was often not at lectures, occasionally failing to turn up for tutorials too. The jammy bugger always managed to get away with it, and pass exams with marks to rival the most diligent.

Moira turned up soon after with the same sort of news. He wasn't at home, had been there briefly on Sunday, but hadn't been seen since. It didn't mean he had vanished, not yet anyway.

They sat outside the Union eating salad from plastic trays.

Danny told her of Tasgo's desolation and anger.

She turned to Tasgo, *'We need to get you somewhere more comfortable...'* she started.

'I don't need comfort Moira,' Tasgo interrupted, *'I need to get back. I have already spent too long here.'*

'I'm sorry,' she told him, *'that's going to take a while. At least we know where it happened, though not how.'*

'How does not matter. The gate must be opened, then I shall return.'

Moira smiled at the direct simplicity. *'The HOW is how we open the gate,'* she told him. *'I'll need some...'* she paused and chose, *'Druids to help work it out. You can't help with that Tasgo, any more than Dannaigh can.'* She was moving into the decisive, she was smoothing out the plan as she spoke. *'I'll take charge of the 'how'. Dannaigh, the best place for Tasgo is my home. The town is small, and there's open land behind the house.'*

It seemed a good idea, but again the problem was how. It would take days to walk there, now the countryside was all fences and fields and villages. There was no straight way, and the footpaths were so convoluted it would double the distance. *'You'll have to drive him there,'* Moira decided.

Danny mentioned quietly, in the modern, the wild anxiety brought on just by the sight of a vehicle. Moira took Danny to task, in the ancient.

'Tasgo is stronger than that, Danny. He will control his fears, and you will show him how exciting a modern chariot can be.' Then dropping quickly back into the modern, 'I suggest a convertible, keep the top down.' She passed him a credit card. 'You've got expenses up to a twenty

thousand on that, the insurance will be expensive. Make sure he keeps his seat belt on.'

Tasgo eyed the card. *'What is that?'* he demanded.

'It's a modern chariot,' Danny told him, getting up, *'or will be soon.'*

Ride

Tasgo stood beside Moira and just looked at Danny in the driver's seat of the car. Danny unclipped the seat belt and got out to join them.

'Very pretty,' said Moira, then 'How much did that cost you?'

'Nine k' said Danny, pretty pleased with himself, looking at the car rather than at Tasgo. It was a pretty car, a Mazda MX5 roadster in black, a bargain at that price, even given its age. It looked sleek, it looked sporty. It looked expensive. He had got it from a dealer on the outskirts of the city, where an old school mate, Grant, was polishing vehicles on the forecourt, and was proud to show Danny his influence with the salesmen.

'Insurance?' Moira asked.

Danny couldn't help the grin, it was preposterous, a joke. 'Nine k,' he said. He was twenty, and the clean licence meant very little next to that. He held out the credit card for Moira to take back. She waved it away, there wasn't much left on it anyway. 'Glad I got a cheap car,' he said, still grinning.

Now Danny turned to Tasgo, *'Have a look,'* he invited. *'It's my new chariot.'* Turning, he went back to stand by the car. To make a point, he ran his hand over the smooth lines of the bonnet. Moira said, *'Go ahead, Tasgo, it won't harm you. It's Danny's.'*

It wasn't as hard as Danny expected. Maybe Moira's magic words earlier let Tasgo overcome his fears. He was fighting them down, showing that he was, indeed, stronger than them. He asked all the delaying questions he could think of. Danny got in and out of the vehicle a few times, to show how easy escape was, and, after all, it was open-topped, Tasgo would be as good as free at any time.

Students passing by were having a good look. Tasgo could see the envy. When at last he got in, taut as a drawn bow, Danny showed him how to put on the seat belt, and how to take it off again.

'Why?' he demanded.

Danny grinned, *'You'll see,'* he said, then relenting a little, *'It's necessary.'*

Then, both buckled up, he put the car into gear and pulled gently away, with Moira's command of 'Be careful!' following after them.

'How?' demanded Tasgo, tersely, trying to hide the fear he so obviously felt.

'Later,' Danny told him, carefully avoiding looking at Tasgo as they drove off, barely at walking pace, into the traffic. He could feel the tension beside him. He could see the legs thrust hard against the front of the foot well, keeping Tasgo safely wedged into his seat. After the traffic lights they had to speed up, but Danny soon turned off into a side road, where they dawdled along for a while, letting Tasgo get used to the motion.

They were soon out of town, into fields and green pastures, things that drew Tasgo's attention despite his deep-seated fear of a chariot that moved by itself. The size of the fields, the various sorts of fencing and hedges, the massive size of cattle, the whiteness of sheep, all needed thought. Danny stopped where he could pull off the road, and they both got out to look over a gate at a field of corn. Tasgo vaulted easily over the interesting grey metal gate to inspect the crop. He was amazed. He was bitten by envy. The grains were still small, new, not yet developed, but the number of grains to a head, the lack of weeds, the yield per square foot, they were all marvels to him. For someone who would have been shocked to be called a farmer, he was only too well aware of the wonders before him. Danny could see him recalculating Seahome's wealth if only he could take some of these seeds home with him.

'Wait till you see Moira's home,' Danny said, leaning on the gate as he watched Tasgo overcome by wheat and wonder. *'Come on!'*

Tasgo vaulted back over the gate, he got into the car cautiously but quickly. Danny left 'dawdling' behind as they set off.

By the time they reached a town Tasgo was hunched down in his seat but enjoying it, in the way that rollercoasters are enjoyed, with excitement and trepidation. But Tasgo had faith in Danny's assurance that Danny could subdue the beast, that he was in control. As they flashed down the highway, Danny kept to the speed limit. He knew how well the little car stood out, especially with two young men in it. He didn't want another encounter with the police. There wasn't much traffic on the road though, and no sign of a police car or a speed camera. They topped a rise with a long vista ahead of them, and only a couple of vehicles in sight. The temptation was too great. He wanted to know just what his new car could do.

He gunned the engine, and heard it roar, felt the sudden surge, saw the needle climb.

Air rushed wildly past them, buffeting them from both sides. He felt Tasgo hunker down beside him, his face wild with terror and delight. They sprinted past a dark car that had been content to sit behind a lorry at low speed, passing it as if it was at mere walking pace.

In the rear-view mirror Danny saw the car pull out and accelerate after them.

It was a fast car, a newish saloon, with two figures inside. Either they wanted to race the sports car that had just roared past them or... could it be an unmarked police car?

Danny took his foot off the accelerator. He let the roadster coast, losing speed as he dropped back to the speed limit, ready to let the others win if it was a race. Now was not the time for that sort of play.

The other car lost speed faster, hanging back. Danny checked the dial, a stately fifty. The dark car behind them was keeping the same distance between them, still no blue light, he was probably being over-cautious. What was the chance? He knew from Ken Raynes how thin the police were stretched. Better to be cautious though.

He slowed down for the oncoming town well in advance of the 30 sign. Better safe than sorry.

The car followed them through the town and out onto the open road, always keeping its distance, and Danny was beginning to worry that his suspicions were true. But when they reached his home town and turned off to take the shorter route through the houses, the car sailed past on the main road, without even a glance from the men as they passed the turning.

Now that they were moving more slowly, and houses lined the streets on either side, Tasgo gave up excitement, growing at once warier, more oppressed by the man-made environment. Scudmoor Road, its bungalows fronted by neat gardens, might have been more of a relief if

137

they were not blessed with so many flowers beginning to bloom. In Seahome sometimes women wore flowers in their hair, hedgerow blossoms, or daisies made into chains. No-one bothered to grow the flowers, they were jewels of nature, enjoyed where found, but not worth any effort, unless they were good to eat as well.

Danny stopped outside the house where Moira and Ken Raynes and their daughter Lily lived, and said *'Here we are, Moira's home.'*

Tasgo looked about him rather surprised. It looked the same as every other building in the street. True, it was at the very top of the road, where it turned to go back down the hill again, if that meant anything. He looked at the low roof and the glass windows with dismay and turned to Danny. *'You are sure?'* he asked. *'They are all the same.'*

Danny had already got out of the car, he smiled. He knew Tasgo was expecting Moira's home to be more like a roundhouse, grand, outstanding, as befitted a chieftain or elite warrior. *'Only on the outside,'* he said, moving towards the front gate. Tasgo unfastened his seat belt warily and followed.

Danny had the key amongst others on his key ring, but he rang the doorbell first, in case someone was at home. There was no answer.

Inside, Tasgo's fears that Moira and Ken were not important and wealthy were obliterated. They stepped into the living room. It took up most of this floor. Polished wood was the base on which Persian carpets glowed between the comfortable sofas. A low table and easy chairs faced out through the back window at the heathland beyond. On the wall was a huge flat-screen, and a gladius in a boxed mount.

Tasgo stopped at the doorway, looking at it all with awe. It was simple, clean and clear, a place where an honoured few could sit while others must stand. Danny walked into it with the modest arrogance of one who knew his place here. He stopped by the soft chairs and table in the window, so Tasgo followed him in. Through the window he could see the landscape he had been yearning for. Despite the huge expanse of clear material between him and the view, it felt like coming home. Then his eyes dropped to the land below, and his sense of comfort lurched. Beneath them was a structure of that same magical material, a pyramid of triangles which met at a high apex. Under it were more spaces, all in that same sparse rectangular shape. He looked about him suddenly anxious again.

'Where is everyone?' he demanded.

'It's just Moira, and Ken and Lily,' Danny told him gently. 'This is their home.'

'Where are the farm hands, the women who weave, the workers?' demanded Tasgo. It would take a small army to create the wealth that was needed for a room like this. Already he was realising how stupid his question must sound. Obviously the workers must live in the structures below.

Danny had already worked out a simple way to put that complex answer.

'Far away,' he said, and before Tasgo could put the next obvious follow up question, 'There are overseers to deal with all that.'

At last Tasgo looked almost satisfied. The family were overlords, so far above the average that tribute meant that they could live in luxury.

An hour or two later Tasgo seemed more relaxed. The empty beer bottles gathered around the two chairs where they sat looking out over the distant hillside might have had something to do with it. Tasgo had been surprised by the bottles, so small, so perfectly formed of clear coloured glass, and so cold, while the room was so comfortably warm. He had been surprised by the liquid inside, bubbly, beer but tastier, more bitter and much more alcoholic.

After the second bottle he had confessed to a dream-like state, where everything seemed to be a smoother, sharper, better version of things he might already know. But where nothing was exactly as it should be, everything transformed into something he hardly knew how to deal with. Like a dream, or a nightmare.

Danny smiled. 'I know that feeling,' he said.

Tasgo looked at the bottle he was holding, held it against the light from the window. 'It is glass,' he suggested, 'like the jewels some women wear?' Only their beads were small, tiny droplets of the material, not uniform and stretched over so wide an area. Tasgo could only gaze at the window in wonder, so clear, uncoloured, so uniform, so almost invisible. And, remembering his first moments of imprisonment in a box he could not see, so strong.

When Danny rose to get more beer, he found Raynes just this side of the door to the hallway, watching them.

Raynes had the opposite of swagger. It was one of his knacks. He would somehow be in a room without ever seeming to go through the process of entering it. By the time anyone noticed him, it would be uncertain how long he had been standing there, how much he had witnessed of what was going on.

Danny welcomed him with 'Hello, Sir.' It was their private joke, ever since Raynes had married his aunt Moira, and become an official Uncle, and an unofficial guardian. Raynes liked it because it gave him a spurious authority, which the unwary could misinterpret at their peril. Danny liked it because it reminded him that Raynes embodied the law and knew where the bodies were buried.

As always Raynes just treated him to a slight nod, he was busy taking in Tasgo, a bigger, more filled out, more mature man than the one Raynes remembered. Even with the dressings on his wrists, and bruises on his face, he had become an imposing figure, standing now to greet him.

'Welcome to our home,' said Raynes, approaching Tasgo. 'It seems we haven't treated you well, so far.'

Tasgo waited, tense, for the translation before he answered, formally, his right hand over his heart, 'Greetings Ken, Keeper of Lore. I regret I have unwittingly behaved as I should not. Thank you for allowing me into your home.'

Danny translated it as precisely as it had been spoken, formal, apologetic, hurt and challenging. A man unsure of just how welcome he was.

'You're welcome,' Ken repeated at once with added warmth, surprising them all, himself included, by stepping forward to put his arms round Tasgo and drawing him close.

Danny was surprised that Tasgo let him, he was surprised that Tasgo fell into that embrace as if suddenly relieved of a great burden, returning it almost tentatively. Then he remembered the 'killed three times' by men who might well be associated with a 'Keeper of the Lore', like Raynes.

Ken released Tasgo, and motioned them to the chairs, as he drew up a third. He wasn't going to pause for small talk. He looked at Tasgo and

140

said, 'Tell me how you came to be here.' Danny started the translations, Raynes asked the pertinent questions. Moira might have told him it all already, but Raynes wanted it straight from the horse's mouth. Danny could tell he was picking up the gist of some of what Tasgo was saying before Danny gave it to him complete. Raynes hadn't forgotten what language he had learned in those brief months when the portal was still open, but he still lacked the accuracy that Danny was careful to give him. He was after the details that would help him piece everything together. He was watching Tasgo's face as he spoke, seeing there all the emotions tamped down under tight control as Tasgo tried to hide how unsettled he still was. He was putting on a front, but Raynes was too good a detective to be fooled.

At last Raynes ran out of questions, and leant back in his chair, mulling it over. It gave Danny enough time to ask the question that had been puzzling him. 'What took you so long?'

Raynes settled his gaze on Danny, taking time to register everything encapsulated in that question. At last he said, 'Never simple, once Intelligence gets onto something. Even the possibility that Tasgo was some sort of terrorist was enough to set them off. That brushes off onto everyone connected, you, me...' He paused still looking at Danny, before adding, 'I've been busy.'

Danny heard the deliberate understatement. Was that some sort of warning? Were they out of the woods with the police? Or was it internal politics again? Raynes had been busted down a rank once before, he was back up to Detective Inspector again now. His career probably wouldn't survive another crash.

'They can't think...' Danny began.

'In that light,' Raynes continued, 'the explosion, your father's disappearance, and yours, it all seemed to add up to something more than it was.' Danny was working his way through that. It brought back something he had been thinking about a lot. Something that now seemed more important than it had then. 'Do you remember,' he asked Raynes, 'when you caught Kelly and me in the ruin of our old house, how I found Freya's earrings in one of the columns?' It felt strange saying the words, as though he was there again, nearly fifteen, still in a sort of shock that made everything feel weird. Everything had been weird. Most of the house had vanished except for all the metal, fused into two twisted columns. As Raynes nodded, going with it, Danny went on, 'I found them because they were just below something else, something my father had been handling, earlier that evening before...' before the world had blown up and changed everything forever.

Raynes waited, knowing the rest would follow. Danny went on, 'It was a metal thing, like an egg. Like Kuillok had when he was on the hill, when Tasgo and I caught him. My Dad had it, he had it that night. Mum gave it to him. A present from a student.'

'Freya didn't have students, as such,' said Raynes, immediately questioning it. It was true, students worked with her on some of the digs, but it was a come and go thing, never a long-term engagement.

'That's why it was odd,' said Danny, mystified himself. He didn't know why it was suddenly such a strong memory. That, and the blue sparks that had come from Kuillok's hands as, half mad with fear and despair, he had tried to do something, up on the hill above Seahome, the night that he and Tasgo had set on him, and taken him, a prisoner, down to the others in the iron age village below.

He could see Raynes absorbing that, accepting new information, keeping it for later when he could try and tie it in to other things. Now the detective went back to what he had come here to say. 'I'm afraid Moira was wrong to offer you a bed here. Visiting is alright, but you had better sleep at Freya's.'

'You don't want him here?' asked Danny, surprised.

'I know he's a good man, not a terrorist. But a police officer can't 'associate' with criminals, or suspects.' Danny already knew that the trouble with the police couldn't be over so soon, he had never believed it would be that simple, but now he was worried. Raynes was being cautious with his choice of words, almost as if he thought the room might be bugged. Danny had better do the same and was choosing the right words when Tasgo leant forward, interrupting.

'I yam so ree,' Tasgo told Raynes, 'I donut speak in Glish.' He had picked up the increased tension in Danny, and the cautious gaps between speaking. He was a chief who needed to know what was being said.

Raynes leant forward with a sudden smile, he met Tasgo's gaze straight on, with warmth 'I'm glad you found us Tasgo. *You will be safe with us,* until we can find a way to get you home. Tonight you and Danny will sleep in Freya's house, *Freya is looking forward to seeing you again.'* He had definitely been speaking with Moira, she had taught him some necessary phrases.

Tasgo asked the question, the one question, as far as he was concerned the only question. *'How do I get back home? It is already too long a time.'*

Farewell

Days had turned into weeks, and Danny was finding it hard to fill Tasgo's days without letting him stumble on wonders he could never understand. He was grateful when Moira and Freya offered to take over for a few days, so that they could catch up with what had happened in Seahome over the last few years, and find out more about what had happened to bring him here.

Danny drove back to Sheffield. He had made appointments, but he wasn't looking forward to any of them.

When he got there, he knew he was badly unsettled, more than he had expected.

He arranged to meet Chrissie for dinner, at the Rajput in Crooksmoore. She liked Indian, and they knew him there. It was a nice restaurant, he thought she would appreciate him taking the effort, but he wasn't looking forward to it. He thought she might be thinking of a longer-term arrangement, of staying together, maybe marriage and children. Just a few weeks ago, he might not have been scared off by that. He liked Chrissie. He more than liked Chrissie. She was great. She was fun, but not superficial. She was fit, and great in bed, enthusiastic and inventive. But more than that, she was warm and generous, with a quick take on things, and always ready to step in and lend a hand, to get things done. She was loving and kind, and just a few weeks ago he knew he could have lived happily with that, even though he wasn't ready to take those sort of steps yet.

He had too much history, that was the truth. While it was just that, history, locked off two thousand years ago, unattainable, he could think of a long-term arrangement. She wouldn't need to know the things he had done then, the situations he had had to cope with, how they had changed him.

Tasgo's arrival did away with all that. Tasgo was a secret he couldn't share, didn't dare share. If they succeeded in opening another gateway, a portal, Danny knew he would go back with Tasgo. Tasgo would need his help. He would need all the help he could get, after vanishing in the middle of a battle.

He couldn't tell Chrissie that. He couldn't talk about the portal, if there was to be one, nor time travel. He wouldn't be able to tell her where he was going when he left for days or weeks at a time. Because he knew he would do that. Impossible not to. He would have to lie to her, and he couldn't live a lie, not with Chrissie. She held too great a place in his heart.

The interview with his tutor that afternoon was easier. Despite missing most of a term, he would be allowed take the exams. His tutor was very positive, he made it clear that he thought Danny would make a good paramedic. His results so far had been excellent. The reports back from the paramedics he had worked with were even better. He assessed danger well, but was not afraid to step in where others, more timid, might have waited for back-up. He had shown himself calm but assertive when needed. He had been equal to aggressive drunks and hysterical relatives. His assessment of the order in which to do things was remarkably good.

His tutor was assuming that once the family emergency was over, Danny would be back for the third year. Danny couldn't see quite how that would happen, but since it was a possibility, he let it stand, and took down the dates of the exams.

Bolstered by his mentor's good opinion, Danny went back to his digs, and packed up everything he had there, leaving only an overnight bag of essentials for when he came back for the exams. Luckily no-one was home, so he took a quick shower, got changed into something more suitable for his date, and left a note to tell his housemates.

With the car boot packed it was time to go to the Rajput. He was already late as he parked the car in the only space available, on the other side of the wide road.

Chrissie was already there, waiting for him.

'Nice car,' she greeted him, 'When did you get that?' as if it were a happy surprise, or a secret he had been keeping from her for some time.

'It's new,' he confessed, looking out the window at it. He was glad it was in full view, he had all his computing devices in the boot. The fact that he was leaving was already bearing down on him. Chrissie was his

145

best friend, as well as his best girl-friend ever. As they took their places at the table he was wondering if there could be any way of saving this relationship. If they couldn't open another portal, to the right time and place, he would never have a better friend. Apart from Tasgo.

The two would never be compatible. Tasgo would need his help. If they couldn't find a way for him to go back, Tasgo would really need his help. There was no escaping that.

They ordered food without the usual toing and froing that went with knowing they would share everything. The waiter brought cobra beer for them both.

'You're very quiet,' Chrissie told him. 'How's your cousin?'

'Things are difficult,' he muttered. He had hoped to keep things light to start with.

'He's been arrested?' she surmised.

'No, they've been persuaded...' what he feared was true. He couldn't lie to her, not even to try and put across that Tasgo was vulnerable and in need of care.

A party of six was settling in to a table further into the restaurant, making the restaurant feel full and lively. He wished he had asked for a table tucked away in a corner.

'I don't want to talk about him,' he told Chrissie.

'That sounds bad,' she said, and then with sympathy, 'Are you alright? You're not in any trouble?'

'No,' but a vision of that little round mouth pointing at him, the roar of voices washing over him, reminded him of the trouble he had been in. 'All a misunderstanding,' he told her, as the waiter brought them complimentary nibbles.

She reached a hand across the table and laid it on his. 'Over now?' she asked. Her hand was warm, her touch was comforting. He met her eyes properly at last, and could not help telling her how beautiful she was. That put the conversation on happier lines, and then food arrived, and they busied themselves sharing out the various dishes. He wanted it to be a good meal, a last encounter to remember with warmth. Now he was here, his loyalties were stretching him in opposite directions once again. Once again almost more than he could bear.

146

He was dreading saying goodbye. But if he stayed with Chrissie, he wouldn't be able to tell her where he had been, what he was doing, why he was so consumed with longing to fill an ancient emptiness. He couldn't live with her and lie to her.

She knew something was wrong. She wasn't afraid to ask. They told each other everything, everything about their lives here and now. He told her he had to go away, he had to help sort out this family problem. She was concerned about his course, his qualifications, so he told her that all that had been sorted. He would come back to take the exams, but, basically, he was leaving.

'I know, it's family, they need you,' she said, 'I'll be here, when you come back.'

He might not be coming back. If they couldn't open a portal, there would be Tasgo to look after, to explain. She would see through his lies. If they could, he would go back into the past with Tasgo. One way or another, he could easily die. Or at least, be unable to return. They couldn't afford to have her waiting, asking questions, wondering where he was.

He said, 'I might not be back.' He smiled, as if it didn't matter. 'It was always only going to be a bit of fun, wasn't it?'

Clearly she had thought it was more than that. She had thought that it had changed, she was thinking long-term, making a home, making a family. She told him so, still expecting him to agree, to see sense, to stop trying to protect her from - whatever it was.

If Tasgo's unexpected arrival had not metaphorically torn apart Danny's sense of time and space, he might have agreed with her. Now that separation was in front of him, happening, he knew that without Tasgo he would have agreed. Instead he pushed aside his plate, still half full, and told her, 'No, you've been wonderful, it's been fun, but it's run its course. Time to move on.'

She looked at him, colour beginning to rise in her ashen cheeks. 'I don't believe you,' she said. She knew him that well. 'You're not that kind of cold-hearted bastard,' sounding cold herself.

He forced himself to shrug and look careless. 'I never meant to fool you,' he said. 'I thought you knew it was just a bit of fun that was never going to last.'

'This isn't you,' she told him.

'Sorry,' he said. 'I was hoping for a gentle goodbye.'

She got to her feet, the chair rocked back violently. She snapped 'No you weren't!' People were looking, she was grabbing her coat off the back of the chair.

He stood up himself. 'I'll take you home.'

'What did you think?' she demanded, 'Sorry? Goodbye, little wave? Really? Bastard! Take me out for a meal and drop me, so I'll just walk away? Found someone else, have you?' He managed a 'No' to that, but she wasn't listening. 'Bastard through and through!' She still didn't believe it, but she was angry now. 'Don't you come near me!' she snarled as he took a pace towards her. She was leaving. There were tears in her eyes, and she didn't want anyone to see them. 'Leave me alone,' she snarled as she turned and ran. The waiter hurried but was too late to open the door for her, she was through and running.

Everyone else was looking at the bastard through and through. The bastard was too full of hurt to care. The customers were taking sides, against him. The staff were all concern, but seemed more anxious than usual to see him pay the bill and go.

Chrissie was gone by the time he got outside, possibly on the bus that had just moved off.

He stood, a broken-hearted bastard, and phoned Chas to tell him that Chrissie might need a shoulder to cry on. He knew Chas was smitten. He felt he needed a shoulder himself. Chrissie's would be the one.

He had been unsettled when he arrived. He was in tatters as he left.

It was nearly nine o'clock when he got into the roadster and started driving out towards the motorway. He felt drained, exhausted. By the time he joined the M62 he knew he was driving badly. He was just too tired, and his concentration was shattered by what he had done. Home was too far away, Hull was closer. He could make it to Moira's bedsit. She wouldn't be there, she was at home, treating Tasgo like a king.

When he got there, tugging aggressively at the wheel to turn in, another car was in her drive, but he guessed it would belong to one of the post-grads.

Once again, the front door was not locked, though surprisingly the door on the first floor that led up the stairs to her attic room was. Danny had the key, and as he went up he called 'Hello?' up the stairs. There was no reply, but as he turned on the light there was a sharp squeal, and someone sat up on the futon, wielding a baseball bat.

Danny stared in astonishment. 'Kelly?' leapt from his mouth. What was she doing here?

Kelly stared right back, full of indignation. 'Danny,' she shot back, heavy with resignation, as if only he would burst in on her just as she was falling asleep.

He found his voice. 'Sorry,' he said, 'I thought it would be empty.'

Kelly lowered the bat, pulling blankets further up against her more than demure nightie.

'Nice to see you too,' she said, miffed.

'I'm sorry,' he said, 'I can go...'

'You look like crap,' she told him.

'Yes,' he confessed, ready to go. Maybe he could sleep in the car, he really couldn't face driving any further.

'Sit!' she told him. 'I'll make coffee.'

Indecisive, he hovered in the doorway for a second. Then, like an obedient dog, he took the only chair. He was too exhausted to argue.

She made coffee and offered to lace it with vodka. He accepted. She did the same for her own, then sat on the futon, with the duvet wrapped round her.

'What's happened?' she asked. He told her.

At least, he gave her a version. He couldn't let her know they were trying to open another portal. Five years ago she had gone with him, when they found the cool blue flames in the cave beneath Moira's house. She had shared all that heady, tumultuous, violent first encounter with the past. She had been more sensible than him. Once she got back to the present she had stayed away, urging him to do the same. He had no secrets to keep from her, not until now.

He told her he and Chrissie had split up. He owned the fault of it himself. She watched him with all-seeing eyes, looking into the heart of him, feeling his hurt.

'You can be bloody stupid sometimes,' she told him. He acknowledged it, and drank deep of the coffee, feeling the vodka do its job. She didn't try to make him feel better.

'You'd better sleep here,' she told him, tossing a pillow onto the floor at the foot of the bed. 'You look all in. We'll talk in the morning.' He had always liked that about her. Never mind the whys and the hows, she just got on with things. In no time there were blankets and bedding enough to make him comfortable on the floor.

'What are you doing here anyway? What's wrong with Oxford?' he asked, putting his shoes together by the wall, taking off his jumper and his best shirt.

'Trying to get a good night's sleep,' she told him, snuggling into the more comfortable futon, 'busy day tomorrow.'

Rebuffed, he lay down, and surprised himself by falling straight into a deep sleep.

There was no ignoring the morning alarm, and Kelly stepping over him to get to the bathroom first. He had time while she showered to get himself presentable, and to put away his makeshift bed. He was noticing that Kelly must have been here for a while. She was a neat and tidy person, but there were books on economics with bits of paper sticking out to mark important pages. A small pile of clothes had collected in a corner, and three notebooks were tucked neatly by the futon.

She returned, looking clean, fresh and only too lively from the shower, towel wrapped round her demurely. He opened his mouth to speak, but she cut across it quickly. 'Your turn,' she told him, clearing the door to the shower room, 'And don't dare come out till I knock to say you can!'

He gave her a grin at that, remembering how she had come up the stairs at Moira's house dressed just as she was now, and the effect it had had then. He entered the small cubicle, no toothbrush for his teeth, and already dressed so not wanting to go through the hassle of stripping for a shower. He was intrigued now. What was she doing here? Had something happened at Oxford? He couldn't imagine what might send her back up here, to Hull. Last night he had been too wrapped up in his own distress to consider what might have happened with her.

When she at last knocked at the door, he burst out full of questions. If Kelly were in any sort of turmoil it didn't show. She looked cool, calm, collected and full of energy. She looked wonderful. He told her so.

'We'll have breakfast at the Dancing Goat,' she told him by way of reply, stuffing her notebooks into a carry bag and grabbing her coat. 'Busy day,' she said, opening the door to the stairs.

'What are you doing in Hull?' Danny managed to ask her, following down the stairs with a clatter. Mr Uptight had heard them coming and was on the landing with a smile for Kelly, and then a glare for Danny as he realised she wasn't alone. What sort of idea was he getting of Danny? Danny didn't care. Kelly gave the man a cheery 'Good morning,' as she passed. Danny gave him a leery grin as he chased Kelly down the next flight.

She was moving too fast for conversation, but once they were seated, with coffee and sandwiches, it was possible to talk. Kelly had gone for chicken with cranberries, Oxford was having an effect on her. She got in first, 'If you love her so much, why did you break up with her?' He couldn't tell her. She should have been the one he could tell everything to, she had been through the portal, she knew about the past. But then again, she had fallen in one hundred percent behind the idea of closing it. She didn't need telling how dangerous meddling with the past might be, she had worked it out for herself. Also, he was beginning to get the idea she was trying to hide something of her own. He ignored the question.

'What are you doing here Kelly? Why are you here, rather than with your posh mates in Oxford?'

She looked at him as if he were an idiot. He was used to that. 'Not everyone who goes to Oxford is posh,' she told him, 'the criterion is clever.'

'Criterion,' thought Danny, very posh.

'Nor all too-clever-by-half either.' Kelly went on. 'There are some really nice people.'

Danny lifted an eye-brow provocatively; had she fallen for someone?

She went on, 'I'm up here for research. Social outcome of industrial decisions. Industrial outcome of political decisions. Maggie Thatcher amongst other things. Why the docks got so important and then why they ceased to thrive. What happened to industry. It's going to be part of my final thesis.' She sounded as though she could go on forever, but there was a cheeky glint in her eye, as if she were sending herself up at the same time.

'Sounds – interesting,' Danny said.

She laughed. 'I'll have to think up some clever angle to get it up to scratch. Do you still ride?'

'In Sheffield? I row,' he told her, keeping quiet about the martial arts. She didn't need reminding about that sort of thing. 'How's your Mum?' he asked, always a tricky subject.

Kelly tossed it aside, 'Doing really well. You know Patricia Paxman has joined Bradford Braithwaite?' Patricia Paxman was his family's lawyer, an ever ready resource. Kelly was warbling on, 'It's Bradford Paxman and Partners now. Mum's working for her, legal secretary. She loves it.'

Why did that rankle with him? What was wrong with that? Kelly had once, a very long time ago, saved his mother's life. Of course they were funding her through university. Her mother was an anxious person, she needed an ordered life-style. Why shouldn't she work for their lawyer, she was a legal secretary after all? Somehow it made him feel unsettled. He felt his grandmother's interfering hand in it, even though she had opted to stay in the past. It made him so unsettled that Kelly had time to finish her sandwich and was ready to run.

'Important meeting,' she told him, getting to her feet, glancing at her phone to see the time. He hadn't asked her half the things he ought to have done.

'Talk later?' he tried, but she was on her way.

'Leaving soon,' she told him, making for the door, 'lectures, tutorials, things...' she told him, opening it. Then she was gone.

Leaving him feeling even more unsettled.

Urgency

Weeks had turned to months, and Danny was finding it hard to keep Tasgo occupied.

Matt had turned up again, returning from a quick 'holiday' as innocent as if butter wouldn't melt in his mouth. When Moira had talked to him on her own, he had denied everything. Never been there, knew nothing about it.

When Raynes arrived and flashed his warrant card at Matt, Matt caved in instantly. He knew nothing, he shouldn't have been there, he was just trying to impress the girls. He shared digs with Kevin Wilcox, and it was Kevin's research lab, but he had come along with Kevin a few times and knew how 'to make the sparks fly' as he put it. He had no idea what had happened that night, it was 'all Greek' to him, he had no idea who the strange guy was or where he had come from. Yes, somehow the bar had started to give out drinks to everyone, but that wasn't his fault, it was nothing to do with him, ask the guy who did the ordering.

He was relieved to discover the bar bill had been paid, though of course, it had never been his responsibility. He had no idea what Kev's research was about, nor did he know that the funding for it had dried up and that Kevin had had to give back his key to the lab. He certainly did still have a key to the underground labyrinth, and yes, he, Matt, had borrowed it while Kevin was away. But no, he didn't still have it, ask Kevin.

Raynes had warned Matt of various offences he might be found guilty of, but that it was unlikely he would be prosecuted, provided nothing further came of it. He was heavy-handed enough to make sure that Matt wouldn't be chatting about it to anyone.

Danny was angry that Kevin was involved. He was furious, even though Moira told him that she had removed funding, given him other work to do and taken back the key five years ago after they had worked out how to close the gateway. It seemed Kevin had chosen to make a duplicate key and to keep working on his 'space-time anomaly' project.

'Perhaps,' she said, looking sharply at Danny, 'it was just as well, because that gives Kevin some of the most advanced knowledge of practical wormhole theory.'

Danny kept silent on the obvious fact that Kevin was also the person who had used his knowledge to send a band of Iron Age warriors into his home five years ago, destroying the house, maiming his Mother and taking his father.

It was obvious now that they were using Kevin Wilcox to find a way to open another wormhole. Danny hated the idea, but he couldn't complain. Not with Tasgo trapped here, with his urgent and ever present need to get back there. There was no way Tasgo was going to fit in here and now.

Chrissie sent Danny a text. >You told CHAS! You thought I needed THAT! What is wrong with u.<

No need to answer then.

Time passed.

When asked, Moira sounded optimistic about opening a wormhole somehow, but there was never much evidence of progress. But if they did succeed, Tasgo would need to be in top condition ready to go back. They kept to a punishing routine of training. Tasgo had only come to the fitness Gym with Danny once, and was amazed at all the machines and weights, the many exercises.

'Why?' he had demanded. 'What is wrong with felling a tree, teaching the youngsters how to fight, building a house, planting a field? Doing things. Useful things.' He was getting tetchy.

They hadn't gone back. Instead they ran in the morning, then swam in the pool in Freya's house or went to Brazilian Jiu-jitsu classes, or the boxing gym, where Tasgo sneered politely at the mouth guards, gloves and belts.

154

Chrissie sent Danny a text. >It's your cousin, isn't it? Somethings gone badly wrong hasn't it? Call me.< He blocked her number.

There was a climbing wall in Middlesbrough and Tasgo allowed himself to be roped up, on the grounds that it would be stupid to fall off just over a bit of fun. Though having been put on the rope, he deliberately fell off more than once, just for fun.

Tasgo asked often about Bethany, and whether they shouldn't go back and see that no harm had come to her. He couldn't understand the total lack of women eager to catch their eyes. Danny asked who Tasgo had in Seahome, hoping to distract him. He had Freda, the woman with the lovely voice, mother to his two sons, though not exactly his wife. That position might yet be held by a woman from another village, even another tribe, to seal some treaty. Danny didn't ask how Freda felt about that.

Chrissie sent Danny a letter, at his mother's house. He stood for a long time holding the envelope, wondering if there was any way he could save the situation, get back with her. If they made a new portal, to the right time, and it worked, and they weren't slaughtered as soon as they got there, he could take her through and make her part of the secret. When he was only fourteen he had been eager enough to do so with Raynes. Being honest, he could see the odds were stacked against him getting that far. Then he wouldn't be coming back, and if they had got back together, she would ask questions. Being Chrissie, she would never stop.

There was absolutely no way he should open that envelope, containing her last words to him, whatever they might say. He stood, unable to just bin it, but knowing that opening it would only cause more pain.

The fire was already laid in the living room, safe behind a glass screen. On a sudden impulse he was moving towards it, the envelope in his hands like an offering. He knelt before it, opened the glass door and laid the envelope, incongruous, across the top, making sure it was level and

155

would not slide off the moment flames approached. He took a match from the box below, and carefully lit the paper under the kindling, closing the door as the flames began to lick upwards. He watched it burn, feeling the heat of the blaze like a wound in his heart. Thinking of Chrissie, he forced himself to wish, with all his heart, that she would forget him quickly, without bitterness, that she would move on, unharmed, as Tasgo would say.

All the old feelings of desolation and of loss welled up inside him, threatening to overwhelm him. He yearned again for his father, a loss he still grieved for. He longed for his mother to be unharmed, for Chrissie to be unhurt by his choices. Things that could never be.

As the paper shrivelled and burned, he became aware he was not alone. Once all traces of the paper were lost forever, he took a breath, got up and turned. Tasgo was in the doorway, tense and puzzled. Danny could see he was unsettled by what he must see as a ritual he didn't understand, but knew better than to ask questions at a moment of importance. Just as well, Danny wouldn't have been able to answer.

It was hard to find new and interesting things for Tasgo to do, and Tasgo was getting tighter and terse. He had only one thing on his mind, and although Moira and Freya and even Raynes told him again and again that they were working on it as hard as they could, he was getting more and more impatient.

Tasgo was looking out of the window into the garden as Danny trotted up the stairs from the laundry, ready for their morning run. Only Tasgo was dressed in his brecks and tunic, the broom handle with which they sometimes sparred was in his hand, upright like a spear. There was something about the way he was standing, the stillness of him, that slowed Danny. Then Tasgo turned his head slowly to look at him, and Danny knew something was very wrong.

Danny stopped two stairs from the top. He could almost smell the tension in Tasgo, the immediate danger.

'What happened?' he asked carefully, coming slowly up the last two steps then stepping to one side, so there was not a dangerous drop behind him.

'*Nothing,*' Tasgo told him, hard-edged, unyielding. '*Nothing has happened, Dannaigh.*' He turned his whole body to confront Danny, and went on, anger and impatience deep within the words. '*Every day, we get up and we run. We run, and we run, for miles, to get back to where we started. Day after day we work on your complicated fighting skills to keep strong. We eat, and we sleep, and nothing, NOTHING happens.*'

On other days Danny had tried to reason with Tasgo, to explain that Moira and Freya and their skilled experts were working hard on opening another portal. He didn't need to explain they were calling it an experiment in mathematical hypotheses.

This was not going to be one of those days. Tasgo had reached the end of his patience. Weeks had turned into months, and Tasgo had run out of patience, nothing could take his mind off the fact that he was still here, and not there, where he needed to be.

Tasgo glared intently at Danny as he went on, explaining as if Danny had never understood the urgency. '*We should be at the gate now, smashing it to pieces, setting aside any who stand in our way, destroying all obstacles. I have been here too long. I have to get back. Now. Today. We make it happen, today, Dannaigh.*'

On other days Danny had tried to explain that it wasn't that sort of gate, that no-one was standing in their way. Not today. Danny wasn't going to risk Tasgo seeing him as an obstacle to be overcome. This time he said, '*You're right. Though it may take more than a day.*' He took a breath, making decisions. '*We'll have to use my chariot. I'll get it ready, you grab us some food.*' This last with a nod towards the kitchen, where bread and cheese should be easy to find. Tasgo knew his way around the cupboards by now.

It gave Danny time to phone Moira and warn her they were on their way before he got the car out onto the road.

Sometimes Tasgo took terrified delight in the speed of the car. Today it merely fitted his purpose, taking them swift and sure on their way. Danny parked as near to the library as he could, and they walked in.

The receptionist looked up, tried to hide a smile at Tasgo's outfit, and told them Moira had said to let them in. They went through the 'Staff Only' door, and entered the darker realms of books below stairs, winding their way through the narrow spaces between the densely packed racks of books and then into the tunnels. Danny could feel tension ramping up in Tasgo as the light seemed always to be leading them on, ahead of them, while darkness dogged them at their rear.

The light in the corridor in the next section was already on, as Danny tapped in the code to let them through. Tasgo suddenly surged closer to the glass pane in the door with a cry of *'Kelyn'*. But as the door swung open, there was nobody there. Tasgo was looking round, puzzled, but both the door ahead and the loading door to their left were closed.

'She isn't here,' Danny told him, thinking it must have been a trick of the light, a reflection on the reinforced glass. How tense must Tasgo be, to imagine that? Though he suddenly remembered his encounter with Kelly, that now distant night, how she had been staying in Moira's bedsit. Had she been evasive? He had been so upset that evening...

Moira opened the door ahead of them, and the proximity of that dark room where Tasgo had arrived wiped everything else away. They went in, Danny first, Tasgo lingering a moment at the door, looking for potential dangers, knowing he probably wouldn't recognise them as such even if they were there.

He followed Danny in, makeshift weapon ready in his hand, alert for anything that might cause harm to any of them. He stayed close to the door, ready to guard it should Danny and Moira need to escape.

At first glance it looked the same as it had the first time they had found it. But Danny could see some changes, the black boxes with dials set closer together in a neater array, the wires strapped together in neat bundles. There was more of it, and there were clipboards heavy with pages of what might be instructions or settings.

Tasgo gave a firm look at the glass box he had arrived in, as if to put it in its place, under control.

From here he could see that it was, as Dannaigh had said, not the sort of gate you could batter down. For a start there was no way out of this room crammed with things he did not understand. But then, there was no sense to the small room in Freya's house which you entered in one place and came out of in an entirely different part of the house, usually somewhere above or below where you started. But nothing about Freya or her house made sense to him. Despite the terrible injuries she had suffered so long ago, she had survived. Even though her hand had transformed to metal, it still worked as well as any made of flesh and blood.

Moira was explaining that they had made progress, but still the gate was being stubborn and wouldn't open. She was using words he didn't understand in ways that made no sense. What he did notice, with some surprise, was that, in the middle of the cage in which he had landed, was a stand, on which rested the memento Danny had given him four years ago, just before he and his family had left the real world forever.

When he was taken by the blue fire every other thing made of metal that Tasgo had carried had been left behind. But here was that metal object which he had worn in a pouch round his neck ever since Dannaigh had given it to him. He was fairly sure it had protected him from all misfortune, until he landed here. Somehow it too must have come through that unearthly blue fire.

He stared at it, mesmerised, no longer hearing Moira's words. Why had it come through, when his sword, knife and torc had not? How had it got into this place of display? Had it been there when he had tried so frantically to fight his way out of a trap that could not even be seen? He felt panic try to rise up in him again as he remembered how he had fought, how he struck more than once that device that now held the metal tracery of the egg. He forced himself to think panic was no longer needed, but he could not remember how the memento had got where it was.

Danny touched his arm and he turned sharply, hands raising to – well, to do whatever might be necessary, he told himself, seeing Danny's face and stance suddenly ready to fend.

'It's the thing you gave me,' he told Danny abruptly, with a motion towards it. *'How did it get here?'*

It was Moira who said, *'You had something like that, Tasgo?'* and Danny explained to her how Kuillok had dropped it when confronted on the hillside, and how Brec had repaired it so that Tasgo should have something to remind him of their victory that night. (When he spoke the name Kuillok, the words 'Evil Sorcerer' remained unsaid, though never unthought. He would never forgive Kevin Wilcox for the damage he had done, the damage to his mother, Danny's father forever missing, and the battles that had raged across the countryside.)

Moira's face lit up as she heard what Danny said. Her eyes were bright as she turned eagerly to Tasgo. *'You had it, you had it on you when this thing happened? You were wearing it when the blue light took you?'*

Tasgo nodded stiffly, he touched the ripped carry pouch he had been carrying it in, the one from which it had escaped so violently. Moira turned to the little object on its plinth. *'That's it,'* she breathed excitedly. *'That's the trick. That's what we have been missing. There has to be one at each end for it to work properly!'* Then her face fell. *'How do we get one there?'*

It took Danny a moment to understand exactly what she meant. Then, *'We don't have to,'* he told them both. *'Tasgo's is still there. It couldn't come through with you Tasgo, it must have dropped to the ground, like your sword, and your torc. It's still there. This is one that Kuillok had made, here.'*

'Then why aren't we making a connection?' Moira demanded. *'If it's still there why aren't we…'*

'It won't be there,' Tasgo told her bitterly. *'Jago will be wearing my torc. He will have my sword and my knife and the keepsake you gave me Dannaigh. He was there, and he will have taken the lot.'*

There was a moment's silence.

Then Moira said, full of purpose, *'Where will Jago be now, Tasgo?'*

Progress

They were back in Moira's tiny apartment in the top of the house in Newland Ave. Danny glanced about him, but there were no signs of Kelly. Somehow that was a relief, Tasgo's sudden cry of her name had unsettled him. The thought that she was somehow involved bothered him far more than it ought.

Danny concentrated on feeling positive, they had made a huge leap forward. It seemed that the portal needed one of those egg-shaped concoctions of many metals at each time zone to make the connection between them. He didn't understand it, it seemed to him they were far too flimsy to create that rift through time. Moira pointed out that they would merely be anchor points for a wormhole. The energy to create the wormhole would come from tensions already in the fabric of space-time, something that could be exploited by Reimann Curvature Tensors, initiated using a massive amount of electricity to make the correct electromagnetic forces.

But her mind wasn't on the mathematics and the physics. It seemed the egg-shaped tracery of metals, the memento Danny had given Tasgo five years ago, would form the Iron Age end of things. But it was in Jago's possession, not where Tasgo had been, near Cynmar. Moira now turned to Tasgo, full of purpose, *'Where will Jago be now, Tasgo?'*

Tasgo looked back at her bleakly. *'How could I know where that man is, being here as I am, rather than there.'* Then he tried to be more helpful. *'He would have gone back to Seahome, to try and make himself chief.'* He stopped to put this carefully. *'He would have some support. He has his favourites, who he treats well.'* He was becoming gloomy, *'Margan might oppose him, but he is too old to be chief. Marrec is no leader, and Pinner,'* he took a breath, *'Pinner would not put himself forward.'* He had thought through all of this before, many times. The conclusion was unavoidable. *'He is chief now.'*

He faced up to it and answered Moira's question. *'He will be in Seahome, overseeing the work. Maybe going out to see the outlying homesteads, maybe visiting Judoc in Stonewall to make alliances there. If you had asked me this,'* he went on gravely, meeting Moira's eye, *'many moons ago, when I was newly arrived here, I could have been more sure of his whereabouts. It would take time to win over all of the homefolk. He would have to stay there to work at it. At night he would have been in the roundhouse, MY roundhouse. Sleeping in my bed!'* A heavy conclusion.

Moira ignored the implied criticism. She was more worried about where Jago might be now. Tasgo's new roundhouse, bigger and better than the last, would have been near the old one. It would have stood where now the shopping centre and town administration stood, right in the middle of town. There was nowhere to set up any equipment without folk noticing. It was not a good place to set off an electromagnetic explosion that might wipe computers clean.

She was hunting for some sort of solution, and not finding any.

It was Danny who asked, *'What about Gamma, Tasgo? Dugal is gone, but Gamma – she was still strong, wasn't she?'* His grandmother was not the sort to sit back and let things happen round her. She was a bossy, interfering busybody. She had a lot of experience to work with, and she had always been flirtatious with Jago. Danny could see Tasgo was thinking along the same lines.

Moira was the one who had brightened up though. *'She told us she would leave things in the cave for us, to come the long way round,'* she said. She meant - lying there for two thousand years or so until now. *'Might she do that Tasgo?'* she asked hopefully, *'Might she leave the keepsake there?'*

Tasgo thought about it. *'If she could get hold of it,'* he said thoughtfully, *'If she could get it away from him.'*

Tasgo read their faces and took hope from Moira's enthusiasm. He allowed Danny to take him back to Freya's house, with its puzzling lift between floors, and amazing internal lake, rectangular of course, water held in a box and smelling unpleasantly of magic.

When they went to check Moira's house, no carefully wrought egg lay waiting for them in the cave, only the remains of the equipment they had

162

used to close the portal. If Gamma had put Danny's present to Tasgo there, it had not stayed there for two thousand years. Refusing to be downhearted, they had taken that as a good sign.

Danny was nervous though, taking Tasgo for a run, or down to the boxing gym. He could sense the growing impatience, the suppressed anxiety and anger that could so easily be provoked and unleashed. Instead they visited the cave almost every day, hacking the old melted equipment to smaller pieces that could be removed more easily.

Coming up from the darkness of the cave, Danny was always careful to make a quiet unobtrusive exit from the cupboard that hid the secret passage, even if he was only going up for a drink to take down to where they were working. When he heard voices, he paused at the bottom of the stairs until he could make out who it was. It was Raynes and Moira, talking quietly. He was about to call out, to let them know he was there, when he heard the name Kevin. It stopped him where he was, listening intently.

Moira was asking if Kevin could be released into Raynes' custody.

'Even under my supervision,' Raynes answered, 'they'd be unhappy about letting him off the premises, especially without a member of the staff.'

'They told me,' Moira answered tautly, 'that he seemed to be improving.'

'He's still grade A,' Raynes told her. 'Still down as highly dangerous and a risk to the public.' They were talking about the older Kevin Wilcox, the one who had been into the past, causing trouble everywhere. The one who had already, five years ago, sent men into the modern to kidnap Danny's mother Freya and to take Danny's father Tom from him for ever.

'Delusional,' Moira was saying dismissively, 'so long as there's someone to keep him to reality. We need him Ken. He's already done it once.' Her voice became softer, 'He's the only one who could understand what we're trying to do, and why.'

'We don't know that's what happened, Moira. Just because his younger self has disappeared now doesn't mean...'

'Of course it does!' Moira was short with him. 'We've already seen him there! Kevin's trapped there, and five years ago we rescue him!'

Listening, Danny felt dark emotions rising in him, a dread of the inevitable.

'We don't know that he's gone there now,' Raynes told her firmly, 'If he did, it's not the same distance back as you were used to. It's an extra five years previously, in the past. He might have fallen anywhere, in any time. If he did indeed vanish into the past. Things can change – you said so yourself!'

'Which is why we need him out of that hospital and helping us now! Kelly knows him well enough by now, she can handle him!' Moira retorted.

Danny had been mounting the stairs to the top floor slowly as they spoke. They were in the kitchen, and now Raynes saw him, and got to his feet. Moira saw the look on Raynes' face and turned.

A silence stretched between them in which icicles could have formed.

Raynes broke it. He spoke quietly, no doubt he had been in worse predicaments in the course of his work. 'Young Kevin's vanished,' he said.

'No-one mentioned he was involved,' Danny shot back, trying to keep his voice as low key as the detective. His heart was hammering though, his pulse racing with anger and mistrust, his mind leaping ahead through all the details. Kelly in Moira's flat. Danny and Tasgo back here, out of the way. The younger Kevin Wilcox wilfully included, learning everything he needed to know about time travel, and nothing at all about the havoc he would release in the past.

As in the night when his parent's house had exploded, his home demolished, his father whisked away forever, his mother, Moira's sister, torn and maimed, Danny was in a turmoil of ignorance. But this time he could work things out. No wonder Kevin Wilcox had trusted Kelly, back then, five years ago, and about two thousand and another five years ago. He already knew her!

'Why do you never tell me anything?' he growled at Moira.

'Because you react like this!' she snapped back.

Raynes was wiser. 'You can't give away what you don't know, Danny. It kept you innocent.'

'Ignorant!' Danny corrected him. Violence lay under his skin, ready. He knew that feeling. He kept it in check. There were more important things to deal with than their distrust and lack of faith in him. His voice was taut, reined in but strong. 'You think he's gone through, back then?'

Moira said, 'Yes,' but Raynes said, 'He's missing.'

'No blue flames burning anywhere?'

'Not that we can find,' said Raynes. Moira kept silent. Danny hoped she could see how he was taking it, how he was rising to the challenge.

'And Kelly's been helping,' Danny said, his voice heavy. She hadn't told him. Kelly was studying economics and politics. There was no way she could be helping with the science. No. Kelly was there to deal with Kevin Wilcox, to lure him in and keep him on track, to stop him running amok and letting the cat – the whole litter of cats – out of the bag.

When Danny had encountered her in Moira's flat, he had thought he was keeping things from her, but she now he saw she had been keeping them from him. He wondered if, at the crucial moment, he had told her the truth, let out the secret, his secret, their secret, would she have told him her own secret? He hoped she would have. She must already have known that he was lying.

Danny got out his phone and called her. If anyone knew what to do now, it would be Kelly.

As the phone rang, Tasgo came up the stairs, wondering why Danny was taking so long.

He didn't need to understand the words to know that something had gone wrong. He didn't need to be told there was conflict, he could see it in their faces, he could taste it in the air.

Danny shut down the phone. The last thing they needed now was for Tasgo to know that Kelly was involved. Not after the way they had parted company the last time. One complication too many. He turned the phone off, so that Kelly couldn't call him back.

He turned to Tasgo and said, *'The gate seems to be working. We need to get it set up here, in the cave.'* Since he was facing Tasgo he didn't see the startled look on Moira's face, as she realised that he had just cut through all the complications to the solution.

She said, *'There will be some adjustments to work out as well, but that will move things forward.'* Danny, like Tasgo, heard only the promise of more delays.

Strange Storm

It took weeks to move all the new equipment down into the cave, to set everything up, and for Moira to experiment with the final adjustments. At last everything was ready, and they had all gathered in Moira and Ken's living room, at the top of the house. Freya had joined them.

Tasgo had been amazed the first time he saw Freya. He could hardly believe his eyes. He had been certain that no-one could survive the wounds she had. The last time he had seen her she was so badly damaged he was sure they were taking her Underhill to die, but here she was, walking and talking, upright and very much alive. Even more beautiful than before, as he was quick to tell her. Then, once he had got used to this miracle, she had taken off her gloves and he had seen the metal hand, working as any ordinary hand might but transformed into metal. It had left him speechless for quite a while, trying to believe what his eyes saw, trying to understand what sort of magic could work such a wonder.

He had got used to it by now, but always he felt the presence of magic when he looked at her, and was uneasy.

It seemed everything was ready, but Ken Raynes was not.

'For a start,' he told Danny, 'we don't know that it will work. Tasgo shouldn't get his hopes too high.' He was speaking in the modern, and Danny was translating for Tasgo. 'If it succeeds in making a wormhole, we can't be sure that it will take you through to the right era. There could be some glitch that lands you in some other time. You might not be able to return. It might not be as easy to go through as the old one, it might tear you apart. And even if you get there, and the time is right, you still might not be able to get back again. Whoever goes through will be stepping into the unknown.'

After he had translated, Danny didn't need Tasgo to open his mouth to know that they were both of one mind. They both spoke at the same time, each in their own language, 'We'll go together,'. Neither had looked at the other as they both spoke, each was committed to the task.

But only Danny went on to say, 'If it works, it'll need two of us, and when things are fixed, we'll let you know.' They could work out the other outcome themselves. But together the danger would be less.

Seeing them side by side on the sofa, facing the detective, they looked a formidable pair. Young, strong and fit, they could have been brothers rather than cousins. They had heard all his dire warnings with thoughtful intensity, taking on the possibilities, seeing the danger clearly, and accepting it.

Meanwhile Freya had known what Danny and Tasgo's response would be. She was saying, *'I've collected a few* re-enactor's *spears, with bone blades tied on with waxed threads.'*

Tasgo got his feet as a gesture of honour. *'You are your mother's daughter,'* he said, with a wide grin. She laughed.

Raynes accepted that, but he had a bone to chew, and he wasn't going to let it get away. He asked Tasgo, pressing him to realise it was not just the journey that was uncertain, but also the arrival, 'If the portal does work and takes you to Seahome, what do you expect to face? What will you have to do?'

Still standing, Tasgo looked down on the Keeper of Lore, and was polite enough to answer, *'I will assert myself as Chief. If Jago is there, he will challenge that. In the end it will come down to a straight fight between us. He will yield or die.'*

Once Raynes might have thought 'cocky', but looking at Tasgo as Danny translated, 'over-confident' was closer to his fears. Tasgo looked formidable, strong in his self-belief, confident of his ability to wrest back command. 'Hubris' was what worried Ken Raynes.

Freya kissed both young men, it was time for her to leave them. Her new hand was powered and controlled by tiny chips which translated her movements and electric impulses into motion. She needed to be far away before the huge electromagnetic pulse spread out.

The week before, they had organised a massive information day in the town, on computer and internet security, with free advice on storing important and sensitive data in the cloud, or backed up in some distant location. Experts had toured the town, giving free assistance to save data elsewhere. They had done all they could. But there was no backup for Freya's hand, she would have to be far away.

The doorbell rang, and the taxi was here to take her to the station. As she left, Freya reminded Tasgo that he could always come back, at any time. He would be welcome. If things were not as they hoped and expected, the best thing would be to return here. To Danny she simply said, 'Stay alive. If it's all wrong, come home.' Having already kissed him, she turned away, as if it was no great thing, like going out for the evening or something like that. She walked quickly away and didn't look back. She was keeping her fears from him, she was letting him do what she knew he would do anyway.

There was a lump in Danny's throat that stopped him from speaking, of even calling out a farewell.

He was silent as they set the timers.

Then they all went down to the chip shop on the quay. No party was needed to take the neighbours safely out of the danger zone. Mrs Arkwright was in a home now, and everyone else was at work.

Danny kept a weather eye open. When they had closed the portal, there had been a violent storm. This time it was already raining, a damp drizzle, that was getting steadily colder, and heavier. The sea was choppy and grey green, and the sky was darkening in an ominous way. Danny remembered how, on that day five years ago, he had clung to a steel railing set deep in the earth, and wondered whether the world was about be torn apart, so violent was the storm that tried to tear him from the ground and send him sailing into the maelstrom. It didn't feel the same today, though he did wonder if a steel shutter over the glass window might be a good idea.

They ate their food sitting in the shop on high stools, with a shallow shelf as table. Drizzle turned to heavy rain, falling vertical, drumming on the road and the cars outside. Even with coats, they would be drenched in seconds.

With a sudden increased clatter, rain turned to ice, hailstones bounced and splattered, dancing violent along the pavement, large as peas, larger now. They vanished into puddles made furious by the onslaught, and soon were enough to blur the road to a white surface, uneven and still dancing. People still outside were taking shelter

168

anywhere they could, and the chip shop was now filled with folk exclaiming in amazement about the sudden change, their voices barely audible above the din.

Raynes suggested they keep back from the window, and the hammer of ice on tarmac persuaded most of them to do so. Tasgo watched with an ominous eye, still eating his chips. The first time he had tried chips he had been suspicious of their unnatural shape, and their unusual texture. Now he just accepted them as food, and he was taking on fuel as a tanker might, preparing for a long and arduous journey in rough seas.

Gloom had set in, outside it was almost as dark as night, despite the white glaze over everything. As suddenly as it had started, the hail stopped. Lights from shops and cafes reflected pale from the thick layer of hailstones which glossed the ground. Tasgo was licking his fingers clean. *'There was a storm like this,'* he told Danny, *'the day after you left us, we thought forever. Only then the wind howled like banshees, trees broke, and branches fell.'*

In the harbour waves had been battered to restless billows, and the air seemed deathly still, as if the world was holding its breath. Traffic had been forced to a standstill. Nothing moved. Into that silence, slowly as in a dream, snowflakes, huge and soft, began to float gently down, like feathers after a pillow fight. It seemed unreal, almost ghostly. Excited chatter amongst those sheltering in the shop died to nothing as everyone came under the spell. At first it was just a few flakes, but slowly the amount increased, filling the air, blotting out the far hillside and Gamma's rock. No pillow fight scattering this, the air was full of falling snow. The sea wall was no more than a shadow between the falling flakes. The boats sheltering beneath it were blurred from sight, it nearly blotted out the rail above the harbour, just across the road. A white veil of falling flakes obscured the world.

Someone said, laughing, 'Bloody Hell, I thought it was global warming we were worried about!' but there were few laughs. It was beautiful, but weird. And, even inside a fish and chip shop with the vats of hot oil, air was turning cold.

The church bell was chiming the hour when, suddenly, the lights went out. Everywhere. A shocked consternation ensued. Suddenly it was no laughing matter. Folk were dressed for drizzly autumn, not bleak winter.

169

A white blanket lay outside the door instead of dark tarmac. Day had turned to gloomy evening, all light lost. Muttering had started about power cuts and past storms.

Moira said suddenly, 'If this goes on for much longer, we won't be able to get back up the hill. We'd better go.'

'Better wait,' countered Raynes. Danny thought so too. If it was this cold here, how cold would it be in the house, in the cave? Raynes gave up his seat to a pregnant woman, and Danny made way for her mother and their tribe of children, staring out at the snow with wonder.

Time passed, it seemed like hours, but gradually skies became clearer, until the few remaining flakes floated flashing reflected sunshine from a sky of azure blue. Clouds still massed gloomy in the distance, but here they had been turned to ice and snow, and now lay prettily on the ground, virgin and untouched, leaving a circle of blue above them, bright with light. The epicentre was over the higher part of town, Scudmoor Road to be exact.

Others less fortified against the cold were deciding that the freak storm was over. They were ready to leave the warmth of the shop and make a dash for home through the snow. Raynes bought another bag of chips for the family to share. They had to wait for them to cook, because the shop had sold out to the sheltering crowd. It had been a good day for the chippie.

At last, having gorged again, making it last because they could feel the cold draught from the door, they set off. They all had good coats on. It was just as well.

They went out into air so cold it seemed to cut. Collars up, shoulders hunched, their feet stamping inches of fluffy snow down to mere wafers, they hurried up sloping streets towards their home. The last flakes were still swirling, held up by tiny movements of air. Snow drifted against skin, caught against eyelashes, collected against the fronts of their coats as they ploughed through the cold air. Haste made heat, but not enough to keep cold at bay. It was just as well that the air was so still, though it seemed so cold it might even set solid.

Inside, the house was as cold as a deep freeze. Electricity was still unavailable, but Moira lit the gas hobs and boiled milk to make mugs of hot chocolate to help warm hands tight with cold.

170

Outside, though the last flakes hung in the air as if reluctant to reach the ground, the view was clear. By the time they had drunk the chocolate, sunshine lit a landscape transformed into white.

Danny longed to dash down the stairs to the winter sitting room, snug at the very bottom of the house, tucked into the ground, but Moira had voiced her opinion that it might be exceedingly cold in that place, the centre of the sudden freeze. She made them wait, watching the snow outside melt into nonexistence, the heathland and fields appearing bit by bit from underneath as if cautious and a bit ashamed. Light was fading again, and the town in the other direction was unusual in its dark state.

At last, carrying candles, they went downstairs cautiously to the icy rooms below, and down again into the winter sitting room. Hidden switches turned cupboards into doors and allowed them down through the dark cleft into the cave below. Surprisingly it was less cold here, despite the cool pulsing light that now hovered in the middle of the cave, painting it blue.

With relief Danny felt the long forgotten ache in his shoulder, from when he had first found the flame and stupidly put his hand into it. That first time he had fought the intense pull of it until pain was so great he had to leap into it instead. Ever since the mere proximity of it was enough to waken the old injury.

The plan had worked. This was the portal. Danny quietly blessed his Grandmother Gamma. Whether she knew what she was doing or not, she had somehow got the metal-wire egg from Jago, and placed it in the cave. Danny hoped she had placed a few sharp weapons in there too!

Turning, he found Tasgo, tense and still as a statue, staring at the blue light, face hard.

Moira was the one to tell him, *'This is the gateway Tasgo, though we can't be sure it leads to where you want to be. You have to get ready first.'*

They had tried to think of everything, which would have meant a mountain of stuff to take through the blue flames with them. Tasgo would have whittled it down to just the spears and a warm cloak. Danny insisted on enough food to last them a couple of days. In addition Moira gave him a small pouch, containing little bags of diamonds, rubies and pearls, saying they would be almost as good as money for most of history if somehow the other end of the portal were not in the Iron Age. He and Tasgo refused any other burdens.

Moira tried to warn Tasgo again, that it might not be the home he recognised on the other side of the portal. He shrugged it off. The gate was open, they should go. He was glad Danny was going with him, though secretly he might have worried that Danny might be more of a hinderance than a help.

Now, with Tasgo dressed in the clothes he had been wearing when he was snatched from battle, and Danny in more recently acquired re-enacting clothes, they stood together. The spears were bundled together and tied with heather bindings, but they were still cumbersome. The two of them stood together in the faint light of the cave, Tasgo looking at the blue light as if it were an enemy to be conquered.

'We jump through,' Danny told Tasgo, grabbing one of his arms, 'together. That's all. On Three'

'Three!' Tasgo commanded.

They leapt.

Tasgo was surprised to find himself landing in the same cave, on the other side of the flames. 'Don't touch them,' Danny warned him. 'We'll go round to the cleft carefully.'

Back on the other side of the flames, Danny gave a cry of delight. There on the ledge where the candle and matches stood, was a sword in a scabbard, three knives and a lovely bronze torc. Tasgo grabbed them with growled thanks to Lugh and to Taran, and called on all the gods of house and home to bless Gamma, while he fastened the sword carefully about him, and found niches in his torn pouches that would take the knives, adding the torc to his neck last of all. He offered a knife to Danny, but Danny wanted to start as he planned to go on, without weapons of any sort.

Danny surprised Tasgo by lighting the candle with a match, a small display of Underhill magic. Then they clambered through the cleft with the same difficulty as when they had come down, but now it came out not into the hidden parts of Moira's home, but into a more cavernous space, very dark. Danny pointed out the faint glow of light that marked the cave mouth, and they found their way over the rocks towards it.

172

There Danny put the candle on the shelf built there, snuffed it and with a finger to his mouth for silence, rolled out into the open air.

The Unknown

There it was, an older landscape. Scattered clouds let sunshine dapple the valley, no roads scored the hill beyond. Trees filled the valley bottom and the air was scented with heather and herbs. Danny crouched as he took it all in.

Tasgo rolled out of the cave to join him, standing and looking about him, hope and relief showing on his face. Surprise also as he looked about him, and back at the overhang of rocks that hid the cave.

'This is it?' he said, looking with disbelief at where he had come from, checking it against the shadows below other rocks, where rough grasses grew, looking exactly the same. He looked at Danny as if disappointed. *'All this time – it was just a cave that our eyes have been blind to all this time?'*

Danny gave him a twist of a smile, *'That and a gate of blue flame,'* he said, *'Never give it away,'* he added, *'it is after all Underhill.'* While he spoke, he was looking anxiously towards the curve of woodland that lay above what should be the village and was rewarded by a haze of smoke drifting through the trees. If this wasn't the exact time, it was close. Maybe close enough.

On his own territory, sword at this hip, spears in hand, Tasgo took control. He passed the spears to Danny to hold. As Danny slipped the carry strap over his shoulder, Tasgo too was looking towards where the village should be, but he turned away from it, looking down the hill towards trees bare limbed against the sky.

Down at the fence line there were people, doing something with the fence. *'We'll go this way,'* he decided, starting down the hill towards them. *'It feels like Imbolc, the promise of summer,'* he said as he walked.

'Yes,' Danny answered striding with him, *'Our seasons and yours are always out of step.'*

Tasgo nodded, as though this made some kind of sense to him. His eyes were on the figures below them, intent on their work. Margan, his

174

hair grizzled like an old man, was aided by a few young lads. Danny had to remind himself that it was five years since he had seen any of them, that Margan had been old then, something like forty years old. He must remember that they would all be older now, as he was himself. He was no longer the ignorant youngster he had been then, as they would remember him.

The group were replacing one of the fence posts, so deeply engrossed in the task that they failed to see the two men coming down towards them until they were quite close. The taller of the youngsters looked up then, and took a moment to realise what he was seeing. He pulled on Margan's sleeve and pointed. They all looked.

Tasgo kept on walking, Danny at his side, both steady and collected, watching the group's reaction as they approached. The older boy, maybe ten years, or twenty seasons as they would say here, took a step away, his face suddenly pale and frightened. Without taking his eyes off the approaching men, Margan's hand went out to grasp the boy's shoulder and steady him. One of the younger two boys took a step closer to Margan, eyes wide as they took in exactly who it was.

Margan spoke a few words to them. His sword in its scabbard was hung round another fence post, a few strides away from him, but Margan made no move towards it. He waited until Tasgo and Danny were an easy spear's throw from him, then raised his voice to ask, *'Is that you, Tasgo?'*

'Indeed,' Tasgo called back, still walking. *'Who else would it be?'*

'Do you still live?' Margan asked, strong and bold, a challenge.

'I do,' answered Tasgo, as if this were a normal sort of conversation, *'Why would you think otherwise?'*

Margan passed the hammer he was holding to one of the younger boys. *'Jago said you were dead,'* he answered, taking a step through the gap in the fence towards Tasgo, his hand still on the older boy's shoulder. *'Dead and taken Underhill, in a flash of blue light. He said the trader killed you.'*

'I was untouched,' Tasgo told him, slowing to a standstill just a few feet from the man. *'I slew that trader. It was no choice of mine to go Underhill.'*

'Nor of ours,' Danny put in. *'It's been a struggle finding a way back.'*

'How do things stand?' Tasgo asked, getting at once to the essentials.

Margan, still keeping his hand on the older boy, said to the wide-eyed one standing nearer to him, *'There are women in the pool. Go down and tell them they are needed up here at once. Nothing more than that, then come back quickly to let me know they are coming.'* As the child raced off, he called after him, *'And don't waste time gawping!'* Turning back to Tasgo he answered the question, grim faced. *'Jago is chief. Your disappearance at Cynmar shocked them all. They were afraid. Jago made them give their word to support him. Back here, he told everyone you were dead, killed by the trader, your body taken by grey folk. He called on all the warriors to pledge themselves to him as chief. Leir had already done that, so Marrec had no real choice. Some of the young bloods had pledged themselves before I arrived at the scene.'*

'And you?' Tasgo asked quietly.

'He already had half the warriors. He had your sword and your torc, so I said Seahome needed a good chief, a wise lord, and I would back him until you returned. He pretended it was a jest, but he didn't like it. Mokan did the same and the rest did too.

'Pinner?' demanded Tasgo.

'Dead.'

That shocked Tasgo. 'Pin?'

Margan was grim. *'Ran off a cliff chasing deer,'* he said.

It shocked Danny too. That wasn't right, surely not possible? Pinner knew this land like his own skin. They all did. How could he not know he was close to a cliff top? There was a long moment of silence, then Tasgo, equally grim, asked, 'Who saw it?'

'He was with Carod. They were supposed to scare the deer towards Jago, Cadryn and Leir. '

'Did they see the body?'

'At the bottom of the cliff, sea washed.'

'Did he still have his sword?'

'Waves washed him, it was hard to tell.'

It came to Danny like an unwanted vision, Pinner, broken, far below on the rocks, waves breaking over him, stained with his blood. The others looking down from above, shocked and suspicious. They had looked to see if his sword had been taken from him. At least one of them was thinking murder, because if you'd murdered a man, you might take time

176

to take his valuable sword off him before throwing him off a cliff. He shook his imagination free of the sight. Why kill Pin? Why would anyone want to kill Pinner?

'*When was this?*' Tasgo demanded.

'*Two moons after you vanished.*'

'*Morven?*'

'*Same as me.*'

Tasgo nodded his relief at that '*Kelwyn?*' was Tasgo's next.

Margan shrugged, '*Paid man,*' he said with some distaste.

Tasgo considered that for a moment, then pressed Margan, '*Did he give his word?*'

'*Not in my hearing. Stands with him though.*'

Tasgo nodded, then continued the roll call, '*Freda?*'

'*Took the children and ran, while Jago was still calling the pledges in. I'd guess she's with Kennis. Jago hasn't bother to hunt for her.*'

'*Cynwrig?*' This question surprised Danny. Cynwrig had been an unruly five-year-old when Danny had last seen him, he would be ten going on eleven now. Why ask about him?

'*I took him to Coraith's, told him his job was to protect their family.*' Margan said, then he realised what was missing and added quickly, '*Jago didn't ask Coraith to give his word. They left a few days after.*' Danny could understand that. Coraith was lame, but he still carried a sword. He would have taken offence at being discounted. But where would he go, with his wife and – and his family. Danny's heart skipped a beat, remembering his wife Seren, taking on the fact that they now had a family.

'*Gamma?*' was next, which brought a sharp look from Margan, a look that included Danny in its compass.

'*She's ill,*' he said. '*May be dying,*' he added, then went on cautiously, '*She took it badly, first Dugal, then you.*' He faced Tasgo then, his hand still on the boy's shoulder. '*Jago was furious when she...*' his eyes slid from Tasgo's to the torc about his neck, and then to the sword strapped on his hip. Coming back to Tasgo's face, his words turned to tentative question, '*when she gave your torc and your sword as offering to the gods...?*'

Tasgo merely cocked his head a little to the side, still listening, so Margan went on, gaining strength again, *'but he got over that when he realised how ill she had become. He's been…'* again the pause, choosing his words carefully. *'He looks after her himself, won't let anyone else bother her.'*

Danny's hackles were up. This sounded out of character to say the least. His brain fizzed with questions How ill? What ill? What sort of tending? Why no-one else? He didn't ask. This was Tasgo's task, he had to gain back control by himself, his own way, and it was looking increasingly difficult.

But then the boy Margan had sent as runner was flying up from the woods, though Tasgo went on collecting information, martialling his forces in his mind. *'Cunddu?'* he asked, a name new to Danny.

Margan grimaced. *'Dead. Jago tried to call him to heel, and he bit the man. Jago beat him to death in front of us all.'*

This startled Danny, until Margan went on, *'You trained him well, never saw a dog defend an absent master before.'*

The boy was approaching fast, calling breathless, *'They're coming, they're coming.'*

As he puffed up to them, coming close to Margan, Margan turned to the lad still held by his hand. *'Suinney, you tremble, what ails you?'*

All this time the boy Suinney's eyes had been on Tasgo, as if transfixed. Now he took a step as if to hide behind Margan as he tried to speak. The words were less than a whisper. *'He's dead.'*

Tasgo gave something like a laugh. *'No I'm not, never was. Here,'* stepping forward and holding out his hand, *'feel for yourself.'*

But for the hand on his shoulder the boy would have shrunk back, maybe he would have run. Having stopped him, Margan let him go, and with a warm voice, said, *'I'll take that hand,'* doing so, stepping forward as he did, embracing Tasgo suddenly and warmly with, *'Welcome back!'* Stepping back he gave a nod to Danny to include him in the welcome. At last he stepped over to his sword and began to strap it carefully in its place as he spoke to the boy. *'Never be afraid of your Chief Suinney, for you are a good, strong lad, and have nothing to fear. Shake his hand now, like a man.'* This last without looking at the boy as he worked the leather strap through the ring buckle and pulled it tight.

178

Tasgo favoured the boy with a smile, *'I remember you winning the race across the ford and back, last summer. You were fearless that day too,'* he said, with a slow offer of his hand. The boy's hand came fearful forward to meet it, found it warm to the touch, and gathered strength. Gaining courage, he did indeed shake the hand of his chief like a man, and his chief smiled on him.

The younger boy spoke up quickly, *'Can I too?'* and Tasgo shook his hand too, and then that of the youngest. The boys' eyes were sparkling now with excitement.

Now armed, Margan asked Tasgo, *'What's the plan?'*

'We go down past the pool and through the village,' Tasgo told him calmly, *'until we find Jago.'*

Margan may have had his doubts on the wisdom of that plan, but he joined them as they started to do just that. Tasgo was walking with that same steady gait that he had used before when going into conflict. Steady, determined, looking unstoppable. They were half way to the shade of the wood when figures emerged from it.

As they came closer Danny recognised Bahee, Pinner's daughter, a shawl wrapped round her to cradle what must be a baby, and that must be her sister Treva. Treva had been about ten when Danny had saved her from being carried off, now she had changed almost beyond recognition. Still the same intense look on her face, but she had filled out, she was a woman, shapely, but less lithe in her movements, and she had put on some weight. An older woman followed her, stopping when she saw who it was ahead. Bahee didn't. She ran forward, her voice sang across the open space. *'It's you! It is you!'* Her delighted eyes took in Danny as well, *'I knew he lied!'* she cried, coming to a stop, and looking back at Treva who was following her at a slower pace. *'I told you, didn't I?'*

Treva was not overjoyed. She stopped beside her sister and snarled, *'You're late! You're too late!'* angrily. She was looking at Danny not Tasgo.

Ignoring this, Bahee went on, *'I knew you'd be back, sometime. About time too!'* she added. Their father was dead, unburied, unburnt, no funeral rites at all, taken away by the tide after an untimely death. They would be no friend to Jago, Danny thought.

'Where were you?' Treva demanded of Danny angrily and somehow tearfully too, not like Danny remembered her at all. *'Where have you*

been? Why weren't you here?' Anger taking over again, she suddenly flew at Danny, fists raised to beat against him. Tasgo stepped aside out of the way, so did Margan. Danny did the only thing he could, he caught the flailing fists, got his arms around her and hugged her tight to him, so she could do no real harm.

She burst into tears then, collapsing against him, not like herself at all. She had always been fierce, strong, feisty. Anger was her first resort, rather than tears. As he held her thin arms, and her bony ribs he realised she hadn't gained weight at all, she had lost some, and that thickening of her waist was something else entirely. He leant his head into her hair, still wet from the pool, and made hushing noises. He had no idea what else to do but hold her tight and make sympathetic noises. Over her head he could see Bahee, all sisterly concern, but standing back from them, meeting his eyes. They confirmed what he now knew. Treva was pregnant, and it was no joy to her.

Tasgo said, down to earth, *'We are here now,'* as if that were all that mattered.

Bahee answered it with, *'Ailiese is with us, she's coming, and she'll be armed too,'* but sounding as though that were a good thing, that Ailiese would be on their side.

Tasgo was moving on, but Danny was encumbered. *'Treva,'* he whispered, trying for comfort, warmth and urgency all at the same time, *'I have to go with Tasgo, I...'*

Her head went back, and she looked up at him, back to anger, eyes red rimmed and narrowed to slits. *'Kill him,'* she hissed. She was pushing herself off him, standing on her own two feet, *'Rip his heart out! Slit his throat!'* She surely didn't mean Tasgo? The older woman came forward then, as Tasgo and Margan passed her with Bahee and the boys in their wake. The woman made to put her arms round Treva but Treva was having none of it. She was taking in the fact that Danny had the bundle of spears, still tied together. She made a grab at them, she wanted a proper weapon, better than the knife Danny knew she would have about her. The woman was saying something about the baby, and trying to contain Treva. Treva back-elbowed her in the face, and Danny had to grab her arms again.

The woman stepped back, keeping out of the way, not remonstrating, head bowed. Danny did the next best thing. He said, clear and calm, *'I'll give you a spear, just calm down.'* It did the trick. As he handed Treva the spear, she settled to anger and purpose, and set off after Tasgo. Danny had to bound after them all to catch up.

Ailiese had finished strapping on her weapons and had been coming to meet them. Her surprise to see them was momentary, she gave a cry of thanks to Bel, and kissed Tasgo on the lips with fervour. Taking no notice at all of Danny, she fell into step with Tasgo. *'He'll be in the new Hall,'* she told him sideways, with scorn. *'That's where he usually is.'*

As they approached the horse field, Marrec was leaning over the gate observing the animals with a watchful eye. He turned to see who was coming. His face paled with dismay as Tasgo approached and greeted him. Marrec threw his arms wide, in surrender. He drew breath and said, unhappy, *'I gave him my word, Tasgo. I'm sorry for it, was already sorry for it, but Leir...'*

'I know,' Tasgo told him, *'Margan said.'* He waited a moment to let it sink in that he was laying no blame, as yet, then spoke again. *'What will you do now?'*

Marrec looked at him wild-eyed, his gaze slipped to Margan as if for help, and then back. For a moment his frantic thoughts showed in his face, then he said, a man grasping at straws, *'There's a mare in foal, she needs attention.'* Turning his back on them he mounted the gate, dropped to the other side and walked away towards the horse nearby. He didn't look back.

Leaving him they passed the stake where first Kuillok and, much later, 'TheBoy' who was to become Gatwyn had been tied. There Margan's boys left them, with obvious reluctance as he sent them away.

The forge bed was black and cold when they reached it, it looked unused for some time. Beyond it Brec was working on something being held by his slave Hod, while Gatwyn watched and handed tools as required. Gatwyn was a youth now, grown strong from working the bellows and pounding metal. It was he who looked up and saw the party coming towards them. A word from him brought a quick look from Hod, over his shoulder, while Brec finished what he was doing before throwing a glance towards them. He straightened, setting his tool aside, and picked up the hammer he was never far from.

His growled greeting could have been a challenge. *'Took your time, didn't you?'* In case that were not ambiguous enough he went on, *'All but set on leaving, us!'* as he stepped towards Tasgo with a determined look on his face. *'He's in the new Hall, stuffing himself or some poor maid.'* He turned back to Hod and Gatwyn. *'If things turn bad, and I don't come back, consider yourselves freed, and run,'* he commanded.

Hod picked up the long poker. *'We'd not get far,'* he said. *'If things get bad, you'd need some help. If we're free if things get bad, I'd be free to help you.'*

Gatwyn looked at Hod in some surprise, while Brec told the man not to be so stupid.

Then a smile broke on Gatwyn's face, turning him suddenly into something handsome and happy. *'Sounds like you need some luck,'* he said. *'I've been lucky so far.'* He grabbed the pincers that could snip steel, and came towards them.

Tasgo almost laughed. He said, *'You have unruly slaves Brec, you should beat them more often.'*

'He could try!' Gatwyn countered almost gaily, as if this were some sort of game. With that Brec, still grim, gave up trying to keep them out of the fight.

Danny felt a great relief rise in him, almost to the point of happiness. They were becoming a crowd, though neither Brec nor his slaves were fighters, they gave heft to the group. They all had muscle, but Brec had attitude too, and Gatwyn had raised their moral. Danny was beginning to think that they might win through.

On the exercise field Leir, taller now and more handsome, was training a horse on a long lead, getting it to walk in a circle and stop on command. Bahee rushed ahead to him, and as he saw her his face lit up with love. Then he saw the rest of them.

Danny watched as dread drenched the smile. Bahee was talking to Leir as she came to him, but he was talking too, grabbing her shoulders and speaking insistently, so that they could hear his urgent tones. It was obvious she was arguing with him. As they came closer, they could hear the words, Leir's more clearly, since he was facing them. '*...for the children, take them and go!*'

Her voice was not as fierce '*... can't, not after what he's done. He lied Leir, he lied to you!*'

But Leir was straightening now, looking over her shoulder to Tasgo, and his hand dropped to his sword hilt. '*Go, now!*' he instructed Bahee as he faced oncoming trouble.

Tasgo stopped, still at some distance. '*I know,*' he said, his voice carrying over the matted mud and green grass, '*you gave him your word, and I wouldn't expect you to go against that.*'

'*He saw you die,*' Leir answered.

'*Yet here I am.*'

'*The grey folk took you,*' Leir said.

'*I was not dead, it was not my will to go.*'

'*You vanished, you left your sword, your shield, your torc...*' Leir had his reasons, he was not willing to give up Jago's truth that had settled in him over all these months, not even in the face of living proof otherwise.

Danny stepped forward then. '*It was not his doing. It wasn't ours. Kuillok still has some powers to strike at those he hates.*' Because it was true. That day in the tunnels back in Hull, in the twenty-first century, Tasgo had seen Kelly. Danny hadn't believed it at the time. Later he had remembered how the light had been on ahead of them. How much cooler the air was in that chamber. When he was alone with Moira, he had asked her. She confessed Kelly had been helping. When pressed she told him Kelly had been shepherding Kevin Wilcox out of the way, so that he should not meet Tasgo and Danny. Kevin was the one who had worked out the forces needed to open a wormhole, given anchoring points at each end. As Kelly had said earlier, Kevin was the one person who knew more than anyone else about portals and wormholes through time. He was the only person who could find out how to let Tasgo get home, even if he hadn't realised that was what he was doing.

Danny had been forced to hide his anger. He could see only too clearly how Kevin had learned enough to propel himself back into the past and cause havoc there.

Now Leir looked from Danny to Tasgo, and it was clear how much his loyalties were divided. '*I gave my word,*' broke out from his lips painfully.

Treva broke into it with fury, *'He's a lying filthy bastard raper!'* The words broke on Leir like slashing blades. Pain and shame showed in his face, but still he stood, facing them. *'He's been poisoning Gamma!'* she went on, and this time it was Margan who tried to restrain her with words, *'We've no proof of that, Treva.'*

'Then you're a fool!' she snarled back.

Tasgo went on talking to Leir over the top of it, calm as if it were no matter, *'Jago will want to know that I am here. If you will, you could shout into the hall that I am here, just that. He would thank you for the warning. After that you can stand where you please.'*

For a moment Leir stood in confusion, then *'I want no thanks from him,'* burst from his lips. He looked angrily at Bahee. She had started towards their roundhouse as if to obey his orders, but now she turned and was standing beside Tasgo and her sister. She held her hand out to Danny, and reluctantly he gave her one of his spears. He knew better than to argue.

A mix of emotions on his face, Leir knew better too. He turned on his heel and marched towards the new roundhouse. They all followed.

Confrontation

Ahead of them, Leir bent to shout a warning in through the roundhouse door. *'It's Tasgo! He's here!'*

Straightening he walked on a few paces to where a horn hung near the door. He raised it to his lips and blew a series of blasts. Danny remembered that sound, the call to all warriors, the call to action. It sent shivers down his spine. He had known it would have to be like this, everyone involved. Now it was becoming real he felt the fear, the real, deep-seated dread of battle.

Leir moved away from the door, away from Tasgo and his small army, turning to face them obliquely, but also part facing the doorway. Carod was coming out, belligerent yet puzzled. He stopped dead when he saw Tasgo and Danny, too astounded to take notice of the rest of the crowd. He had put on some weight, it didn't make him look less formidable. Kelwyn had to prod him to move over as he ducked out as well.

Kelwyn was not puzzled, he was not astounded. He had been a paid man, a warrior who lived for fighting. He looked pleased at the prospect as he moved out into the open, facing them, taking in Tasgo and Danny's presence as if it was only to be expected.

Jago took a little longer to appear, and meanwhile young men were running in from the woodland, or from the river's edge. Some of them were as yet unarmed, a few already had spears in hand. A few had long knives half hidden in the sheaths. The sight of their erstwhile chief brought each of them to a halt.

As Jago came out to stand between Kelwyn and Carod, the young warriors began to take sides, and most of them were going to stand behind Jago as he took in the forces opposing him.

Jago ignored Danny, he snarled at Tasgo. *'How dare you come back, after deserting your fighters and your home.'*

'I have never done that,' Tasgo answered, raising his voice so that everyone could hear him, but sounding calm and authorative.

Jago wasn't listening, he railed *'Bringing your grey folk with you, your real family! You don't belong here!'*

Tasgo was dismissive, *'Have you forgotten my father Aod, so soon?'* he asked, *'and my mother, Bel rest her soul. Have you forgotten Dugal, and all he stood for?'*

Jago pointed a finger, *'Deserter!'* he cried, accusing. *'You ran!'*

'I was taken to a greater battle,' Tasgo told him, *'Where I was needed more. The trader was already dead, killed by my sword.'*

Danny watched the faces of the young warriors opposite. They were confused. Danny was not sure about this greater battle of which Tasgo had spoken. He was still unsure what Tasgo had made of the modern world, but fighting a pack of police, armed with Tasers, would probably count as a greater battle. If it was needed Danny was ready to put in a word or two on Tasgo's behalf, but it would be better if Tasgo could be seen to do it all himself. No-one seemed interested in Danny. Some of the older fighters, like Morven were coming to stand by Tasgo, pushing their way to the front, wanting to be seen by his side.

Danny stepped back, slipped away, unnoticed. Everyone was intent on what Tasgo was setting out and what Jago was yelling. Danny moved quietly to the door of the roundhouse and ducked in. Tasgo was right, it was bigger and better than the old one. An inner wall separated the outer area, where things could be stored, from the inner hall, lofty and spacious. There a fire burned brightly in the centre, several sleeping chambers were partitioned off round the edges. Jago's would be the one furthest over, slightly larger and hung with drapes. Blathin was grinding grain by the fire, twisted over her work. When she looked up, bruises showed on a battered face, on which horror was suddenly plastered. She dropped the handle of the pestle-stone, getting awkwardly to her feet, like an injured bird trying to fly.

'Not my doing...' she was stammering, broken voiced, *'I couldn't... he wouldn't...'* She was afraid, mortally afraid. She was afraid of Danny.

'It's all right,' he told her, but she was going on, *'Not my fault, I swear... Bel and Sulis...'* she was shrinking away from him as he approached.

'It's alright Blathin,' he told her softly, *'I'm not angry with you, I could never be angry at you.'*

186

She stopped, cringing, still afraid. *'I couldn't stop him...'* she whispered, as if walls had ears, *'he made me...'*

Danny laid a gentle hand on her arm, felt her flinch. *'Where is she?'* he asked. She looked towards the chief's stall.

In the half-light the bed looked empty, but as Danny came closer he could see a slight form, almost that of a child. The face was that of an ancient hag, wizened, little flesh on the bony face. It took a moment to realise that this was her, his Grandmother Gamma, that confident, demanding, forceful being, full of bustle and command, shrunk to this bag of bones and pain. The pain was in her crumpled face, her closed eyes.

He knelt beside her, touched her cold hand, and for a moment wondered if she were already dead. Then he saw the glitter beneath the eyelids. She was watching him through slitted eyes.

'It's me,' he told her softly, as if a loud voice might be enough to do her harm, 'Danny,' he told her, in case she could not tell. 'Tasgo's here, he's back.'

Her hand trembled as if she were trying to lift it, but the effort was too much. There was a beaker on the shelf by the bed, he picked it up, and saw her eyes flash open in alarm. He sniffed it, to her greater alarm. Her mouth made a mew of dissent. The liquid inside the cup smelt acrid, unpleasant. He saw her relief as he lowered it. Perhaps she had thought he was going to drink it? A knot formed in his stomach, an awful feeling of what had been going on.

'Poison?' he asked, and saw her attempt to nod.

'Jago?' he asked, and this time saw anger and malice flame in her face for a second as she gave a more evident nod.

Danny turned to Blathin, still crouched by the fire. Anger was a bitter flame in his chest. He covered it as best he could, in case Blathin should take fright and flee. *'Get her some ale,'* he told her, *'and then some broth, if she can take it.'* She was still afraid of him. Sweet, smiling Blathin was cowed and defeated.

Hatred blossomed out of anger. It filled him with purpose. *'No one will blame you,'* he told Blathin, *'It's not your fault. Look after her now.'* His mind was racing ahead, to what was happening outside.

He leant forward to tell his grandmother, 'I'll be back very soon,' like a conspirator. Blathin came forward with a beaker of ale. She was still afraid of him, she was expecting blows. He made his voice as gentle as he could, but anger still burned in it. *'When I call for it,'* he told her now, *'bring me out a beaker of ale.'*

He was already striding to the door as he spoke, the beaker of ill will in hand.

Ducking out of the door he felt tension like a physical thing, two angry gangs facing each other. Most of the younger warriors were behind Jago, the older ones who had worked with Dugal sided with Tasgo. It was the presence of Carod and Kelwyn beside Jago that was most worrying. Carod was a brute of a man, ready to do as bidden. Kelwyn was a man who could kill clean and quick, tireless. He was worth a dozen of the young bloods behind him.

Someone had given Tasgo a small shield though, it was held firm in his left hand.

Leir still stood indecisive at the far end of the two groups. The shouting was still going on. The whole village seemed to have gathered round the conflict. Armel and the other folk who mainly farmed were mostly behind Tasgo now.

'You coward, standing with a load of traitors!' Jago challenged. *'I dare you to take on my champion, Kelwyn.'*

'I have no quarrel with Kelwyn,' Tasgo answered coolly, *'and I won't cower behind a champion. It's you I challenge.'*

Jago smiled smugly, *'Kelwyn,'* he ordered, *'kill the coward.'*

Kelwyn shifted weight, not moving a foot, but observing Jago, *'You never asked me to give my word,'* he said.

Smug dropped from Jago's face. *'You are a paid man,'* he snarled, *'Mine to command.'*

'No,' Kelwyn told him.

'You were Dugal's!' Jago countered angrily, *'and so came to me through Tasgo.'*

'Dugal and I had a contract,' Kelwyn answered with quiet certainty, *'completed the day Kuillok was taken. I was never his slave.'*

'Why else would you still be here?' Jago was furious.

'Apart from Braiga?' Kelwyn smiled a crooked smile, 'It's been – interesting.' Braiga was one of Margan's daughters. Jago stared at him full of thwarted fury.

Danny took the moment. He stepped quickly and decisively into the open space between the two groups, and spoke first to Tasgo. 'Credit where it's due, Blathin tells me Jago has been looking after Gamma like a hero, tending her himself, and giving her this medicine.' Tasgo looked daggers at him, but Danny had turned to Jago, and went on, 'For that you deserve a just reward, or at least some credit where it is due.' He raised his voice, 'Blathin, some ale for Jago, I'll share a toast with him, before any ill befalls him.'

He knew he was cutting through the conflict, causing puzzlement and irritation. He did not dare look at Tasgo. The young bloods behind Jago were looking confused, Danny was supposed to be the enemy here, one of the fair folk, in Tasgo's camp. They didn't know what to make of it. No-one did, but Treva wasn't having none of it. Her voice rose shocked and angry, 'There's nothing good about him! He's a blasted raper! Kill him! Just kill him, now!'

Jago wasted a moment to proclaim dismissively, 'Your choice sweetheart, you wanted me then.'

'Never!' she shouted, furious. Bahee had to hold her back. 'It was you, or Carod **then** you! That's what you offered, you bastard!'

Some of the lads beside Jago looked uncomfortable, others looked distinctly cocky and superior. One of them even laughed at her and her anger.

Blathin was ready though, she had heard Danny and hurried out with the beaker, though the limp slowed her a little. She brought the beaker to Danny rather than to Jago, and then shrank back.

Heart thumping, hiding hatred, Danny held out the beaker of ale to Jago, who took it uncertainly. Danny could see him looking for the trap, and not finding it. He knew Dannaigh was an ignorant bastard, but could he really be that stupid? Sneering contempt was hiding in Jago's face as Danny raised the beaker of poison in his own hand, and said, 'Here's health,' holding his arm out towards Jago as he said it.

'Health,' replied Jago, a smile of victory on his face as he brought the ale towards his own lips. Danny could see Jago's pleasure, watching to

189

see Danny of his own free will take the poison meant for Gamma. But Danny cried out, *'No, no!'* pausing Jago. *'Where I come from, we drink to each other with straight arms,'* holding his arm with the poison cup out straight.

It stopped Jago, puzzled. He even straightened his own arm a little. *'Impossible,'* he said, *'no-one can drink with a straight arm.'*

Danny creased his face into something like a smile. *'It's easy enough,'* he said, taking one deliberate step towards Jago, swinging his arm towards him too. *'We each drink from the other's cup,'* he said.

Jago's mocking smile vanished as he saw the trap closed upon him. *'You bastard,'* he snarled.

Danny feigned innocence. *'What? Why would you not drink this good tonic that you have been giving Gamma?'* he asked. He looked at the beaker in his hand as if unable to believe an idea forming in his head, acting it out for all the world to see. *'Is there something wrong with it?'* Looking Jago in the eye, all pretence thrown aside, *'Jago, it couldn't be poison, could it?'*

Jago threw his beaker at Danny's head, ale flying from it into Danny's face, into his eyes. His other hand was at the hilt of his sword.

Kelwyn's hand got there before him, holding it in place. Kelwyn had closed in hard and fast, was right behind Jago now. He made no other move than to hold the sword in its place.

Danny dropped all pretence of innocence and ignorance. He leapt furious at Jago, thrusting the beaker of poison at his face, grabbing his tunic with the other hand. *'Drink it and prove me wrong,'* burst from his angry lips as he forced the beaker towards Jago's mouth, while Jago tried to knock it from his hand, and to retreat. Kelwyn blocked him, keeping him in place while Danny forced the metal between the man's lips, crying *'Drink it! Drink!'*

No-one tried to stop it. Most of the liquid went flying as Jago fought against it, but it was clear to everyone now. Jago had not been tending Gamma, the liquid in the cup was something foul. Danny tipped it up so that the liquid splashed over Jago's face, though only a little made it into his mouth. Danny leapt back, and Kelwyn let Jago loose.

'You lying, murdering bastard,' Danny told Jago roundly, making sure that everyone had got the point. 'Poisoning an old woman because she would not bend to your will!'

As others took it in, Tasgo said, clear and loud, coming back to the main point, 'Enough! It is simple. I am chief here, but you think it should be you. We will fight for it, on the exercise yard where everyone can see, and one of us will be chief, and the other will die.' It was a simple answer, easily accepted by all. Not that many still backed Jago on merit, some of the young men were obviously confused, but still, they had given their word, and many felt they could not go against it. Much better for the best fighter to win.

Danny had no doubt who that would be. Jago could talk the talk, he could teach the method, but when fighting was in the offing, Jago was usually the one to stay in Seahome, to guard it while Tasgo was out doing the real fighting.

Jago must realise the outcome too. Danny wondered what he was going to come up with, to skew things in his own favour.

Already folk were streaming ahead of them towards the exercise ground. They would form a human ring around the fighters, so every move of thrust and parry would be witnessed. Jago gathered himself, and started forward, Tasgo went with him, at his left side, pace for pace as they moved together towards the battle ground. Folk gave them room, staying clear of immediate conflict. Already they were spilling into the open space where the fight would take place, choosing their spots for the best view.

As the throng ahead opened out into the exercise area several yards away, Jago struck. The sword seemed to leap into his hand, and swing towards Tasgo. His other hand was pulling his dagger free of its sheath.

Tasgo was quicker. He must have been expecting it, he was so fast. Though the shield was in the hand further away from Jago, it came up to parry the sword, thrusting it aside. Only then did he draw the short sword at his side. It came up, striking Jago's dagger and pushing it back as the sharp sword flashed into Jago's side between his ribs.

Surprise filled Jago's face as he staggered under the blow. His sword drooped in his hand, the knife twisted away and fell. Jago stared at Tasgo as Tasgo thrust the blade even deeper. Jago wasn't yet ready to believe that Tasgo had killed him, but the sword had done its job. Jago's knees began to buckle, he was falling away, and Tasgo was half supporting him with the blade as he struggled to pull it from Jago's chest. With a sideways wrench the sword cut its way past ribs and came free.

Jago fell, and so did silence. Tasgo held the dripping blade, eyes on Jago to see if he might rise again.

Everything became very still, as if no-one could take in the sight before them. The crumpled body lay in a space of its own.

Then Morven, who must have been able to see how it happened himself, called out loudly, *'Who drew blade first?'*

A dozen or more answered him, *'Jago!'*

Margan added, *'Sneak attack,'* in disapproving tones.

Cadryn raised his voice, sounding shocked, *'Sword and knife without warning. Coward.'*

They could all see where it had happened, not in the exercise yard yet, without any of the ceremony that should have ensured a fair fight. Most of them had seen how it happened, but it had been so fast it was hard to be sure. Tasgo walked forward, into the open space of the yard, turning to face the crowd, so that each and every one could see his face in turn.

'For one who seemed to set honour so high, this was a poor end to his life. He was less than he might have appeared.' Blood still dripped from his sword as he went on, *'But if any would wish to fight on his behalf, or to challenge me for my rightful place, I am ready.'* That much was obvious. They could all see it.

Danny was surprised that it was Margan who answered that, with *'He told us you died at the hands of a trader.'*

'I did not die,' Tasgo told him. *'I killed that rogue. He died by my blade. Did none of those at Cynmar see that?'*

A silence followed, those who had been there had all been fighting their own part of the battle. Then Cadryn, who had been on Jago's side, spoke again, thoughtfully. *'I saw Jago pull a sword from his body. But now, I seem to remember, there was a sword sheathed at his hip as he did so.'*

Another of the young warriors, Danny thought it was Corraith's youngest brother, said, more haltingly, *'It was Tasgo's blade he had in his* hand. *The one he had pulled from the body. He showed it to us as proof of Tasgo's death.'*

Morven asked Tasgo a different question, *'Where have you been all this time then?'*

'Underhill, but not dead,' Tasgo answered, turning to look at Danny.

Danny took his cue, *'Kuillok still has some powers. Though he is punished, he still managed to reach out and drag Tasgo Underhill. He hadn't the power to kill him, but Tasgo was trapped there until we could find a way for him to return. All this time we have been striving to get Tasgo back here, where he belongs.'* They had discussed this, back in the twenty-first century, what to say about the long delay. He raised his voice a little stronger. *'There have been battles there, that only the strongest could survive. They speak his name with honour there, they praise his strength.'*

Another of the young men challenged Tasgo, more hostile, *'Are you Grey, then?'*

Tasgo gave something like a laugh, *'Would you say such a thing to Gamma's face?'* he asked. Then to forestall an answer, *'You have known me all your life. I am as everyone else here.'*

Danny spoke up then, trying to make a joke of it, *'And I am wearing blue and green, nothing grey about me either.'*

Tasgo glared at him then, for being flippant when this was all deadly serious. Danny made a contrite face, and threw his empty hands wide in surrender, taking a step back. He was hoping it would remind them all that he had given up on weapons, that he was just a friendly fool. He was trying to remind them that to be Fair could be a good thing, sometimes. He was hoping it would not bring to mind what someone had once said, that he didn't need weapons, he could kill with a look.

Ailiese spoke up then, stepping out of the crowd towards Tasgo. *'I'm glad you're back, Chief,'* she said, her voice warm. *'Standing in for you went to Jago's head, a little. He was always a proud man, too full of himself.'*

'Aye,' Margan agreed, *'He had his place, he was well connected, but he overstepped himself.'*

'*He was always good to me,*' put in one of the lads who had stood behind Jago, perhaps the one who had laughed at Treva. It sounded more like an excuse than an epitaph.

Suddenly everyone had words to say, coming slowly to an agreement from both sides. Jago had served to hold the village together while Tasgo was away, but Tasgo was their chief. They were getting used to the new situation. No-one was willing to make a challenge.

The muttering about Grey Folk was muted, like the murmurings about Jago's favouritism. When Treva was forceful about blasted rapers, another woman said loudly that no woman had been safe. '*Warped sense of honour,*' and '*No respect for others*' seemed to fit the general mood.

Danny thought he could pick out the young bloods who had been given a false sense of entitlement, they were looking less than easy now.

Tasgo raised his voice a little. '*Cadryn,*' he called out, and '*Leir,*' both of whom had given their word to support Jago. '*Take Carod to help you and bring Jago's box out here, will you?*'

They exchanged looks, but did as they were asked. Though Carod was in obvious turmoil, having seen his master killed, and not knowing what was to become of him, he went with them, suddenly rather cautious, somehow looking smaller than he had before.

As the young men moved off, the tone of things changed. Expectation had crept in.

Jago's body lay where it had fallen, no-one stood near it. Danny couldn't help but keep looking at it, untended, blood seeping from it into the soil. Tasgo was asking Margan about who had been favoured by Jago, who had been slighted. The young warriors seemed more and more uneasy. Things were not yet settled.

At last Carod came out, holding one end of the box that was Jago's while the two lads took the other end. They set it down in front of Tasgo, and a space cleared round it. Tasgo told them to open it, and they set the lid down next to it.

Tasgo picked up Jago's best tunic, lying on the top, and tossed it on the lid. The clothing below he used to wipe his sword blade clean, making sure to remove every fleck of blood, polishing the blade to a shine before stabling it in his scabbard. While he did that Leir and Cadryn did as he asked, moving all of the clothing and blankets to the lid, revealing the rest of his goods below.

'Do you see Pinner's sword?' asked Tasgo.

Cadryn reached in. 'I should have known,' he muttered softly, shame faced as he brought it out, still in its scabbard Showing it to the crowd, he said more clearly, 'We should have known.' He looked unhappily at Tasgo. 'We should have searched,' he said.

'But you didn't want to believe it,' Tasgo told him, 'And he would have taken it ill.'

Cadryn's face confirmed it. Tasgo took the weapon from him, held it in both hands. Then his taut facade of control burst, anger and sorrow welded into one. He held the weapon high, proof of murder. 'How could you?' he demanded in anguish. 'How could any one of you have believed it, even for a moment, that Pinner, our Pin, had run off a cliff!' Faces dropped under his gaze. Most of them couldn't meet his eye.

He turned suddenly to Carod, more anger than grief now. 'How did this sword get into your master's box?' he asked.

Carod was not bright, his strength was in his muscles. He wasn't stupid though, not that stupid. 'Put it there,' he mumbled.

'Who put it there?' asked Tasgo, less accusative, but sharp for the details.

'He did,' Carod countered quickly, 'his box, he put it in.'

'But you fetched it for him,' Tasgo stated.

'Yes,' Carod leapt at an excuse, 'He told me where. Where he'd hid it.'

'But you were the one who hid it,' Tasgo said, as if to remind him, then gave him the let out, 'he told you to hide it.'

'He told me to hide it,' echoed Carod, grateful for the get out.

'He told you to hide it, after you killed the man,' said Tasgo.

'No, no!' Carod wiped the palms of his hands against his tunic, 'Not that, I didn't do that!'

'Who else?' Tasgo asked. 'Carod and Leir were with your master, they couldn't have done it. You were the only one who could have killed him.'

'No! he fell, he ran off the cliff and he fell!'

'He ran off the cliff and he fell, and then he took off his sword and gave it to you.'

'Yes!' Carod flustered then realised, 'No! he must have... he must have took it off, yes he took it off! Before, that's what he did.'

'He stopped running, took off his sword, and then ran off the cliff?'

'Yes,' but even Carod could see that this was beyond belief. He searched desperately for some other way, some other thing to say, then gave up. 'He made me! Jago! Jago told me! I have to do what I'm told, I can't – I can't not – I have to...' He ran out of words.

'And the women?' Tasgo asked him, all pretence of calm dropped. 'It wasn't just Treva was it? Did you get your share? Did you hold them down? Did you help beat Blathin? Did you beat her for him?'

Carod dropped to his knees. He knew he was defeated. 'I have to – have to do what I'm told.'

Tasgo leant forward, and spoke clear and loud, 'Didn't have to enjoy it, did you?'

It was there in Carod's face, he was found out, he was guilty, through and through.

'Don't,' Carod pleaded, seeming to shrink, 'please don't...'

Tasgo didn't answer. He looked instead at the gaggle of youngsters who had stood behind Jago. 'This was the strength that you supported. This was the freedom you thought right! To kill and rape where you should have protected!' At least one of them was ready to protest, but Tasgo did it for them. 'It wouldn't have seemed like it at first. Seahome needs a strong leader. You believed his lies. You liked being his strong-arms. You felt the power. We need strong-arms, and strong minds.' His eyes fixed them where they stood. 'You don't need a Druid to tell you what is wrong, even if you don't know how to stop it or put it right. You are men of Seahome, I have faith in you. But I'm going to need you to show me I'm right.'

Corraith's young brother spoke up suddenly, 'I give you my word...'

'I don't need your word.' Tasgo cut him off, 'We need deeds. You'll show us.' Then to Carod he said, 'You can strip your master of his weapons and jewellery, toss them in the box.'

196

Just Rewards

All the finery, and the jewels that had adorned Jago's body, were in the box now. When Carod started to strip the corpse of its clothing as well, Tasgo said nothing to stop him. When Carod was going to put the bloody tunic on top of the other clothes, Tasgo told Carod to throw it on the ground, the brecks too. Jago lay now, lifeless, pale skin naked on the ground, without any trace of status or of power. Just a man, somehow vulnerable even in death.

Only then did Tasgo call on Bahee and Treva, and their younger brother Erient, not yet of fighting age. Tasgo motioned Cadryn closer as he spoke to the boy alone, as if they were the only two there. *'Your father did not run foolish and heedless off a cliff. He was a brave man and true. Never was there one braver. He was murdered by that man lying there. Carod was his tool, Carod dealt the blow, but Jago ordered it.*

'This was your father's sword. It is yours now.' He gave the sword to Cadryn, who in turn gave the sword over to Erient, holding it in both hands like a ceremonial gift, bowing as he did so. The boy stood there, his father's sword cradled in his arms, looking awkward, not knowing what to do next. Tasgo went on, *'All that Jago owned is in this box, or on its lid. It now belongs to you, and to your sisters. You can choose for yourselves whether you want to continue to live in the home you now have, or to move into Jago's place in my Hall. Let me know later what you decide, and men will put the box there. All his wealth, and more if he had it, is not enough to compensate for the cowardly murder of your father, but it is yours.*

'Tell me now, Erient, what do you want to happen to Carod? His blow killed your father, but the will was Jago's, and Carod had to obey. What do you want me to do with Carod?'

Treva got in first. *'Kill him! Stick knives into him until he is dead!'*

Bahee put an arm round her younger sister, and said, her voice small but determined, *'He killed Pin. He should die.'*

But Erient, his arms still burdened by the sword, his face open and either empty of all emotion or too full of it to show, was looking at Carod. His lips thinned, and then he spoke. *'Carod was his slave. He owned Carod, didn't he?'*

'Yes,' agreed Tasgo.

'He is mine now?' the boy asked.

'Or I could take him, since I killed his master.'

'What is the punishment for a slave who murdered?'

'Depends on the circumstances. In this case he was obeying an order. I'd say willingly obeying.'

'So?' Erient was looking to Tasgo for guidance.

'Anything from ten lashes to death.'

Erient was silent for a long moment. *'Fifty lashes wouldn't kill him, would it?'*

'He's strong,' Tasgo told him. *'He should survive. Wouldn't be much use for a while though.'*

'And then he would have to do what I told him to?'

Tasgo nodded.

Danny felt his skin creep as he wondered what the boy was thinking.

'Who would do the lashing,' Erient wanted to know next.

Tasgo must have been getting worried too, he took time to think. *'Who would you want?'* he asked.

The boy's eyes darted towards Treva, and then back. *'Kelwyn,'* was what he said then. *'Forty lashes,'* he specified.

Tasgo looked at Kelwyn. Kelwyn gave shrugged consent. Carod still crouched by his master, his face too stolid to show what was going through his mind, but he was no longer brash and defiant.

Tasgo then took a stance. He was a chieftain, dispensing justice. He was a chieftain, making his position strong.

'I am rightful Chief here, Son of Aod, son of Dugal. If any of you wishes something other, speak now!'

A long silence as he searched their faces for dissent, working his way round the circle that surrounded him. A couple of the young bloods who had stood behind Jago, dropped their eyes in shame. Only one met Tasgo with defiance, though he said nothing. Then Margan stepped forward. *'You always have been chief, since Dugal died,'* he said, clapping a hand on Tasgo's shoulder.

Morven was quick to follow, then both Leir and Cadryn proclaimed him chief, going to his side at once. An inrush of others followed. Even those young lads who had found themselves privileged by Jago followed on. Danny was left outside as they crowded in. He was unsurprised to find Kelwyn beside him.

'Always something happening, in Seahome,' said Kelwyn wryly.

'Jago seems to have made a mess of things,' Danny answered.

'The youngsters loved him, he made them feel like young kings.' Kelwyn was watching the people eager to show their loyalty now Tasgo was back.

'Not all of them,' Danny countered.

'Enough,' was Kelwyn's answer.

Danny couldn't make him out. He seemed to have been content with Jago's rule, even though he had seen Dugal's style, and Danny guessed Tasgo would have been much the same as Dugal.

'What about the women?' he asked. *'It wasn't just Treva was it?'*

'Mostly they didn't mind. He let them think they were special. His choice, chief's consort. Till the next one took their place. Too late then.'

Danny was shocked. So many ways in which that was so wrong. He blinked, and then picked the major point, *'Mostly?'* he asked.

'Mostly,' Kelwyn agreed, moving off suddenly. Near his dead master, Carod was outside the scrum of people keen to make their own loyalty noticed, and he was getting to his feet with a crafty look on his face. Everyone was busy welcoming Tasgo back as leader, and for the moment forty lashes were a distant thing that he could perhaps escape, if he ran fast, while they were all too busy to see which way he went. Kelwyn scuppered that thought, coming suddenly too close to be ignored.

Carod sank back to the ground, and Kelwyn stayed there, between him and the elusive temptation of freedom.

Treva too was outside the group, where Tasgo was now asking questions, and giving orders. Her eyes were on Jago's body, and Carod once more kneeling beside it. She came over, her face tight and still angry. Even Carod shrank from her. She stood for a moment looking down at the figure lying face down on the trampled earth. Her arms were tight around her body, and Danny wondered whether he should go to her. He didn't know what he could say to her, he didn't know whether he would be a help or would just make things worse.

She prodded the body, still oozing blood from the slash across his chest, as if testing whether he was really dead. Then she drew back her foot and kicked him, hard. *'Honoured, are you now?'* she growled, and kicked him again. She was wearing footbag shoes, they had no hard sole. She might as well have been kicking him with her bare feet. *'Privilege is it?'* she demanded kicking him again, and this time bringing her heel down hard on his ribs afterwards. The body heaved at the blow. Carod was crawling away from her. Kelwyn was watching only Carod, he didn't seem to mind Treva's rage, and the violence of her attack as she stamped on ribs and flesh that could feel no pain. She was working herself into a rage.

Danny strode forward to her, unnoticed.

'You like it like this, don't you!' Treva snarled at the dead man, this time kicking at the head, stamping on the face turned sideways away from her, as if he was too ashamed to look at her.

Danny caught hold of her. Her rage was mounting, but it was her own feet that were going to get damaged. He hadn't reckoned with the fury inside her. She twisted towards him, raining blows on his chest.

He caught her as gently as he could, *'He's dead,'* he told her unnecessarily, *'He can't harm you anymore.'*

She came to a quivering stop, not looking up at him, eyes level with his throat. *'It's not enough,'* she whispered.

'He's dead, though,' Danny reminded her, *'dead enough.'*

She was still looking at the corpse, he realised. *'Not **enough**,'* she said again. *'He didn't suffer, **enough**.'* The words were quiet but drenched with venomous emotion. He let her wrench her hands free of his.

'He's gone,' Danny insisted, trying to keep matter of fact, *'He's humiliated, deposed, put down... forget him.'*

She looked up at him then, eyes flashing with anger. *'He's not gone,'* she told him, as if it were his fault. *'He's still inside me.'* Then, as if he were deaf or a simpleton who could not understand, she yelled it into his

200

face, *'I want him dead, ripped apart, cut to ribbons. Hurt like he hurt me!
I want him dead! Not inside me!'*

For a moment the violence of the words stopped Danny from realising what she meant, then it was obvious. *'The baby isn't him,'* he told her, *'The baby is innocent...'*

'His child!' she snapped back. *'His flesh!'*

'Yours too,' Danny got in quickly.

Her eyes flashed with uncontrollable anger, but for a moment she was lucid, torn between anger and despair, but lucid. *'I don't want it,'* sobbed from her. She couldn't understand why he didn't see it for himself, *'I don't want it inside me. I don't want him.'* Somehow a knife was in her hand now. Where had that come from? He hadn't even noticed the movement of her hands. She held it out to him, handle towards him. *'You do it!'* it was somewhere between a plea and a command. *'Do it now! Kill it! Kill it for me!'*

She meant it. She wanted him to stab her, now, to stick the blade in deep and kill the baby now. He felt worse than he did in battle. He had no idea what to do. Part of his mind was realising that he didn't even know where in her abdomen the baby might be – as if he might somehow actually do that terrible thing. There was no way he could make this better.

Keep it calm. Keep it real, that was all he could think of. He kept his voice low, while grabbing the hand with the knife. *'I can't do that Treva,'* he told her, feeling fury rising in her again, but he went on, overriding it, *'I can't kill it without hurting you , and I can't hurt you Treva. I won't. You don't deserve that!'*

Treva exploded into anger, was screaming at him, *'He's inside me!'* she snarled then wailed. *'He's still inside me! Get it out, get it out! I don't want it in me!'* She was strong and determined in her effort to break free of any constraint. Danny wondered if constraint was anything like the right thing to use, considering what she must have gone through, but he daren't let her go,

'I'll do it myself!' she cried, struggling harder.

In the distance Bahee had seen what was happening. She was coming towards them, the older woman who had been with her at the pool following her like a shadow. Danny tried looking at Kelwyn, to bring him in to help, but Kelwyn wasn't interested. It was Carod Kelwyn was keeping a watch over, although he couldn't ignore the violence so close to him.

A glance over to the crowd showed that, despite the noise and the ruckus, just like Kelwyn, they were ignoring it.

Time to try something else. Danny said quickly, firmly, *'I can do something better.'*

She was beyond hearing him, she was beyond wild. Hysteria was a word Danny had heard used, but never of behaviour quite as wild as this.

Trying for firm and authorative, he shouted her name at her, point blank. And again, and again, till he was sure she had heard him. *'Look at me!'* he demanded. *'Treva, look at me! I can do something better!'*

To his surprise she stopped struggling and was now looking up at him, still angry and anguished, as if it were Danny who was the enemy, but listening, even though expecting to hear something she must fight against. He dropped his voice. *'Look at me,'* he was still searching for the right words,

He was aware of Kelwyn, suddenly watching with some interest, his knee against Carod's shoulder. Danny lowered his voice, *'The baby isn't just him Treva, it's you too. It's your baby too.'*

'I don't want it!' she snarled, but with less force than before.

'I know,' he said, his voice dropping to a whisper, *'I can't kill it without hurting you. But I can kill the part of it that is Jago.'* She became stiller then, though still wild eyed. Danny kept his voice down, he didn't want any of the others to hear this. They already had the idea that perhaps he could kill with a look. He went on swiftly, making it up as he went. *'I will help you Treva. I will kill what there is of Jago in you. The baby will be all yours.'*

'I don't want it!' she insisted, anger was no longer enough to hold her together. She didn't want to meet his eyes, but he went on talking, low and authorative.

'We can deal with that when the time comes,' he told her. Bahee was running towards them now, despite the baby bound to her chest. The older woman was right behind her. *'I will kill Jago's part,'* Danny whispered urgently as they approached, wondering how he had got

202

himself into this corner. *'I will kill him with a look, and you will be unharmed.'*

She looked at him then, met his eyes, seeking truth within them. Anger gave way and suddenly she was in tears, collapsing in tears against him, sobbing so violently that she shook with it, and her knees no longer held her up. Danny tore the knife from her hand, and encompassed her, holding her up, his tunic soaking up tears.

Bahee arrived then, and the woman with her put her arms around Treva, making comforting sounds. Treva remained uncomforted, she leant in on Danny. Somehow, she had believed him.

When the old woman said, *'Let's get you home Darling,'* Danny said he would come too.

Only a few yards away Tasgo was still talking with village folk, catching up, giving orders. Danny was aware he should stay here, to back up Tasgo, but it seemed that man was well enough in control without him. Perhaps more urgently he should go into the Hall and see about Gamma, she seemed desperately ill, she would need help and support.

Instead he kept his arms around Treva, and the four of them walked away from everything, towards the older huts.

Undoing

Danny left the hut feeling exhausted. The old woman had given Treva something to drink, and that let Treva, exhausted by wild emotion, fade into sleep.

Danny had no idea how long he had spent before that, holding Treva's hands and staring at the low swell of her body that housed her unwanted baby, willing peace and a quiet mind on Treva, wondering whether she was going to believe he could alter things inside her. Wondering how anyone was going to keep her settled for the remaining months of her pregnancy. Wondering what was to become of a baby born to a mother who already hated it.

As he straightened after ducking out of the building, he couldn't help feeling that a pitched battle wouldn't have been much worse, or more tiring.

Outside there was no trace left of conflict. There was still work to do, cattle to feed or milk, cloth to weave, yarn to be spun, wood collected and worked, grain to be ground, a thousand other tasks, and that's what people were doing. Some with contented faces, some looking downcast or worried, even shame-faced. Carod had vanished, and so had Erient but Tasgo was still out on the exercise yard, surrounded by a small group of warriors. Marrec had joined them while Danny was busy, and stood with a hand on Leir's shoulder. Armel, who dealt with the cattle, was there too, while Kelwyn stood behind Tasgo, like a body guard, not taking part in the conversation.

Jago's body still lay where it had fallen.

Danny decided to go to Gamma first, his paramedic course had included practical work. He could be of some help there. But, without seeming to look his way, Tasgo was beckoning him over. For now, Tasgo had to be the boss. Danny had promised Tasgo, just as Tasgo had promised him back in the modern, that he would obey instruction instantly, without question. He trotted over, as Tasgo finished what he had been saying.

'*Is Treva content?*' Tasgo asked Danny directly.

Danny thought it must be self-evident that Treva was anything but content. Content was a word totally inappropriate. He had thought Tasgo had been too busy establishing himself with the men to even notice Treva's raging and weeping. He realised he was wrong. Tasgo may not have the details, but he would have been aware of every subtle play amongst the villagers.

For answer, Danny said, '*She's sleeping. She'll live, but she'll need watching.*' seeing Tasgo's nod that that was enough about Treva, Danny went on quickly, '*Gamma is very ill. I think he's been poisoning her for some time.*'

'*Can you deal with that?*'

'*Can try,*' answered Danny, he had no idea. With a twitch of his head, Tasgo sent Danny off to do just that, turning back to Armel to ask, as Danny left them, '*Who else deserves compensation?*'

Inside the new grand roundhouse, a couple of women were with Blathin, whispering together. They fell silent as he came in, looking to see who it was, and what he might want. He went towards them first.

'*How badly are you hurt Blathin?*' he asked, and saw them group themselves in Blathin's defence.

'*it's nothing,*' she protested.

'*Clearly,*' he said, '*spry as an acrobat. If you don't want to tell me, that's fine, but I'd ask you women to lend a hand if you can. Excitement will give everyone an appetite tonight.*' He didn't know the names of the women, but by the looks of them it was a mother and daughter.'

In tones of willing obedience, but actual dismay, Blathin asked, '*Is it to be a feast then?*'

Danny had no idea if that would be the right thing to do. He asked them what they thought. '*Not tonight,*' the mother put in, and the daughter, an uppity lass, added, '*Perhaps tomorrow, when things are more settled?*' she was hopeful.

'*Just plenty of food tonight, ordinary food,*' Danny suggested. Blathin wasn't going to let anyone think she was less than capable, and it seemed she had helpers. Where was Eles? She used to run the everyday doings in the hall. She had been old when Danny was last here, but surely not so old as to have died in the interim? But he was preoccupied with Gamma, he was thinking ahead to what the poisons were, what harm they had done, what he might be able to do to help. He went to the sleeping stall where she lay, in Jago's bed.

She seemed to be sleeping. Her hand was still as cold as death, and he looked to see the rise and fall of her breathing, but it was imperceptible. He spoke her name quietly but saw no flicker of response. How ironic if he had arrived to save her only minutes after she had died. It was unacceptable. He refused to accept it.

He leaned forward to lay a hand on her forehead, cold and dank. He spoke her name loud and firm, searching for a pulse, his mind preparing him for all the actions of Cardio Pulmonary Resuscitation. Her eyes opened before he found the pulse, he saw the flutter of her lids before she opened them wide. Her lips tremored to make a single word. 'Dead?' was the question she wanted answered.

'He is,' Danny told her. 'You're not. And you're going to stay that way.' He would have liked a saline drip to re-hydrate her, and keep the blood right and vital organs working, but there was nothing like sterile water, or tubes of any sort. A beaker of ale, thin and weak, stood where the cup of poison had been. He moistened an edge of his tunic and held it to her lips to suck. He called for honey to sweeten the water, to get some energy into her, and some furs to tuck against her now scrawny body to keep her warm, to give a feeling of comfort and of hope. He held her hand and told her that Tasgo was back in control, that Jago was dead and could do her no more harm. His face was wet with tears.

Tasgo had been right. He should have listened to Tasgo's rants, and taken him back to the tiny lab hidden under Hull's busy streets sooner. They should have worked harder, they should have got here sooner.

He dried his face with his sleeve. He was translating his modern training into actions that could be taken back here in the iron age. Without equipment there were limited things he could do, he was going to have to find simpler ways of getting them done.

He looked at the cauldron hung by the fire. There would be warm water in that, but no way to put it into a hot water bottle.

He left Gamma, to ask how many pots there were. Plenty of pottery ware to sit on low embers it seemed, fewer metal ones to hang over the flames. He commandeered one anyway, half filled it from the bucket near the door, then put it over the fire to come to the boil. Then he ducked out, looking for some help.

A group of children were quarrelling over who had collected the most fleece earlier. Danny picked on the eldest, a lively lass with a serious manner. He didn't know her name. The last time he had been here she would have been no more than five, just one of the noisy brats getting underfoot.

As he approached, they had all stopped quarrelling to look at him, she was the only one who didn't move away. He didn't blame them, they would hardly remember him, and who knows what sort of tales Jago had been spreading. He apologised for not knowing her name, it had been so long since he had last been here.

She met his eye, standing tall, unabashed, and told him *'Ailliana,'* in a clear voice. Perhaps one of Ailiese's daughters then, she looked commanding enough.

'I need some pebbles from the shore, about so big,' making the shape with his hands. *'Big and smooth and rounded with no sharp edges, just as many as you can carry. I need lots.'*

'Get them yourself?' suggested a tyke at the rear, a tentative challenge. Danny ignored it, the girl was asking, *'What do you want pebbles for?'* without any sign of challenge.

'They're for Gamma,' Danny told her. *'She's very ill. The stones are going to help her get better.'*

Alliana looked puzzled, more than a little sceptical, but she nodded. *'How many?'* she asked.

Good question. It would need quite a few to make Gamma's bed a warm place, and they would need changing regularly as they cooled. He wondered how good they were at counting. *'Three or four each, if you all go,'* he said.

Alliana pitied his simplicity. *'About fifty then,'* she concluded. *'Any colour?'*

'Just smooth and round. And clean, very clean. As soon as you can, she's very ill.'

Alliana nodded, taking on the task, giving orders immediately to what was obviously her crew of wool gatherers. Then with a cry of *'Come on,'* she raced off towards the shore, light as the wind, hair flying. The rest, boys and girls followed like a ragged wake, cries of who was going to get the best stones scattering among them as they went.

Back inside the hall, Danny took stock. Blathin was at the quern stone, grinding flour again. He knew for himself how hard that was, hour on hour. She shouldn't have to do that in her state, bruised and broken as she must feel. He went over and started cautiously.

'Who usually tends the sick?' he asked.

The other woman was mixing stuff in a bowl, it was the daughter who turned from chopping something up *'Dervan,'* she said, *'or Gamma,'* as if he should know that. Of course he did, just rather inconvenient now, as Gamma was the patient. The Druid was obviously not around, or he would have recognised the signs of poisoning and stopped it, or tried to.

'Since she's been ill?' he tried.

The girl looked at her mother. The mother didn't want to look back, but she was a mother, so she did. She said a name, one that Danny didn't know, said it so reluctantly and low that Danny had to ask her again, and then ask where she might be found. An uneasy silence fell, then the girl tossed her knife into a pot and muttered, *'I'll go.'*

She went, so fast Danny didn't know whether to follow her or not. By the time he had decided she was out of the Hall, and would be lost to him.

He went back to Gamma, and wet her lips again. He wondered whether he should crawl into the bed with her, and try to warm her with his own body, but something within him revolted at that. What would folk think, he told himself, but that wasn't what stopped him, and he knew it. He told himself that she was too frail, that it would be enough to suffocate or break her. He was ashamed of himself for picking excuses.

He told Blathin to stop grinding the grains for supper, to come instead to Gamma. He showed her how to wet Gamma's lips with water, so she would not choke on it. He asked her to keep Gamma warm, as much as she could, while he fetched some more furs to cover her.

A child hurried in through the doorway, no stooping for him. He was one of the taller boys, almost as tall as Ailliana, and his arms were filled with stones from the beech, one looking like a small boulder, some mere pebbles. Danny told him to put them by the fire, collecting a few of the smaller ones and tossing them into the water in the pot, now nearly boiling. The boy looked at the pot with some surprise, then at Danny as if in disbelief. Before Danny could explain, he was off at a run. It seemed Ailliana kept taut order

There were two more stone deliveries before the daughter came back followed by another woman. As they came into the firelight, Danny saw it was the older woman who had looked after Treva. He should have guessed. What was she then, Treva and Bahee's mother? Another member of the family? Or something else? For now it wasn't important.

'You help the sick?' he asked her.

She hung back, 'Gamma was teaching me – a few things.'

'She needs someone to sit with her and get a little water into her, a little at a time. Trying to drink from the beaker would probably choke her. I'm warming some stones to wrap in cloth and put in with her. Not too hot or they'll burn her, just enough to warm the bed round her.' He saw her taking it in, looking at the small cairn growing beside the fire. 'Have you got an idea what we can use to counter the poison?' She lowered her gaze, not respect. This couldn't be Treva's mother. Treva's mother would have enough status to face Danny and answer his questions to his face. She wasn't just learning things from Gamma. She would be the village mid-wife, he thought, the one with the handy herbs. Maybe even the witch, though before now Danny had not thought there might be such a thing. He was beginning to wonder whether she might be more of a risk than a help. Then she looked up at him, an appraising look, as if she was wondering the same about him.

He asked, quietly, 'Have you got an idea what sort of poison it might be?'

She didn't duck it, she just went on looking at him, trying to work out whether she could trust him.

Danny wondered whether he should say something foolish, to put her at her ease, to stop her wondering whether he could in fact kill with a look. But she had already made her mind up.

'When she fell ill,' she said carefully, 'Jago asked me what herbs would help. He said he had some skill, but he wanted my advice. I told him. He *thanked me. And then he asked me which herbs should definitely be avoided. He already knew about nightshade, and the mushrooms, but said he wasn't clear on some of the others.'* She was looking Danny in the eye, as if daring him to think ill of her. *'I told him. I told him what herbs would do terrible harm, so he could avoid them. I showed him the plants.'* She knew she was guilty.

Danny felt cold run through him, felt his stomach contract.

When she saw that he was not moving, that the full horror was not yet in his face, she went on. *'Later he consulted me again. He asked me what else he might try, to save her, because his potion was not working. He said he thought it was because she was Grey, not as we are. But he wouldn't let me see her. He seemed so kind.'* She finished bleakly. *'I knew it wasn't right, but then he would be so kind, so thoughtful. But he wouldn't let me see for myself.'* At last her gaze dropped. She said, very quiet, *'I should have known. I should have said.'*

Danny took a deep breath. He was no longer that stupid boy who rushed to conclusions and spoke out when he should have kept quiet. As the silence prolonged, he was beginning to think he was that other sort of fool, the one who, when the right words would put an awkward situation right, failed to speak in case he chose the wrong words. It was already almost too late.

He couldn't help the bitterness when he opened his mouth, *'But he was so kind.'* He was remembering how, in that first week all those years ago, Jago had shown him his scabbard, with pride, but with warmth, and Danny had thought he at last had a friend, someone he could trust.

He shook the memory away. *'He was like that,'* he admitted. *'He could pull the wool over your eyes, so you'd hardly notice.'* They might not be exactly the right words, but they were good enough. She looked back at him, reading his face again. He still wasn't sure how far he could trust her, but he thought he believed her. Unless she was as good as Jago at hiding the truth.

'So,' he said, getting down to the task, trusting her as far as he could, *'what do you think? What would he have used?'* He had nothing he could write it down on, he would have to remember everything she said, word for word. He listened carefully repeating the words.

When she had finished, they stood over Gamma, who was sleeping now. She hardly stirred as the woman looked at the scant vomit in the bowl next to her, before feeling her forehead, taking her pulse, listening to her breathing.

Watching, Danny wanted to believe the story the woman had told. She had seemed honest in her telling of it, but if it was true, Jago had seemed honest in his enquiries about poisons. He had no way of telling if she was innocent or a willing collaborator. He decided to treat her as innocent, but Treva had need of someone to look after her as well, and he could see no reason why this woman might want to harm her. Treva was safe with her either way, Gamma was not, and now he could see a way of killing two birds with one stone.

After a brief discussion of whether Gamma's condition made any one poison more likely than another, and finding it didn't, Danny said, *'Treva needs someone with her. I'm afraid she may try to harm herself,'* not to mention the baby inside her. *'If you showed Blathin how to look after Gamma, do you think she could sit with her, keep her warm, look after her and make her take enough water? Then you could look after Treva.'*

Much better for Blathin to be here, maybe under the covers herself, looking after Gamma rather than slaving over the food.

As Day Follows Night

Tasgo was busy with the farmers, so Danny took his chance to race back up the hill, to vanish unseen into the low slit that was the cavemouth. A candle lit him through the treacherous boulders of the cave, and the deeper hidden crevice that led to the pulsing blue light of the portal. Coming back up through the twists and turns of the crevice in the modern, he had a flashlight to show the way.

With memories of past escapades, he moved as silently as he could through the secret door into the back of the cupboard, so that when he emerged into the winter sitting room, he startled them. His mother Freya leapt to her feet, wielding the roman gladius which normally hung within an alarmed case upstairs. Raynes only had a police baton ready to use. Behind them Moira was closing her laptop before turning to face whatever danger might have arrived.

Very few words had been enough to lessen their alarm. 'Right place, right time, he's back in control.' The last was not as certain as it sounded, but he had no time for niceties. It took longer to explain Gamma's condition, and to relay the possible poisons. To his surprise Moira didn't leap immediately onto the internet.

Danny told them he had to get back quickly, there were still uncertainties. Raynes latched onto those and insisted on details. Danny gave them; Jago dead, Treva pregnant with a child she already wanted to kill, and all the difficulties of a group of teens and older now robbed of their strutting dreams of dominance and doing anything they wanted.

Freya scoffed, 'Little change there, then!' Raynes was taking it more seriously. Moira wanted more details of how ill Gamma was, and Danny didn't try to soften the blow. He wasn't sure how long she would last. He was anxious to get back. He wasn't sure how easy it was going to be for Tasgo to win back trust and support from those who had been favoured by Jago.

212

At last he had given enough information and they let him go back, supplied with a few things that might help, to where everything was happening. He knew they would follow soon enough.

Coming back out the cave into the ancient, Danny found light fading, and a cool breeze rippling heather and gorse. Under low clouds shadows stretched down the hill, blurring the shape of the new large roundhouse. As he picked his way down the easier route, where underlying rocks shouldered their way through soil, and fewer plants plucked at his legs, the scent of smoke mingled with the smells of cooking reached him.

Not a feast, he reminded himself. He hoped Jago's body wasn't still lying in the open, uncared for.

As he made his way towards everything, being careful of his footing in the twilight, he reminded himself that back here in the late Iron Age, the setting of the sun was the end of one day, and the start of a new twenty-four hour period. Just as the year started with the oncoming darkness of winter, the coming of night heralded a new time period, first night, then day.

Fitting then that Tasgo should be bringing in a new regime, starting afresh now. And the new regime would be like the old regime before Jago, the one that their Grandfather had run. One which encompassed all and brought out the best in everyone. At least, Danny had thought it did. He had been almost fifteen when he arrived, and found his Grandmother was consort to a mighty Chief. Dugal was bluff and bold, wise and strategic, not afraid to share his emotions and his worldly wealth. But now, having glimpsed how things had changed with Jago in charge, Danny was wondering whether Dugal's rule could be seen differently. Dugal's wealth was the wealth of the village. Everything the village had was under his control. Everything except the personal effects of individuals and families. Might it be seen that everything anyone worked for was also the chief's, that he took it all?

Danny had been an ignorant child when he had first been here. He had fitted into Dugal's family as easily as an extra arm might onto a body. He had made a fool of himself. He was no wiser now. Maybe all his perceptions of belonging, of fitting in had been mere foolishness. Maybe the urgent need he felt to be at Tasgo's side, to help settle things was as misguided as it had been when he was a child.

A voice hailed him from where torchlight showed the entrance to the village. He recognised Morven's voice, and shouted back, *'Parisi! Me Morven, Dannaigh!'* and felt at once back home, where he belonged.

Coming to the boundary gate, now supported by a higher stone wall on either side, he asked Morven where Tasgo was.

'Still down with the farmers,' was the answer.

Well, they were all farmers in a way. When things needed doing, they got done, everyone pitched in. Danny doubted the warriors saw it that way. Dirtying their hands was not beneath them, they just preferred a different sort of dirt. They did the things that let the farmers prosper, but their strength and fighting skills were a cut above cosseting cows or planting seeds.

As he walked on into the village Danny was unsure whether he should be there at Tasgo's side. Would he be a help or hindrance? Almost all of the village thought Danny came from Underhill, where the dead might well end up. That either made him a ghost, or some sort of denizen of the darkness, though some spoke of the Fair Folk. He thought Gamma would have helped with that image, scheming manipulator that she was. It hadn't done her much good in the end though. He forced himself to think that this was not the end not for her. Somehow, they would save her. Well, he was carrying a precious load of drugs, pain killers for Blathin, something Moira said would help to calm Treva, and some for Gamma, once she was well enough and they were sure they wouldn't interact with the poisons she had been given.

Moira had said that if Jago had wanted Gamma dead, she would be dead. There were a dozen ways he could have done it. Her conclusion was that he wanted her helpless, suffering, under his control. All those years of Gamma sweet-talking him, keeping him under her eye, keeping him on the right track, hadn't gone unnoticed. He was getting his own back. Back then Danny had thought they might really be an item. How stupid could you get?

He went to Gamma. Treva might still be sleeping, and she had Bahee and a nurse of sorts. Tasgo was probably better off without Danny by his side, reminding them all of the close connection with another world.

People were gathering in the main hall. The smell of cooking drew them in, but there was a subdued air. They were more worried than agog to hear all the news. Danny greeted a few by name, but he went on past the fire and the benches, the low tables and the high. Blathin was lying by Gamma, only she was on top of the blankets and skins. She struggled up as she saw Danny, and he knew better than to try and stop her. The beaker of ale was more than half empty, so Gamma was getting her water, though she looked no better. Danny asked Blathin for another beaker of ale, and she went as quickly as she could to get it, probably thinking that Danny was thirsty.

She was surprised when Danny told her it was for her. He had palmed two of the soluble pain killers, and they were dissolving in the drink while Danny explained that now that Jago had gone, the bruises he had given her would mend faster, and this ale would help with that. She drank the ale dutifully, she looked dubious about the taste. He told her every warrior should rest after battle, and so should she. Her smile at that was frankly one of pity for him. She was so far from a warrior it would be laughable, if only she were sure he was joking.

'You did your best to stop him,' he told her then, 'otherwise he wouldn't have beaten you so badly. You fought in your own way Blathin, and we will be forever grateful.' For the first time she looked at him properly, though still she could not hold his gaze.

A sudden rustle of expectancy in the hall caught his attention. Tasgo was coming back, making his way slowly up the hall to his chair at the far end, greeting folk as he came, a hand on a shoulder here, a few words there. Danny remembered Dugal doing the same, working the room, gathering them all together, everyone included. Tasgo left the women who were preparing the food out of his greetings, but they were busy, and Danny guessed he would speak to them later. While Kelwyn loitered by the fire Tasgo came on past his carved chair, to Danny and Gamma.

'How is she?' he asked. Danny had expected tense, but by now Tasgo just looked weary.

'Very ill,' Danny told him, that was obvious, and he wasn't going to say more. No false hopes. Instead he mentioned that Blathin had suffered a lot and needed rest. Blathin of course denied it, but Danny pointed out that she was the best person to look after Gamma, that Gamma would

215

know that she could trust her. The trust they placed in her was enough to brighten Blathin. Six and a bit months under Jago's control, and she had been almost broken. Jago had never hidden his contempt for slaves.

Tasgo nodded his approval, then came closer to the bed. He put his hand on the skins that covered Gamma's shoulder. *'I am back,'* he said, as if she were not sleeping but listening. *'No more harm shall come to you while I am here.'* He kissed her on the forehead, and then turned to go back to the hall.

Danny stopped him. Very quietly he asked, *'Do you want me near you or far? Am I help or hindrance?'*

It surprised Tasgo, almost angered him. When he spoke it was clear, clean and loud, he wanted everyone to hear. It was passionate. *'Without you Dannaigh, I would be dead, several times over. Without you I would be trapped Underhill, perhaps for ever. Without you, who would bring succour to Gamma, while I took charge elsewhere? Who would have seen to Treva? We are going to need you Dannaigh. I am going to need you. You stay at my shoulder whenever you can, for you see things that are hidden from others.'*

Oops, thought Danny, as he heard the last, not a role he was asking for. But he was pleased and slightly surprised that Tasgo had noticed what he was doing. How he knew was another matter. Did he know Danny had been back to set minds at rest back – not back home, he wasn't thinking that – back in the modern? Tasgo would guess that they would bring help for Gamma.

He spoke quickly, low voiced, before Tasgo could move off, *'Moira will be here later, to help Gamma. Ken may come too.'* Would Ken Raynes be a problem? He was so obviously a creature from another world. He might have been accepted by a Druid as a 'keeper of the lore' but that didn't mean that everybody here was comfortable with his presence. Moira and Freya had practically grown up here, they had been known since they were little girls, and they spoke the language like native Parisi.

So did Danny, though his vocabulary was a bit limited, and sometimes he got the nuances wrong. At least his family had taught him the language, even while keeping him in ignorance of the portal and their connection with the past. Five years ago it had seemed to Danny that they were part of the village, accepted, admired even. But he had been ignorant and foolish then.

Tasgo moved off, still working the room. It seemed he had invited everyone from the village, if not to eat, then at least to drink beforehand. Those who could find seats had taken them, some with wives or sweethearts on their knees. The rest crammed in, settling by, or on, the low tables or snuggled up against wall pillars, great trunks of trees, fine-grained, straight and tall. From a lovely tree whose spirit had killed Dugal so Tasgo could be chief.

The room was getting hot and sweaty, it reeked of bodies as well as smoke, it smelt of tensions and anger, worry and expectation. Voices were muted but the thatched roof still couldn't mop up all the noise. A bunch of younger warriors had grouped together towards the top end of the hall, trying to look confident and part of the elite, which only made them seem shifty. Kelwyn lounged against a pillar not five paces from them, but out of their line of sight as they watched Tasgo.

Tasgo came at last back to the carved seat from which Dugal had held court. He stood looking round at all the faces, his own serious but welcoming. In five years he had certainly changed. No longer challenging, he looked as if he deserved his place at the head of the hall. He looked strong, confident, vital, he had always looked like that. Now he looked like a chief, powerful, decisive, knowledgeable as he waited for silence to settle on the crowd.

The silence fell, but Tasgo went on looking at their faces, taking in everyone, meeting eyes. A rustle of impatience came from some of the younger lads, but they fell silent again.

At last words broke out of Tasgo, heartfelt words, full of heartbreak, longing and release. *'I am so glad to be home.'* A ripple of surprise ran through the hall. *'There were times,'* he told them, *'when I thought that I should never see your faces again. Not any of you. Yet here you are. Parisi. People of honour, strong people.'* He raised his hands to them, looking proudly at them, proud of them. It was not what they had expected, but Danny could see people feeling that pride, accepting it, enjoying its warmth.

'I am sorry to have been so long away,' he said then. *'Not my choice.'*
Someone deep in the hall called out, *'Where were you then?'*

Tasgo searched and found the face, and answered, 'Underhill. Not a place to be when you aren't yet dead.'

Another voice raised, 'What was that like?'

'Too much to be told in one go,' he answered, 'but I will start on it when bellies are full, and good ale drunk. It is no tale for empty stomachs. But you have had your own troubles, and weathered them well. We are Parisi,' he told them, showing them again his pride in them, 'and we give tribute to no-one!'

Sounds of affirmation ran through the crowd, but then someone from the side called, 'Jago sent tribute to Stonewall.'

Tasgo seemed stunned. 'What?' he demanded.

'Three cows,' came the voice, and from another, 'Good milkers!' Perhaps from Armel, one of the farmers, lamps had been lit but in this crowd it was hard to tell.

'He sent three of our best cows – to the Brigante?' Tasgo was outraged. 'What did he hope to gain from that?'

A slight pause, then another voice piped up, 'There's a feast coming up, would we have a place at that?'

Anger and determination showed in Tasgo's voice now. 'The Brigante are fine people' he said with scorn, 'but for three good cows we're going to need a whole lot more than a few seats at a feast!' They liked that, the mood was lifting.

Tasgo milked it. 'I can see there is going to be some interesting negotiation ahead,' Though he spoke grimly, he was smiling, confident of gains to be made.

He got back to the main point, though. 'I blame no-one for supporting Jago as stand in. You needed a chief. Though you might have chosen better. Margan, for one. Or Marrec, or Morven.' He paused for a moment. 'Cynwrig?' he suggested, and a ripple of quiet laughter appreciated the joke. A ten-year-old would be no suitable chieftain. He went on, 'Jago was a good second, but he needed leading. He was too full of himself, too intent on his own needs, his own rank.' A murmur of support came for that, most strong from those furthest from Tasgo, nearer the door.

Tasgo gave up on Jago's better points. 'He lied to you. He lied to you about me, he lied about a lot of things. He knew how to lead folk astray.' He was wholly serious now, and came reluctant to the next. 'There are

218

some things we have to put right before we move on. Armel has a niece. How old Armel?'

'*Eleven Summers,*' Armel gave back from the front of the tighter crowd by the door. Armel added, '*She's a cheeky lass I'll admit, but she means no harm.*'

'What happened?' Tasgo asked, though he must already know. Did they all already know?

'*She was playing a hopping game with others, down near the practice field, when Jago chanced by. It was a child's chant, to hop to, they all do it. He took offence.*'

'What was the chant?' Tasgo asked. Armel shrugged, reluctant. One of the young warriors near where Kelwyn was lounging spoke up. He could tell what was coming and he was getting in first.

'*It was rude, she meant it to be. She saw him coming.*'

Tasgo nodded to him, expecting more. Reluctant, the young man gave it. He couldn't help the sing-song rhythm coming through. '*There's a bull, with a cock too big, sleeps all day, like a lazy pig.*' Someone gave a short appreciative laugh.

'A child's chant,' Armel growled loudly.

'What happened?' Tasgo put to the young man.

'He said, '*Needs to learn a little respect, that one.*' She did too.' Tasgo was waiting so he went on, less comfortably, '*So we caught her. I thought he'd just give her a smack or two, she deserved it, no harm done.*' Everyone was looking at him, his voice now defensive, '*He dragged her over to the big rock,*' they all knew the one. Danny remembered it, it was where whoever was doing the training would stand, where he could step up and have a good view of everything. '*He told me to hold her down on it, and,*' he wavered slightly then, '*he pulled up her tunic and – he stroked her. That's all he did. He stroked her.*' He could feel a confused anger rising around him, the taint of disgust. '*He stroked her on the belly, that's all! He didn't hurt her.*'

'While you held her down,' Tasgo told him. 'How did she take that, LLubelin?'

'*She was scared,*' he admitted. Then, '*I told him to stop! I told him it was enough!*'

'Did she kick out at him?' asked Tasgo, as if curious, 'A sassy girl like that, she wouldn't just lie there?'

'He leant on her legs,' the boy let out, and then jumped to his own defence, 'but he let her go. He didn't DO anything. He taught her a lesson and he let her go.'

'You held her down, he leant on her legs, her body all exposed and helpless,' Tasgo was summing it up, slowly, 'and then...'

'I didn't know he'd do that!' Llubelin defended himself. 'I let go of her. I told him to stop. She ran away, she wasn't harmed.'

'Did you tell anyone?'

Danny saw the other lads looking uncomfortable.

Llubelin started to deny it, but Tasgo turned to Danny, and Danny knew what was expected of him. Danny was supposed to be able to read minds, to see the truth in things. Instead Danny asked, 'Did you tell your father, your family?' He was offering a let-out clause. And then Danny realised from the look on the boy's face that there was no father, perhaps no mother. The lad was a youth, maybe fifteen years. He went on quickly, as if he had known it all along, 'You had no family you could burden with it. And when you told the other lads, it didn't sound so bad.'

He could see comfort being taken from that, over there by Kelwyn. He had given them a let-out too.

Tasgo looked to Armel, 'Does that sound like it, Armel. No harm done?'

'She wouldn't leave the house for a week.'

'What do you want to happen now?' Tasgo asked him.

Armel's turn to shift uncomfortably. He bent his head to take counsel from someone nearby, then lifted it to throw forward, 'It was an indication of the man's attitude. Llubelin should have realised. But, he did let her loose himself. An apology will do. To her.'

LLubelin was in a fix. He was a warrior. She was a child. His Chief was looking at him, waiting. It could get worse. He came up with, 'I will apologise, if she will promise to not insult her elders and betters.'

There was a scuffle of movement by Armel. Danny realised he was bending his head towards a child, half hidden behind a woman's skirts. Her face was barely visible, what with the draping of the woman's peplum and the sweep of dark hair that shadowed her features. Some sort of discussion was going on.

220

Armel raised his head and gave a diffident cough. He was more than a little embarrassed. *'She is willing to give that promise, if you will promise never again to hold down a woman for another man.'*

There were some hidden smiles amongst the crowd. This was turning into the farce of a promises auction. Llubelin was caught again. It was the old 'when will you stop beating your wife?' ploy. Damned whatever you answer.

He chose anger. *'I would never do that!'* he snapped, realising only as the words were out that everyone was thinking he had done just that. He found a scapegoat. *'Only someone like Carod would!'* then, realising again, *'Not that he had to. Not that I saw.'*

Tasgo said, stern but patient, *'Just apologise, lad, and let it lie.'*

Over by Armel the girl had taken a step out of hiding. She grasped her mother's hand for courage, but was still ready to duck out of sight again.

Llubelin looked at her, and decided to be a man. *'I never thought he would behave like that. I am sorry I held you down.'* He looked as though he had finished. She looked as if he hadn't. No-one else spoke, so he spoke again. He made a promise, in front of everyone. *'I will protect you, and any other woman of Seahome, against any such insult. For as long as I live. I promise.'*

'Big promise,' said Tasgo. The girl just nodded, solemn, before sliding back behind her mother's skirts. Danny thought her less subdued than she looked. The sassy lass was still there, just a bit more cautious.

There were a few more wrongs to be aired, promises made and broken, mostly by Jago, to some woman, or family, insults felt hard, whether intended or not, often from the lads. Tasgo stopped it before it got petty. Many of the farmers left then, the room became less crowded, though it was clear that there would be more than enough to fill the tables. Brec stood by the door with his two slaves, unsure whether he should leave too.

Tasgo called out to him, waved him closer, indicating a seat not far from himself. Brec gave a word to his men, and as he came forward, the slaves, man and boy, left.

Revelation

It wasn't a feast, but it was a big communal event. They stood or sat, and they ate. They drank. Toasts were given and taken. When they were full, and glad to find that everything seemed to be going along fine, only with Tasgo back and Jago gone, it was Marrec, with Leir by his side, who raised his beaker to give thanks for Tasgo's safe return. The toast came back from many mouths, but it was not a roar.

Then Margan reminded Tasgo that he was going to tell them where he had been. They were all ready. Tasgo sat, silent.

Danny was aware that before the meal, everything had been planned. The seemingly random questions must have been decided quietly beforehand. Any variations had been dealt with. Now Tasgo was silent, looking into his beaker of mead, for that was what they were drinking now. Behind him in the sleeping stall Gamma was asleep, with Blathin there to look after her. Danny had checked on how she was from time to time. She was too ill to take any tablets, but Danny had crushed some pain killers into honey, and moistened her lips with it. He was worried for her. He was hoping Moira would arrive soon with some better equipment. Now he was worried for Tasgo too. He was wondering what he would say.

At last Tasgo looked up, he had their full attention now.

He eased in with the story of the raiders, how the village further up the coast had sent word of being raided to Seahome and to Cynmar. Fortunately one of the young men there was bright, he had been following the raiders on foot, dashing over headlands, trying to stay out of sight. He was sure now the riders were going to try Cynmar next.

Brad was leading Cynmar' warriors. When they met the lad, they turned back, but sent a rider on to intercept the party coming from Seahome. So warriors from both places arrived in Cynmar in scant time to work out a strategy and get into hiding before the boat approached.

Tasgo told them it was a good ambush. Then he called on Leir and Cadryn, to tell the tale of how the raiders had been foiled.

That was a good ploy, they could tell the tale with gusto, making themselves and their leader, Tasgo, into heroes, in a way that would have sounded self-serving if Tasgo had tried. They did him proud. It had been his plan, his deployment, and the trap snapped closed on the raiders with perfection. They reached the point where the sea captain had turned tail and run, with Tasgo hot on his heels, and now they looked, silent, at Tasgo.

He was smiling as he remembered. *'He was running, but I was faster. He saw the way ahead was blocked by the river, and he faltered. I leapt, sword slashing, as he turned towards me. I felt the blade bite, I saw the death shock in his eyes. And then the world was filled with a blue light, like fire, but cold. Everything here vanished into that light, and I fell into darkness.'* They could see by his face the shock and horror that followed. He stopped to marshal things in his mind, to tell it so they might understand, if it was possible to understand.

When he went on tension was in his voice, as if he suffered again the trials that followed. *'I know now that it was Underhill. I didn't know that then. It is a place of wonder, of beauty, and of absolute terror. Full of magic, hidden everywhere, in everything.*

It is impossible. Just when you think you are somewhere safe, and normal, you find the subtle truths of differences so complete...' he fell silent again, then pulled himself together.

'I can only give examples. I fell into a box that could not be seen. A space that looked like open air, but which contained me, trapped. I beat on the walls, I could feel them, but not see them. There were people outside the box. I think they were as shocked as I was. My arrival was unexpected, unheralded, unaccountable. I was not dead. I did not belong there.

'I did not know where I was. I didn't know if I was dead or alive.

'One of the women set me free.' He went on cautiously. All the time he had been in the modern he must have been thinking how to tell this story, working out how he could tell the tale, let them feel the strangeness, without thinking him mad, or a fool, or a coward. It was never going to be easy. *'There was a hall,'* he faltered. *'It was a*

223

celebration, I don't know what for. Perhaps for me, I don't know. The people were possessed by music, not as we know it. Sounds as of the gods screaming and singing, rhythms that made bodies move, a chaos of light and noise and people dancing as if possessed. A place of joy and life, of light and dark, of movement and sound so loud you couldn't think.'

He paused. 'In a box,' he said, heavily. 'A building so huge, it can only be held up by some sort of magic, a cavernous hall. So much in Underhill is boxes. Their homes are boxes, made up of boxes, each big enough for a family to live in. The boxes go on and on, it seems for ever.' He gave up on it, it was beyond explanation. The hall was in absolute silence, they were listening, rapt. Not without reservations, not yet won over.

Tasgo escaped the remembered horrors and delights of the city. 'You have all seen your reflection in polished metal, or in a pool of still water. There I have seen upright surfaces so full of magic that reflection is as clear as if it were the doorway to another world. Underhill, it is like a reflection of the real world; like this world, but everything the wrong way round, everything strangely other. Their houses are made of light, walls made of light, of seemingly nothing. They have summer in winter, and winter in summer, kept in boxes, always ready. Everything is bigger, altered, amazing. Their sheep are large, and they are all white, each one, all white. Their cows are huge. Their crops grow short, but the heads contain so many grains, so fat and perfect they can hardly be real. The fields are endless. It seems perfect. But no-one tends them. Not a soul.

'There are monsters that roar, chariots without horses. Nothing pulls them, but they outpace the fastest horse. I have seen dragons in the distance and heard them roar. I have seen a huge dragonfly, its wings moving so fast they are no more than a roaring blur.' He must mean the helicopter they had seen one day when they were out running, thought Danny, remembering how Tasgo had been transfixed by the sight, struck dumb and motionless. Now Tasgo had at last shown his thinking, Danny could see the imaginative resemblance. Tasgo was still speaking. 'There is terror, there is delight, it is all extremes.

'I did not belong there. My presence was - a difficulty for keepers of the lore. Their warriors were drawn to me like wolves to possible prey. They swarmed at me, in ones and twos, then more and more.'

His face was hard and bitter as he remembered. Danny felt a sudden fear that Tasgo might be once more overwhelmed by the remembrance of being tasered, rendered helpless, as if he were dead. Tasgo went on, *'They have weapons that you cannot imagine, powers that you could only imagine in your worst nightmares.'*

Any moment now he was liable to say that they had killed him, three times. That wouldn't do, that would scare them. They would never follow a man who had been dead but was now alive.

'One man cannot stand against an army, not for long,' Tasgo said, as bleak and bitter as winter's ice.

Despite himself Danny stepped forward, before it got too bad. *'I am sorry it took so long for word to get to me, that you were there,'* he said. Tasgo turned that bleak look onto him, and Danny knew he had stepped in unwanted, yet again.

Tasgo held him in his gaze as he started again, *'One man cannot stand against an army,'* turning back towards the rest of them, *'but two, back to back, will make the enemy pay a heavy toll,'* and now his tone was turning heroic, he was getting to his feet and there was a twinkle in his eye as his hand came down on Danny's shoulder, *'And if one happens to be a local commander,'* a grin was breaking free, *'and both men happen to be Parisi, there is quite a different outcome.'* Turning to Danny with a proud and victorious stance, arms open wide, *'Never was I so pleased to see a man! Dannaigh, you saved my life! You saved my life three times over. I shall never forget it!'*

Danny let himself be encompassed by the massive hug. He returned it in full force, knowing his place now. They were two victorious fighters, who had stood against immense odds and won through. No vain words of victory where there was none. No lies. No complicated explanations. There was a clamour of approval. Someone shouted, *'Parisi!'* and it was taken up, echoing several times over.

Tasgo let go of Danny and stood, enjoying the accolade. It wasn't yet wholehearted by everyone, but it was warm and welcoming. For the first time Danny felt that Tasgo's return might be safe. There were still folk to be won over, but they were a minority. There were still doubts to be stilled, fears to be stifled, feelings to be soothed, but Tasgo was back, in command.

Tasgo raised his arms for silence, and when it came, he spoke again, loud and strong, *'From that moment until today Danny and Moira, Freya, for she still lives, and Ken have worked tirelessly to open a new gateway by which I could return.*

'I am so glad,' he reiterated, *'to be home once more, where I should be, with you, the strongest and the best of the Parisi!'*

Later, when those who slept in other houses had left, Tasgo kept Brec talking as other warriors came in closer to the fire, the inner group of confidants, the ones who had always been Tasgo's advisors. Others snuggled into their beds and tried to sleep, but round the embers of the fire problems were being laid out, and plans were being made.

They had all known why Gamma kept close to Jago, to keep him under her watchful eye, and counter his more controlling instincts. As Judoc's cousin — that was news to Danny — Jago thought himself superior, far above the common herd, and keen to keep others in their place. Once Tasgo was gone, he had sought tighter control over the slaves.

Margan said, with a nod to Brec, *'He even tried to say that Brec's slaves belonged to the village, and so to him, because the village had paid for them.'*

'But everyone who had been at Cynmar that Beltane knew better,' Tasgo remonstrated, turning to Brec, *'They saw you throw your masterpiece into the deal, that marvellous knife you made for Madog.'*

Brec growled low, *'He claimed I was slave still, that Madog never set me free.'* He clearly felt out of place sitting here with the elite, Danny hoped he felt it as an honour, as it was clearly meant to be.

The silence that followed was uncomfortable. The only witnesses to Madog's gift of freedom had been Danny and Moira, and they had been absent these last long years.

'That must have been when he took against Pinner,' Marrec said thoughtfully. *'He spoke up for you.'*

'You all did that,' muttered Brec gratefully, but conceded, *'his voice was the strongest.'*

Marrec was still putting things together, seeing with hindsight more than he had before. Coming to new understanding. *'That and young Treva not showing the respect he expected.'*

226

'How could he have got away with it?' Tasgo demanded, he kept more to dismay than anger, but they could tell he was more than disappointed. 'Ran off a cliff? Pin?'

'No proof,' Margan told him firmly. 'And Carod was firm in his story.'

Morven said, soft as sorry, hard as fact, 'He had all the young bloods sworn to him. He made them feel strong. They'd stand by him, whatever.'

Margan cut in after that, 'They've grown arrogant. He led them astray, thinking they were owed everything they wanted, nothing to earn.'

'Not Leir,' Marrec put in, uncomfortable. 'He believed it all. He thought you'd betrayed us, or, at least, deserted us,' he added unhappily. 'I tried – but...' he looked helpless at Tasgo.

Danny leant forward and spoke for the first time. 'Not Tasgo's fault. We should have killed Kuillok while we had him here.' Though then there would have been no-one to open the portal again. He had their attention now, so he went on quietly, lessening the sense of alarm at that dread name. 'Because of his status Underhill, they could not kill him there. They...' how to explain a secure hospital, where Wilcox could play with his mathematics but never walk outside the walls? 'trapped him behind walls that cannot be scaled, a token space. They took away his magic, but not all of it.' He took a deep breath, he didn't like doing this, but it was the nearest thing to truth that they would understand. 'Kuillok still has some powers. It was his doing, his revenge, to snatch Tasgo from the world, to take him Underhill even though he could not kill him. Underhill is no place for the living, unsummoned, unheralded. It would have destroyed a lesser man.'

An uncomfortable silence crept around them. Before it settled into their bones Tasgo said, matter of fact, 'We had better have a practice session in the morning.'

That was more like it. Morven said, strong, 'Knock a little sense into their heads.'

'Set the lads straight,' agreed Margan.

Marrec smiled, 'Show them you're back.'

The sound of gentle snores from one of the sleeping booths reminded them of how late it was, but there were still some details to arrange. Whether to send out word to the other villages and hamlets that Tasgo was back in control, or let rumour circulate until he could turn up in person? Word would have to be sent to Freda, if she was indeed with Dugal's sister Kennis in her village. And apparently it was important that Cynwrig should be brought back from Corraith's new homestead.

Danny was wondering where he was going to sleep, and Tasgo too, since Gamma was taking up the best bed.

But then a shout came from the doorway, a message from the guard at the gate. Someone was coming down the hill, people on foot.

No need to say it twice, they were all on their feet moving to the door. Danny said, *'Probably Moira,'* but at this time of night, no-one was taking any chances.

By the time they reached the gate they could hear Moira's voice floating from the darkness. She was singing 'The Maid in Moonlight' as she came, a gentle song, lilting and soft with the tones of love.

Raynes was a step behind her, carrying a heavy load.

Stabilising

Since Danny was the one who had training in medicine, he was the one who took the medical stuff inside the best sleeping stall, turfing Blathin out of the warm, back onto her own sleeping mat. Raynes set up a curtain between them and possible prying eyes in the hall while Danny hung the drip feed from a rafter, inserted the canula, and set about stabilising Gamma's condition.

Through the curtain they could hear Moira's gifts being gratefully accepted, a big joint of pork, a leathern flask of some heady liquor, and tasty biscuits. Danny noticed the tone of the voices changing as they tasted the biscuits, and the drink, while Moira flirted with the men.

Already Gamma's pulse seemed a little stronger.

Once Gamma was settled, they played musical chairs with the sleeping arrangements. Moira went in with Gamma, Margan gave up his bed to Tasgo, Marrec took Margan in with him, Morven gave his bed up to Ken Raynes, then hoiked Cadryn out of his cot so that he and Danny could share that, while Cadryn sloped off to bed down with one of the other lads.

Danny snuggled into furs, making sure his feet were not in Morven's face, and that there was plenty of padding between Morven's feet and his own face, and fell instantly into deep sleep, exhausted by the emotional turmoil of the day, and well aware that he was the last of them to have been given a bed.

When Jago turned up in his dreams, whether naked and dead or pale and sneering, Danny ignored him.

One of the things he had forgotten about the past, was the way that no-one gave any slack for late nights or troubled dreams. He managed to sleep through the feeding of the fire, and the sounds of a thin porridge being stirred, but the smells of cooking, and the rising clatter of people waking were too much. Tasgo's voice came through loud and clear, concerning warriors and practice. Morven wriggled out of bed with no attempt to spare Danny, so Danny stood up too, brushing down his clothes, but he moved over to the curtained off stall which held his grandmother.

Moira had already taken down the drip, and Gamma no longer had the deathly pallor and shrivelled skin of one near death. She was sleeping, a deep recuperative sleep, but Danny would be happier when he had seen her eat or drink something. He spoke to her, telling her that she would be getting better now, sounding confident, or at least hopeful. She made no response. Moira packed all the equipment back into concealing bags, leaving only the canula, covered in bandages, just in case it should be needed again. Danny kept watch, fingers on Gamma's pulse, listening for her breathing, while Moira joined Ken Raynes.

Ken was going to leave almost at once. He was taking all the equipment with him, away from prying eyes, while Moira would stay to look after her mother.

A thin drizzle met them outside, hazing the hillside still shadowed by thick cloud. Danny walked with him to the gate. Raynes tried to assure him that he could make his way back without any help.

'You will have an armed guard, as far as the shoulder of the hill,' Danny told him flatly. From there it would be obvious if there was anyone between him and the cave mouth. And the cave was close enough for Raynes to reach it before anyone else could get close enough to see.

'You think that's necessary?' Raynes queried.

'I'll send Kelwyn,' said Danny.

'You trust him?' Raynes asked.

'As much as anyone – more than most.' Danny was looking round for where Kelwyn was, but he already knew. Kelwyn would be where Tasgo was, on the practice field.

'Wait,' he commanded, starting to move, but Raynes held him back.

'Is Moira safe?' he demanded.

Danny smiled at that. Raynes had to go back. He had to take the modern with him. He had to be seen himself, in the modern, rather than give rise to speculation about where he was. There was absolutely no point in the question, there was nothing Raynes could do about it but worry. Or have a very public row with Moira when she refused to go with him.

Danny let the smile widen to a grin, 'Will anyone be safe, now Moira's here?' he asked, then sprinted to get Kelwyn.

All the lads were on the practice field, every man who could boast a sword at his hip was there facing Tasgo. Kelwyn was leaning nonchalantly against a young Ash tree.

When Danny asked him to escort Ken up the hill, as far as the bare rock this side of the summit, before returning, Kelwyn regarded him with a cool eye, not moving at all.

'Am I not needed here?' he asked, entirely not looking at the young men facing Tasgo.

Danny gave a careless shrug. *'I'm here,'* he said.

Kelwyn looked him up and down with amusement that said there was absolutely no comparison. But he unwound himself with a quick look at the combatants on the field, then loped away at a carefree pace that took him from sight faster than Danny might have expected.

'Today,' Tasgo was telling the warriors, young and old, *'we will not need swords. No point in risking unwanted wounds, when today is about power and strength. Hang them on the fence,'* with a nod towards it. Margan led the way, unbuckling his sword as he went. There was some hesitation, there was some distrust. Leir walked quickly over and slung his sword beside Margan's. Cadryn followed a little less pointedly, and so the rest did the same. Only then did Morven and Marrec remove their own.

The moment they did so, Danny knew with horrid certainty what was coming next. He looked across the open space to Tasgo, on the far side and said with dismay, *'Tasgo, chief,'* accusation and plea together.

Tasgo understood. He beckoned Danny to come to him. As soon as Danny's foot landed on the scuffed surface of the training ground, the young lads' eyes were drawn towards him with sullen interest, and Danny knew it was a mistake he would regret.

Tasgo confirmed it. *'Yes Dannaigh,'* he called out loud, *'it is necessary. Everyone must know their place - even you.'*

The lads brightened, their eyes fastened on Danny hungrily. He was entirely without weapons of any sort, they would have a field day. Danny knew Tasgo had meant quite a different thing, he knew Tasgo had meant the lads to take it the wrong way. He had forgotten this feeling, of being put where he did not want to be, of duties beyond his wishes. He was in the middle of the arena now, where Tasgo wanted him, feeling uncomfortable, but only a little angry. He supposed it had been inevitable.

'*Mokan,*' Tasgo commanded offhand, '*would you strike Dannaigh for me?*'

Mokan was the oldest of the younger warriors gathered here under the older men's command. He was Ailiese's brother, and stood by her whenever she fought, never letting her come to any harm, though she always said it was the other way round. He took a leisurely step towards Danny, keeping a respectful distance.

'*I was with you when we hunted Kuillok,*' he said, '*an honour,*' he went on, readying himself, '*you're a brave fighter, though young then.*'

Danny thanked him for the thought, and was ready when he sprang. Out of consideration for the respect Mokan had shown, in return Danny merely made sure that he was not where Mokan struck. Mokan's fist flew past him. The lack of impact threw him off balance. Danny let him stagger back for another go. He got away with that two or three times, but Mokan soon finished his show of respect, and stopped making it easy. Now Danny had to fend, and fend hard, backing and side-stepping all the time. It wasn't like sparring at the gym. Here fighting was always a serious thing, with heavy intent. Their movement cleared a space in the centre of the field, the lads stepping quickly away. Mokan had yet to land a blow that counted, but Tasgo called a halt anyway.

'*Good try, Mokan,*' Tasgo told him, '*but let's let the younger lads have a go, they're fit and fast. Each can do their best, we'll make a tally. You count blows on Dannaigh, Morven will count blows on his opponent. Whoever gets five blows in, wins.*'

Danny glanced angrily at him. Tasgo had been to Danny's training sessions in the modern. He had been impressed by the jujitsu, but thought the whole thing mere play, insubstantial. Now he was pushing Danny to do more than just fend. He was reminding him that here it was no game, it could be life or death, and it was time to get serious, even as practice. Danny wished he had not promised to obey, without argument. He was glad the lads were tough. He hoped he was up to the challenge.

The first lad made a charge at him. He was young, only shoulder high to Danny, and over-excited. The last time Danny had been here he would have been the same sort of age as Cunedag, about ten. Danny stepped forward and to one side, turning. His foot sweep was so small and fast that a stupid, or over-excited, observer might have missed it altogether, seeing only a sudden rush changing suddenly and unexpectedly into a headlong dive to the ground. Danny danced across the lad's back, which Morven took as two hits, followed by two more as the lad tried to rise, and a fifth as Danny whirled away as the lad finally made his furious response. The lad was counted out.

There were ten of them.

After the fifth Tasgo suggested mildly that they might do better with a weapon, and tossed a baton to represent a knife to the next. Danny gave a rictus smile of thanks to Tasgo, he could have done without that. Sessions at the gym or the club had never been as strenuous as this. It was coming back to him, how tough they were.

Morven didn't count light brushes or taps. Neither did Mokan. Danny had managed not to send anyone flying, though he knew Tasgo would have preferred him to do so. It was true, the lads might be on the receiving end of one lesson, but Danny was too. Tasgo knew how soft life was in the modern. He was making sure Danny knew he had to step up, here.

By the time there was only one left for him to face, Danny had only been seriously hit four times, from three different lads. Each defeat had come as a surprise to the youth concerned. Each had thought they were better than the rest. Each had been trained in every move against the others, learning how to counter, how to overcome that counter. Faced with unexpected actions they had done their best. Faced with the man whom they remembered as a slight and unusual player, sometimes a bit of a joke five years ago, they expected to win where others had failed. They were all feeling put out, and were reassessing.

It wasn't just the jujitsu. Danny's father had taught him self-defence since he was a child, and the martial arts classes had honed him. He had known, just as these lads did, that attack was sometimes the best form of defence. He was glad he had kept pushing hard in the sport.

Llubelin was the last of them. As he made to take the baton, Tasgo said, *'You've a knife at your belt Llubelin, perhaps you'd stand a better chance with that.'*

'No!' burst from Danny, angrily. That was too much. *'I don't mind playing,'* he snarled, *'but there's no need for real wounds.'*

Llubelin smiled a wicked smile, he thought Danny was afraid of him. He really did need taking down a peg.

Before Tasgo could answer, Danny was at the boy. Three brisk moves, backed by the reality of danger, the intensity of intent, he caught Llubelin's knife hand and twisted to lock it, moving in fast to tuck his other arm over Llubelin's shoulder, his elbow pressed hard to Llubelin's neck, catching him under the chin. A twist of the wrist and the knife fell free to the ground, where Danny put a foot on it.

Danny leaned on the youth, forcing him downwards. *'Never,'* he snarled quietly, *'ever, use steel against me.'*

Releasing the twisted wrist, his elbow shoved hard, and Llubelin fell away from him.

Keeping anger under control, Danny strode a few yards towards Tasgo. Tasgo stood, that relaxed and ready stance, secure in his own strength and skill. It was Morven who moved as if to protect him.

Danny stopped short, out of instant fighting range. He held his anger in check, Tasgo was still re-establishing himself, a challenge from Danny would be too dangerous. Instead he said, taut and hard, *'I am no longer an ignorant youth, Tasgo. I will always stand at your side, but do not provoke me to unnecessary violence.'*

Tasgo took it well. *'Now that you are a man,'* he countered, *'you need reminding of your power, and your strength.'* He looked beyond Danny at the lads. Llubelin had not picked up the knife. He had backed off, looking shocked and nursing his wrist. All the lads were looking surprised and morose. They had expected a chance to show off their prowess, and instead had been shown up as ineffective.

Tasgo smiled at Morven, and at Margan and Mokan. *'Five of us,'* he said, with a laugh, as if this was pure play, *'ten of them, reckon we can uppy-end the lot of them?'* He meant the young warriors.

234

Margan gave a grimace of mock uncertainty and doubt. *'We're a bit old for that game,'* he said.

Morven laughed, *'They're light, real light-weights,'* he mocked.

The lads, shamefaced and put down, took it as a challenge. *'We're strong,'* countered Llubelin.

They brightened instantly. *'We're fast!'* sang another. This was a game they knew, and they knew how to use numbers to their advantage. One of them shouted, *'Morven,'* and they mobbed him, lifting him bodily, and letting him drop, out of the game. Tasgo tipped one of the youngsters, and Margan another, coming from behind. Mokan knew the game too, he grabbed two of them by their necks, dragging them close to him, away from the others.

Danny caught on fast, anger ebbing as he scythed the feet from under one lad and grabbed another.

With no word spoken, the rest of the lads turned on Danny. He was the one who had shown them up, he was the one to go down next. Danny made a show of resistance, but after a few moments tussling, let them shove him down on the floor. He wouldn't have been able to stop them anyway, even though Tasgo and Margan were peeling off the boys one by one, landing them good-humouredly in a heap with Morven.

The lads leapt up again, but this was a game, and they had all been 'up-ended', ten of them down against only two of their opponents. They were excitedly ready to start again. Tasgo looked them over with a grin. *'Power and strength,'* he told them, *'never underestimate them. Hone them with skill, and you will be unstoppable. Like Danny,'* he said. *'But never forget to use your advantage when you have the numbers.'*

He gave his hand to Danny, to pull him up, before setting the next task, somehow they were all in better spirits now. Tasgo set them in pairs, one to attack empty-handed and screaming like a night spirit, the other to find some new and surprising way to fend or counter. The lads set to it with a goodwill that surprised Danny.

By the time Kelwyn strode back into view, drawn by the banshee screaming, it was almost a standard training session, everyone working together almost like a team.

Home

Tasgo thanked the lads, praising their efforts. They seemed to accept it well, despite the rough start to the session, despite the dents in their self-esteem and their ideas of their own worth. That game of uppy-end, obviously a child's game of rough-and-tumble, had put them in a better mood. As they started to move off, the looks sent sideways to Danny were more assessment than sneer. They weren't going far, little groups were forming. Llubelin had his supporters, they were still not happy, and covert glances were being thrown in Danny's direction.

Tasgo seemed careless of it all, he was already speaking with Margan, there were things to do.

Before they could move off to do them, Danny, still tense, realised he had to do something now. He knew things were no longer as they had been when last he was here, Tasgo was now his chief, a man of power. Danny would always have to give way to him. But for that to work, Tasgo had to see that Danny had changed too. It had to be done now. He stepped up to them. *'Give us a moment, Margan?'* he asked.

Margan could see it was more than a request. He moved off quick and quiet, taking Morven and Marrec with him towards the next tasks of the day. They stopped at the edge of the field, as if to discuss things, looking anywhere but back towards Danny and Tasgo, now standing alone at the centre of the field. Even Kelwyn had melted away to the edge of the field, a movement unnoticed in its quietness.

Danny stood almost at Tasgo's side, but looking grimly past him, towards the sea and the jetty, while Tasgo, head cocked receptively, kept his eyes on the village huts and the people moving among them.

Danny chose his words carefully. *'We are not what we were before,'* he said quietly, so his voice would not carry, *'you a young warrior learning his craft, me an ignorant child. I am no threat to you, never will be. Nor am I your tool. Don't ask me to do that again. I'm not going to hurt anyone just to prove a point.'*

Tasgo smiled, turning his head to look fondly at Danny. Danny could have hit him, only all those people carefully not watching would notice.

Tasgo knew it, his smile grew wide. *'So I see,'* he said. Then he relented, turning entirely to Danny, his face warm and friendly. *'You don't know your own power,'* he told Danny disconcertingly. *'They've been fed lies by Jago. He always knew you were one to watch. He was afraid of you right from the start.'*

Danny started to protest, this wasn't about Jago, but Tasgo rode on over it, *'If you won't carry weapons, then they must know that you don't need to. They no longer look on you as a weak and weedy Grey Man.'*

'No ,' growled Danny, *'Now I'm a dangerous, possibly deadly Grey Man. They'll think I used magic!'*

Tasgo was still smiling, *'Better that than weak and weedy,'* he said, moving on quickly to, *'and once they recognise your strength, they will be pleased to fight alongside you. You will become Fair soon enough!'*

Danny was fair enough to realise that Tasgo knew better than him in such matters.

Tasgo could see Danny accepting at least the logic of it. He added, *'It's your own fault, you should make your moves more obvious, so they can see what hit them, and learn from it.'* Seeing Danny still angry and finding that difficult to accept he went on, *'You should take the morning session tomorrow, show them some of your fancy tricks – without the threat of blades.'* He wanted to move off quickly before anger could take hold again. Instead Danny caught his arm. Careful, he said, *'If I am to stay here, then you have to accept that I have a different counsel, and a different view, worth respect.'*

Tasgo closed with him, his arm coming up but without anger, Danny let his shoulder be clasped. *'How could I ever forget it, even for a second?'* asked Tasgo. It was serious, and it was a joke.

They stood eye to eye.

Then Danny relented, joking but still serious, *'I'll try not to let it show too much.'*

Tasgo gave a huff of a laugh. *'Don't make me remind you.'* he said, pushing him away with a smile, as he walked away.

Unsettled, Danny watched him go, saw the lads look to their chief as he went. No longer truculent, the boys were still conflicted, questioning.

Danny moved off himself, before the lads had time to turn their attention on him.

Danny had still not managed to ask Tasgo the thing that had been bothering him from the moment they met Margan and the boys mending the fence post. *Where's Cunedag?'* Now was obviously not the time. Five years ago Cunedag had been nine years old, and they were all proud of him. He was going to do great things, they were making sure he was known in other towns. He would be fourteen now, of fighting age, but there was no sign of him, and no mention of his name.

Gamma would no doubt know, but she was a long way yet from being able to answer questions. Mokan had been talking with some of the lads, but was leaving them now, walking off towards the new roundhouse, and the gate.

Danny caught up with him and asked. Mokan looked back towards the exercise ground with lads still grouped around it, and Tasgo gone.

'The Druids took him,' he said. Then hastened to make that clearer. *'He wanted to go, in a way. They sweet-talked him into it. All the things they could teach him. All the things he could learn. He wasn't sure, but they promised him he would always be his own man, to come and go as he pleased.'* He gave a laugh, *'He drove the chariot as they left. Almost took out the gatepost. Druid never turned a hair.'* That was Cunedag all right, all knees and elbows, awkward as a March hare. Bright as the edge of a sword.

'What will they do with him?' asked Danny.

'Who knows what druids do?' countered Mokan. *'They'll have their hands full with Cunedag though.'*

Inside the new big roundhouse Danny met with a happy surprise. Now that the sun was high, even if hidden behind drifting cloud and fine misty rain, folk were coming in for breakfast, clothes steaming, filling the smoke-tainted air with the smell of damp wool and mud. Their voices muted as he came in, but he strode past them quickly.

As he neared the end sleeping stall, Danny could hear Moira's voice. When he pulled back the curtain, the figure in the bed moved, and his Grandmother's eyes turned to see him. Her face, pale and drawn, still managed a smile as she recognised him. Relief flooded through him, like a pressure released. He felt suddenly light and floating, he hardly knew whether he needed to drop to his knees in case he fell.

They had been in time, after all. Despite all the tensions, everything might work out, after all. Now that she looked so much more alive Danny had no doubt of Gamma's recovery, though it might take some time. She was tough.

Treva was another matter entirely. He had no idea what to do about her. He was afraid his rash move, faced with her wild distress, was going to turn out to be more of a problem than a solution.

He was worried about Llubelin and the other lads as well. No-one had challenged Tasgo directly, but they were put out by Jago's death. He wasn't sure they were going to accept that they might have been wrong, about anything. Together they could make life difficult, if they wanted to.

Danny still felt uncertain. Here was where he belonged, he knew that, deep in his bones he knew it. He just wished he knew how he was going to fit in here. He just wished it felt more like a home coming.

But now, seeing the light in Gamma's eyes, seeing her move her head and smile at him, Danny was suddenly sure things would work out.

Tasgo was Chief, he would make it work. Danny only wished he knew how.

Post Script

Although this is a fictional story, the author has tried to make the Iron Age as accurate and realistic as possible. It took a lot of research. As far as we know, no time traveller has ever gone back the past, but new things are being discovered all the time. East Yorkshire was an Iron and steel producer well over 2000 years ago.

The Parisi are first known from a description in Ptolemy's Geographica. Their name may mean 'Fighters' or 'Commanders' though alternatives have also been suggested.

The Brigantes lived to the North and West of them, with the Coritani south of them across the Humber. Romans arrived and built or made over a large camp and town at Petuaria. Since this story occurs more than a century before they arrive, I invented Cynmar, also on the coast and a major river.

Life expectancy then was about 36 years, and they were dealing with climate change, population increase, immigration, occasional aggressive trading practices (raiding), and a distant threat of war, spilling over from the mainland of Europe.

If you would like to find out more about the late Iron Age in Britain, including the Parisi of East Yorkshire, you could try the following.

Visiting an iron age roundhouse. **Castell Henllys** or **Butser Ancient Farm** are excellent examples.

Visiting a museum, such as the **Iron age Museum at Andover**.

Reading something like

Parisi Britons and Romans in Eastern Yorkshire by Peter Halkon - The History Press
Or Try any of the following websites.

https://www.timeandagain.website

http://www.megalithic.co.uk

http://www.bbc.co.uk/history/ancient/british_prehistory/iron_01.shtml

http://www.dumnonika.com/weapons-and-armour

https://en.wikipedia.org/wiki/Ferrous_metallurgy#Iron_Age_Europe

https://en.wikipedia.org/wiki/Stanwick_Iron_Age_Fortifications

http://www.cartographersguild.com/showthread.php?t=19730

http://www.bbc.co.uk/history/ancient/british_prehistory/ironage_roundhouse_01.shtml

http://heatherrosejones.com/archaeologicalsewing/wool.html

http://www.teachinghistory100.org/objects/about_the_object/iron_age_horse_trappings

If you would like to delve further into the past to the bronze age, try
Coming Home by Richard Turner,   Kite press or   Kindle.